CAUGHT IN THE
CROSSFIRE

In addition to being a popular and prolific writer for children, Alan Gibbons teaches in a primary school. He is also much in demand as a speaker in schools and at book events. He lives in Liverpool with his wife and four children.

Alan Gibbons won the Blue Peter Book Award in the 'Book I Couldn't Put Down' category for *Shadow of the Minotaur*, which was also shortlisted for the Carnegie Medal.

CAUGHT IN THE
CROSSFIRE

Alan Gibbons

A Dolphin
Paperback

First published in Great Britain in 2003
as a Dolphin paperback
by Orion Children's Books
a division of the Orion Publishing Group Ltd
Orion House
5 Upper St Martin's Lane
London WC2H 9EA

A catalogue record for this book is
available from the British Library

Typeset at The Spartan Press Ltd,
Lymington, Hants
Printed in Great Britain by
Clays Ltd, St Ives plc

ISBN 1 84255 096 9

CONTENTS

'Courage is resistance to fear, mastery of fear –
not absence of fear.'

Mark Twain

PART ONE

A SENSE OF HISTORY

1
Out of the Shadows

There is something in the shadows. Rabia Khan is worried. She has found herself in the wrong place at the wrong time. She sees the long fingers of the night clawing into the alley and gives a little shudder. She ought to know better than to be this end of the Ravensmoor Road after dark. Things have a habit of happening here. This stretch of road has a history. Rabia's father has warned her often enough – warned her until all she could to do was defy him and go there anyway, just to remind him of her growing independence, her right to think for herself and take risks. Now she is regretting the way she has ignored his advice not to go on her own. It seems Dad knew best after all.

Despite everything, this isn't a town that is used to living in fear. Mostly it potters along like a moderately successful TV sitcom. It doesn't get itself in the headlines very often. It isn't stylish or trendy. It doesn't merit many mentions in articles entitled *The Best Of* . . . But you don't get many scare-mongering journalists making the trek from London, so neither does it turn up in *The Worst Of* . . . It's an ordinary sort of place, what you might call a backwater. But one simple fact haunts this town like many others: hatred can be ordinary and evil can be commonplace. They have a way of strolling in by the back door. It seems to take an awful lot of good people to make a place happy, but just a handful of mischief-makers to turn it bad. This time it started to go bad the day two airliners changed the skyline of New York forever. Rabia knows how some people's eyes have flashed at her in the street since that day. She feels instinctively that the rules of her life have changed.

'Why did the meeting have to go on so long?' she groans, pulling up the collar of her coat against the shower of needle-sharp raindrops that has just whipped against her face, stinging her eyes shut.

There is something in the shadows. She's sure of it. But she doesn't turn her head. She has trained herself to look straight ahead at moments like this. Looking back is the last thing she should do. It is better to hurry on down the hill towards the safety of the Triangle and home.

'Stupid meeting,' she mutters.

The rain is coming down more heavily now, and it is turning to sleet.

'Stupid weather too . . .'

The words die in her throat. There is another sound in the wintry twilight, the thud of footsteps behind her. There are two pairs of footsteps – yes, definitely two – and they are falling in behind her. Two figures have detached themselves from the darkness. She can hear the swish of their nylon jackets, they are that close. Her breath catches. It could be innocent, of course, but she's sure it isn't.

About the same time John Creed is cresting the motorway's highest point. He is listening to Wagner's *Lohengrin*. Already a handful of dim yellow lights are blinking in the valley below, announcing a string of small towns. They were cotton producers once. Creed sighs. The names of these places bring to mind clattering machinery and cobbled streets, clogs and shawls, wake-up calls and corner shops. That's all in the past now, of course. First they made cotton, then, like the fragile cotton threads themselves, they broke. If that sepia, cloth cap Britain really existed, it is gone forever. A new age has dawned.

'Brave new world!' Creed says out loud.

It is at this moment that he sees the sign for Oakfield. He checks it with the junction number on his handwritten directions. He notes the local representative's spelling mistakes and snorts with indignation. The peasants he is forced to deal with! Still, the journey of a thousand miles starts with just one step.

'This is it,' he announces to nobody in particular.

Michael Kelly is on the bus about half a mile away from where Creed is coasting slowly down the hill road. He is looking out of the window, but he is not thinking about the lights of the town or the ghosts of Oakfield's industrial past. His mind is full of the dark-eyed girl he saw across the table at the meeting. Her skin was somewhere between light toffee and brown. In that little conference room something made her stand out from everyone else. And to think he almost gave it a miss! That long, glossy black hair, those oval brown eyes . . . If only he'd been able to get her name!

Michael slips into a daydream where they are walking hand in hand through rainswept streets – *these* rainswept streets. But a dream is exactly what this is. Imagine if he were to bring a girl like her home – an Asian girl! His old man would blow his top. There was that time when he was at primary school. The teachers had them making decorations for the Muslim festival of Eid and giving each other the greeting *Eid Mubarak*. When Dad saw Michael's on the kitchen table he ripped it to shreds. Whose country is it anyway? he demanded of his son. Michael didn't know. It isn't the sort of question you can answer when you're eight years old.

Next morning Sean Kelly had stormed down to the school, demanding to know why Christian boys and girls had to have all this Islam stuff rammed down their throats. Christian? Mike thinks – that's a laugh! When was the last time Dad was in a church? One thing's for sure, they've never seen eye to eye since. Still, Mike thinks, the old man can't stop me dreaming.

––––––––

Rabia quickens her pace. Boys are far from her mind – the sort of boys who might ask you out, anyway. She is preoccupied with the footsteps behind her. They are coming closer. She isn't imagining it. The gap between her and the two strangers is narrowing. Night is tracing patterns of fright down her spine. The Triangle has never looked more inviting. It is the down-at-heel district of cramped terraced houses at the bottom of Ravensmoor Road, bordered on three sides by a dual carriageway, a railway line and a canal, hence the name 'Triangle'. It's nothing much to look at but it's home. That's where Rabia wants to be now – in her terraced house in the middle of the Triangle.

Home.

Something hits her on the neck. It is only a sweet or a peanut, but it makes her start. She has been concentrating on keeping an even pace, not so slow that the strangers will catch her up but not so fast that they will know she is scared either. She has been so intent on maintaining the right kind of speed that the sting goes through her like an electric shock. It has obviously had the desired effect because her followers burst out laughing.

'Aw, what's the matter, *Fatima*? Did it hurt?'

'Watch you don't eat it. You're meant to be fasting, aren't you?'

A few hundred metres away Creed presses a button and lowers the electric windows. The Wagner fanfare blares into the falling night. Creed feels the rain on his face and sniffs it like a wolf. This wind is heavy with rain. It could even snow tonight. Creed checks his watch. It is

16:30. They should be waiting for him by now. They should know what a stickler for punctuality he is. Surely they want to make a good impression? It is his first evening in Oakfield. He cruises down Ravensmoor Road, past the branch library where Rabia and Michael attended their meeting. 'Foulshurst Avenue,' he says, consulting the letter on the driver's seat. 'This is it.'

As he corners slowly he sees the dark outlines of two youths. They are following an Asian girl, taking a rise out of her. Creed smiles. Well, what would you expect from a couple of eager young patriots? He carries on along Foulshurst Avenue until he reaches a Netto supermarket. There are two men in their thirties accompanied by another in his late teens or early twenties. Creed frowns. He expected more of a reception than this. Nothing too showy, of course – no drums beating or flags flying, but a bit more than three men skulking in a supermarket door-way. After all, he is the man who is about to change the face of this town. He consults his watch. It is 16:35. The start of Ramadan.

_____

Suhail Khan glances at the kitchen clock.

'She should be back by now,' he says.

'You worry too much,' says his wife Diane.

Suhail doesn't say anything, but he isn't reassured. Even after all these years, he and Diane feel differently about this town. She is a white woman married to a British Muslim. She doesn't feel automatic hostility when she visits her family up the Ravensmoor Road, but her husband does. Her children do. They've all heard the shouts of *Paki*. Of course Diane doesn't ignore what they tell her. What mother would? She suffered her own share of hostility in the early days. Even in the eyes of her parents she has committed the cardinal sin of marrying *one of those people*.

'I think I'm going to take a run up to the library,' he says.

Diane doesn't try to stop him.

'What's the matter, *Fatima*?' says one of the youths, flicking another peanut at Rabia. 'Not talking?'

No, she isn't talking. Not to the likes of him. Fatima indeed! For a moment she feels defiant but it doesn't last long. She is too scared for that. Some of the other girls at school have been pushed around this way. Shahnaz from Rabia's maths set was walking round Oakfield Park wearing the Muslim headscarf, the *hijab*. Somebody tore it clean off. That was just after the World Trade Center was hit. Rabia feels uncomfortable. More than uncomfortable, she is scared. If only she had taken Dad's offer of a lift. If only her best friend Sofia wasn't in bed with the 'flu. If only her mobile phone wasn't sitting on the kitchen work surface, on charge.

'Hey!'

One of them grabs hold of her around the upper arm. Feeling his fingers digging into her flesh, she shrinks back.

'What's the matter with you?' he asks, feeling her reaction. 'Do you think you're too good for us or something?'

She wants to spit back some smart reply: *A cockroach would be too good for you!* But the words choke in her throat. She feels so alone, alone and vulnerable. He is trying to swing her round, to make her look at him. He wants to see the fear in her eyes.

'Come on, love. Don't you want to do us the dance of the seven veils?'

'Maybe she'd rather give us a kiss.'

Finally her reply breaks loose.

'Let go of me!'

She tries to pull free. It only makes him tighten his grip on her arm. She hears the words *brown bitch* and braces herself. But just when it feels as if the whole thing is about to turn nasty the second youth calls out to his friend.

'Daz, knock it off, will you?'

'Are you kidding? I'm only just getting started.'

'I'm serious,' says the second boy. 'Didn't you see who was in that car?'

Rabia feels Daz's grip loosen. 'You mean it's him?' Daz says.

'Yes, and you know what he thinks of people who turn up late.'

Suddenly the pair of them are racing down the street towards Foulshurst Avenue. Rabia hears a familiar, gruff voice. 'There you are, I've been up and down this road twice. I don't know how I missed you. The council should do something about the lighting along here.'

'Dad!'

Suhail Khan hears the relief in his daughter's voice. 'Is something wrong?'

Instinctively he looks round in the direction of the two white boys he has just seen running up the hill.

'Don't go after them,' she says.

'Why? What's happened?'

'I'll tell you about it on the way home,' she says.

It is a quarter to five when John Creed recognises the local organiser.

'Good to see you, Colin.'

Colin Stone sees his glance in the direction of the small reception party.

'I know it isn't much of a turn-out, John,' he says, 'but you said you didn't want to attract too much attention.'

Creed smiles. 'I don't think you needed to take me quite this literally,' he says. 'Would I be right in thinking the troops are a bit thin on the ground then?'

Colin Stone returns the smile sheepishly. 'You could say that.'

'How many branches?'

Stone pulls a face. 'Just the one.'

And, he thinks to himself, it's more a sickly twig than a branch.

'Don't worry about it,' says Creed. 'From small beginnings . . .'

He is interrupted by the sound of running feet. It is the two youths who have been whiling away their time following Rabia Khan. Stone introduces them.

'Here are a couple of our young foot soldiers now,' he says. 'This is Jason Hughes and that's Darren Wright.'

'Daz to my friends,' says Darren Wright brightly. He is still flushed from their little game with Rabia. 'We saw you turn off the main road. We recognised you from your picture in *The Patriot*.'

Stone looks at Creed. He is anxious to make a good impression. Creed puts his mind at rest.

'See,' he says, provoking appreciative laughter, 'we've started growing already!'

A hundred metres down the road Suhail Khan is pulling up outside the house. He's been listening to Rabia's story.

'I've a good mind to go looking for them,' he says.

'Don't, Dad,' says Rabia. 'They're not worth it.'

'You're right, of course,' says Suhail. 'They're not worth it. It just makes me angry that they can go round picking on teenage girls. Master race, eh? Why don't they try it on with a grown man like me?'

He remembers a night twenty years ago. He was a young man, little more than a boy, and he lay frightened and alone on a rainswept pavement while half a dozen men drove their boots into him. He hasn't forgotten the fear and humiliation that thudded through him with every kick. The memory makes him determined that his children will never feel that terror. This town is their home. They were born here. Surely that's enough to make them British! They should be able to go where they like without being threatened or abused.

'Forget them, Dad.'

'I'll do my best,' says Suhail. 'But why should I? We work hard. We keep ourselves to ourselves. Why should my daughter be threatened by such people?'

Rabia shrugs. He knows the answer as well as she does. You can hide your views or take off a badge, but you can't disguise the colour of your skin.

She has her key in the front door when she hears someone calling her name. It is her twin brother Tahir. He has just turned the corner and is striding towards them smiling broadly. He walks with a swagger though Rabia is close enough to him to know what's behind the tough exterior.

'Dad,' Rabia whispers hurriedly, 'don't say anything about this to Tahir.' Suhail is locking and alarming the car and Rabia can't see his face. 'You know what he's like. You won't, will you?'

Suhail turns round. He knows that boy of his, all right.

'No, I won't say a word.'

At the stroke of five Creed is also locking and alarming his car.

'So where's this watering hole you've told me so much about?' he asks.

'The Lion?' says Stone, suddenly desperate to knock back a pint of best bitter. 'Just down here on the right.'

They walk back to Ravensmoor Road and go into the pub. They are greeted by half a dozen young men in the bar.

'So where were you lot when John arrived?' asks Stone, his face betraying his impatience. 'At least Jason and Daz made it along to the car park.'

There are guilty looks all round. Unexpectedly, it is Creed who breaks the ice.

'Cut the lads some slack, Colin,' he says, speaking with the authority his position in the movement gives him. 'After all, I did say no fuss. Tonight we relax.'

Stone buys a round of drinks and brings them over on a tin tray.

'To John Creed,' says Stone. 'Tonight we have some fun.'

'Yes,' says Creed, the smile fading from his face. 'But tomorrow we change the world.'

Rabia is talking to Tahir in the living room, trying to make him understand what she was doing halfway up Ravensmoor Road on her own. She doesn't mention the two youths.

'It's the Oakfield Book Award,' she says. 'I'm on the panel. We're meant to choose the best children's book of the year.'

'Books!' says Tahir, glancing at the slim volume in Rabia's hand. 'You never do anything but read.'

'It wouldn't do you any harm to read more yourself, Tahir,' Rabia says, opening her book again, 'then you might understand how other people live.'

'I don't care about all that,' says Tahir, 'so long as they let us live the way we want.'

Rabia grimaces. He's been talking this way a lot lately, sneering at this *they* of his and what *they* do to *us*. He won't listen to the teachers at school. All white and middle class, he sneers. As if he's forgotten his own mother is white.

Diane Khan isn't listening to her children. She is in the kitchen with Suhail, and she is more interested in what he is telling her.

'It's a good job I went for her when I did,' he says, keeping his voice low.

Rabia isn't the only one worried about the way he might

react. Tahir is becoming quite the hothead, a real worry to his parents.

'Two boys followed Rabia from the library.'

Diane's hand flies up to her mouth.

'They didn't do anything,' says Suhail hurriedly. 'One of them grabbed her arm but it didn't go any further than that. They ran off for some reason.'

Diane glances in the direction of the living room. 'Is she OK?'

'She's fine, but she was really glad to see me.'

Diane shakes her head. Like Suhail, she has lived all her life in Oakfield and she knows what it's like up that end of Ravensmoor Road. After all, she was brought up there on the Moorside estate, which is where her parents still live. It's the kind of place where even the rats go round in packs for protection.

In a bleak corner of the Moorside estate Michael Kelly is rummaging for his key. Finding only loose change in his pocket, he walks round to the back of the house.

'Is that you, Mike?' his mother calls, hearing the poorly hung door scrape open.

'Yes.'

'You haven't seen Liam, have you?'

'No, why?'

'He isn't in from school yet.'

Mike consults the clock. It's gone five o'clock.

'I wouldn't worry. He'll be knocking round with Jason or Daz.'

Mike knows she won't find that very reassuring, of course. Jason and Daz see themselves as cocks of the estate and have hardly been out of trouble since they could walk.

'I just wish he'd at least call in before he goes about his bother,' says Mum. 'You'd think he could check in once in a while.'

Mary Kelly walks into the kitchen. She is a greyish woman, forty going on sixty. She looks as if all the life has been sucked out of her. Her blonde hair is dragged back in a pony tail, making her face look even more pinched. The strain shows in her eyes, on her drawn, parchment skin. Of the three men in her life, husband Sean and sons Liam and Michael, only Mike has ever given her any peace of mind. In many ways he is just like her. Slim and blonde, he is a quiet boy, a good student too. He is as calm and considerate as the other two are brash and thoughtless. He spends more time around the house than his father and brother put together. To Liam he is just a nerd. Mary thinks differently. But for Mike, she would have gone mad years ago.

'Do you want me to go looking for him?' Mike asks.

'Better not,' says Mary. 'You know what he's like if he thinks I'm checking up on him.'

Mike nods.

'So how was your meeting?' says Mary, happy to change the subject.

'Fine. They're going to tell us how many books we have to read at the next one.'

That won't be until the New Year. It can't come quickly enough. Mike is definitely interested in the dark-eyed girl.

'They can't give you too many books to read, can they, son?' Mary says proudly, cutting across his thoughts.

Mike grins. 'You've got that right.'

He watches as she walks out. The moment she's gone his

smile vanishes. There are fresh bruises on her arm. The old man's been at it again.

At six o'clock Liam is leaning against the wall of a bus shelter on Ravensmoor Road, trying to keep out of the freezing rain. His hands are deep in his pockets. He has been looking for Jason and Daz for hours. He's tried all the usual places. There is one more possible haunt – the Lion. Though only sixteen, his two friends can pass for eighteen. Not Liam. He's the baby-faced one of the group, and the youngest by twelve months. In fact, he's lucky if he can pass for his fifteen years. He kicks a polystyrene tray half full of curry and chips and turns for home. No sense hanging round here if Jason and Daz are in the Lion. He is crossing Foulshurst Avenue when he hears somebody shouting his name.

'Liam. Hey, Liam!'

He turns to see Daz and Jason jogging towards him.

'Where've you two been?' Liam growls. 'I've been looking for you everywhere.'

'John Creed's in town,' says Daz.

'Who?'

'John Creed. We've told you about him.'

Liam looks none the wiser.

'John Creed. Leader of the Patriotic League.'

'And who are they when they're at home?'

Jason exchanges a knowing look with Darren. 'The Patriotic League. We've *told* you. Britain for the British.

Send all the immigrants and asylum-seekers back where they belong. It's the party of the future and its leader John Creed is the man who's going to set this town on fire.'

R abia isn't thinking about setting the town on fire. She sits at her bedroom window on this first night of Ramadan, letting the afternoon's events come creeping out of the back rooms of her memory. She remembers the two figures emerging from the shadows. She hears their foot-steps echoing through her thoughts. She feels the boy's fingers digging into the flesh of her arm. And for what? Because they saw a dark-eyed, dark-skinned girl walking home from the library. She is what this country is supposed to be looking for: an integrated Asian girl, modern, west-ernised, complete with regional English accent. To cap it all she has a white English mother. She probably visits Next nearly as often as the mosque. Rabia is a British Asian or British Muslim, or whatever other silly label they want to put on her. But it will be some time before she walks up Ravensmoor Road on her own again. Next time Dad offers a lift she will say: 'Yes please.'

And she will mean it.

John Creed fastens his seat belt and turns the key in the ignition. He glances at Stone. The younger men have gone. It is just the two of them now. After a five-hour drive up the motorway, including long tailbacks on the M25 and Junctions 7 to 10 on the M6, Creed is looking forward to his bed.

'Which way?'

'Up Ravensmoor to the top of the hill.'

Stone is worse the wear for drink. He gives a bleary grin and stretches out his heavily-muscled right arm. There is a British bulldog tattoo peeking out where the shirt sleeve is rolled up to the bicep.

'Sieg Heil!' he says, chuckling drunkenly.

Creed stamps on the brake and stops the car. His head snaps round.

'What the hell do you think you're doing?'

Stone shrinks back. For all his size he knows his master's voice when he hears it.

'I thought—'

Creed is furious. The veins stand out on his temples. His eyes bulge threateningly.

'It isn't up to you to think, Colin. Do you understand? You don't think.'

Stone looks shaken.

'Leave that to me,' says Creed. 'This isn't a game. There'll be no dressing up in brown uniforms. There'll be no German marching songs, no Hitler birthday parties, not even a mention of the Führer. We're mainstream now. That's the way power lies, not with your childish antics. We want to be the third party in this country within a decade. We want MPs, councillors – and with every mosque that's built and every Islamic school that's opened the Muslims are paving the way for us. We're going to play it straight, all the way to Westminster. Do you understand?'

Stone is staring back, wishing he could crawl inside his own skin. Creed's voice hardens. This is the side he is careful not to show in his TV appearances. There is more than a touch of steel in it.

'I asked you if you understood me, man?'

Creed knows that, if he is to build any sort of organisation in this town, this two-bit bully is the miserable excuse of a man he has to knock into shape.

'Yes, John,' Stone stammers. 'I understand.'

'Now,' says Creed, his features relaxing, 'clear your head and direct me to your house. There's work to do and tomorrow I want to be rested and fresh.'

As the car's rear lights disappear over the hill at the top of Ravensmoor Road a group of youths are gathering round the mosque at the bottom.

'What are we stopping here for?' asks Liam, glancing up at the building.

'What do you think?' says Daz.

He pulls out a spray can and starts to spray a slogan in foot-high letters: R . . . E . . . M . . .

'What are you writing?' asks Liam, looking nervously up and down the road.

'Remember September 11th. You know some of these characters agree with what happened? They think old Osama Bin Liner's a hero. I bet half of them actually cheered when the planes hit.'

Liam doesn't answer. He isn't political, never has been.

All he wants is a laugh, a good time with his mates. But this is Daz and Jason's kick now. They seem to get a buzz out of it. Liam wishes he did. The old man rants on the same way they do from time to time, but Liam doesn't pay much attention to him either. He supposes his dad makes some kind of sense, but he can't see why he has to get so excited about it. It's just boring, like everything else.

The slogan is taking shape:

R . . . E . . . M . . . E . . . M . . .

But Liam has spotted a police car.

'Coppers,' he says, shoving his elbow into Daz's ribs.

Daz looks sadly at his handiwork. He doesn't want to leave it unfinished.

'Get a move on, will you?' says Liam. Mum cracked up the time he got caught shoplifting. Imagine what she'd do if he was picked up again!

'Better go,' says Jason, adding his weight to Liam's plea. 'I think they're watching us.'

A moment later the three of them and two others from the Lion are walking briskly down the road. The police car slows, cruising alongside the youths for a moment before driving on.

'That was close,' says Daz.

'Fancy going back to finish the job?' says Jason.

'Let's give Liam the casting vote,' says Daz. 'Are you up for it?'

Liam winks. He has just experienced the danger rush. It was fun.

Mike Kelly is reading in the living room, enjoying the peace. If Dad and Liam were in the TV would be blaring by now. But it's only him and Mum so the set is switched off. Mum's ironing the old man's Oakfield Town shirt. Mike remembers when Dad used to take him to every Oakie home game. Even after the time with the Eid decorations, he gave the old man a second chance. That's what love is all about – second chances.

But his love for the old man died the night Mike walked in on him slapping Mum all round the house, reducing her to a mewling, sobbing animal. That night, as ten-year-old Mike cried himself to sleep, he swore that he would never go anywhere with Dad again. He even prayed for him to die in his sleep – that's how desolate he was. But his prayer wasn't answered. They never are. That was six years ago. Single-minded and self-disciplined as ever, Mike has kept his word about his father. These days it takes him all his time to even talk to him. The old get makes it easier by going out on the ale most nights, pickling his rotting, soured brain in alcohol.

'Worried about our Liam?' Mike asks.

Mum nods. 'I can't help it. I never know where he is these days or what he's getting up to. He doesn't tell me anything.'

'I know what you mean.'

Mike and Liam are as different as chalk and cheese. Mike's the mummy's boy. He is in the top set in every subject, one of the bright stars at Moorside High, on target for straight A grades. Younger brother Liam takes after Dad. He thinks with his fists. Baby-faced as he is, nobody crosses him. He has taken on and beaten lads two years older. At school he has completely switched off – a teachers' nightmare. Mum dreads parents' evenings. There hasn't been a single item of good news since Liam was twelve.

'He won't be long,' says Mike. 'Are you sure you don't want me to have a scoot round the usual haunts?'

Mum hesitates for a moment then shakes her head. 'Better not.'

The words are no sooner out of her mouth than the door goes.

'Liam?'

'That's me.'

'Why didn't you come home after school? What did you do for your tea?'

'Chippy.'

'Who've you been with?'

'Mates.'

Mum looks wearily at Mike then tries one last question.

'What have you been doing all this while, Liam?'

'Hanging round. The usual.' He tosses his jacket over the arm of the settee and walks to the door.

'I'm going to bed.'

'Goodnight, son,' says Mum.

'Goodnight, Liam,' says Mike.

Liam doesn't answer.

A mile up Ravensmoor Road John Creed is standing in the spare room of Colin Stone's three-bedroomed semi. He wrinkles his nose with distaste. Another folding bed. Still, it's better than the child's cabin bed they gave him in Coventry last week. The mattress was covered with a plastic sheet and smelled of pee. He slips off his coat and punches his home number into his mobile.

'Hi, Angela,' he says. 'It's me.'

His wife's voice crackles into the mobile.

'The local branch? Complete amateurs. Stone? Built like a brick wall, but he's a sad case, complete loner. Yes, he belongs to the old school, living in the past. Streetfighting's about all he's good for. It's a wonder he isn't sporting a little black moustache. No, there are no major problems. I'll soon lick them into shape.'

She asks how long he will be in Oakfield.

'This time? A week, maybe two. I've been through back issues of the local rag. The place is a powder keg. I just need to find a few people who know what they're doing. You never know, Colin might be able to learn. Funnier things have happened.'

At the end of the call there is time for a personal note.

'Yes, I love you too. Give the kids a hug for me. I'll call you tomorrow night.'

Mike is brushing his teeth when the old man comes staggering in. Listening to his father banging around downstairs, Mike brushes so hard his gums bleed. He curses and washes his mouth out with water from the tap.

'Drunken old beggar,' he says.

He steps out on to the landing and listens, half-expecting to hear the sound of a slap. But Sean Kelly is in a good mood tonight. Mike hears him singing. It's an Irish ballad.

Odd, that, thinks Mike – the nearest the old fool has ever got to Ireland is a day trip to Liverpool. Mum is giggling. They're dancing! Hasn't she got any pride? All the grief she has taken from Dad and she lets him take her in his arms. How the hell can you love somebody who is just as likely to knock you into next week? Mike stamps up to his room in disgust and throws himself on his bed. But as he looks up at the cracked ceiling and the dingy, cobwebbed lightshade, he remembers the dark-eyed girl from the library. Life is so ugly but there has been one moment of beauty in this dismal evening. That's enough to live another day.

A mile down the hill Rabia says goodnight to her parents. At the top of the stairs there is a small window that looks out on to the north side of the Triangle. Between the terraced houses she can see the end of Ravensmoor Road. In her mind's eye she is back there willing her father to come and get her. She relives the boys running away and the wonderful sight of Dad pulling up in his car. But behind Suhail Khan's broad shoulders the rivulets of darkness are still spreading, moving through the streets, spilling into the main roads of the town. Hatred and mistrust stalk the darkness. At the beginning of this holy month of Ramadan, when Rabia should be focusing on how lucky she is to have her health and be living in a warm, loving home, thinking of the millions who starve every day of their lives, something mean and wrong is being born out there, threatening to break into her life. Fear did not leave when those boys ran. It's still there, crouching in the shadows of the town, and it is growing.

2
Grievances

It is just after nightfall five days later and Diane Khan is starving or, as she has just told Tillymint the cat, 'I could eat two tabbies on toast.' Tillymint seemed to get the gist, scampering off in the direction of the railway line.

Diane has never converted to Islam, but she agreed early in her marriage to have her children raised as Muslims. Though her parents only ever manage to get to church for weddings and funerals they still went ballistic when they heard the news. In spite of their protests Diane has stuck to her guns. Seventeen years on, however grudgingly, the family has had to learn to live with it. Diane has made her choice. When Suhail, Tahir and Rabia fast, she fasts with them.

Still turning memories of past quarrels with her parents over in her mind, Diane drinks a glass of fresh orange, picks at the bowl of figs and looks forward to breaking her fast. They will eat as soon as Tahir gets home from the gym.

Diane smiles as she remembers what he was like when he first started fasting. He was still at primary school at the time and he didn't find it easy, especially when he knew his mother had occasional lapses while he was out at school. He was always outraged if he found biscuit crumbs where she had been sitting.

'How come you can cheat?' he would wail, roti, chappatis, dhals, samosas and tikkas marching temptingly over his taste buds.

Then he would drone on about how hungry he felt. In the end Diane was forced to keep her fast as strictly as Suhail and the kids.

Rabia walks into the kitchen and finds her mother staring out at the little back yard smiling to herself.

'What are you smiling at?' she asks, already smiling herself. They are about as close as mother and daughter can be. One smiles and the other smiles with her. One cries and they end up weeping together.

'I was just thinking about Tahir,' Diane explains. 'Do you remember what he was like when he first started fasting?'

Rabia laughs. 'Do I? He was so miserable.'

'I know,' says Diane. 'He wasn't a very good Muslim at that time, was he?'

She allows the smile to fade slowly. Her son is a good Muslim now, and getting better every day. In fact, it is Tahir who pushes Suhail to go along to the mosque. For some reason, though she hates herself for thinking it, that scares Diane. Her son is growing into a proud, single-minded individual. Carry your head as high as Tahir does and somebody is bound to want to knock it off.

'He's so different these days,' she says, remembering the loving, impulsive boy he was. 'Such a serious young man.'

It's true. Over the last couple of years he has taken his obligations seriously. He never complains. When he fasts for Ramadan he does so with astonishing self-control for somebody who loves his food so much. As he has grown into a young man he has shown greater and greater pride in his Pakistani ancestry. Painfully aware that Oakfield's communities are pulling apart, he seems to be drawing his Muslim identity around him as a protective cloak. That other part of him, the part she gave him, seems to be shrinking by the day. Diane sometimes wonders if she hasn't become something of an embarrassment to him.

'Tahir's all right,' says Rabia. 'Just a bit *earnest*, that's all.'

'That's a nice way of putting it,' says Diane, winking. 'Now say what you really mean.'

Rabia grins. 'OK then, pompous. You know that new top I bought?'

'For Sofia's birthday party?'

Rabia nods. 'Do you know what he said to me?'

Diane shakes her head.

'Only that I was showing too much.'

'Never!'

Rabia nods. 'He did. He meant it too. He thinks I'm *immodest*.'

Diane shakes her head.

'He's just getting that from his friends. Honestly, you'd think he never looked at a girl. Remember last summer.'

'The girl on the beach?'

'Yes, the one in the bikini. It was lust at first sight. His eyes were out on stalks. He didn't think *she* was showing too much.'

Tahir walks in at that very moment. He is wearing that studied, serious expression he has been perfecting. Rabia and Diane immediately burst out laughing.

'What's the matter with you two?' he demands.

'Oh, nothing.'

He gives them both a suspicious look, then adds: 'When do we eat?'

That only sets them off again. They laugh until they have forgotten why they ever started.

John Creed is also eating. He is finishing a cheese and onion roll at the Lion. He doesn't enjoy the laddish, smoke-filled atmosphere of the place. He hates the thud of darts and the arguments about football. He would rather be listening to Wagner with a tumbler of whisky than sinking bitter with these oiks. The things you do for the cause! He sips his warm beer and watches Colin Stone shepherding the dozen or so faithful upstairs. Stone feels Creed's eyes on him.

'Not much of a turnout,' says Stone, glancing at his watch.

Stone hates all these meetings. What he wants is action. But the papers seem to say the Patriotic League is going places, so he bites his tongue and gets on with the boring stuff.

'I expected Daz and Jason to be here at least,' he says.

Creed looks none the wiser for the mention of Daz and Jason.

'You met them the first night,' Stone explains. 'The foot soldiers.'

'Oh,' says Creed, unimpressed. 'Them.'

He finishes his roll and follows Stone up to the function room. It is an all-male audience.

'Gentlemen,' Stone says, opening the meeting, 'welcome to tonight's meeting of the Oakfield branch of the Patriotic League.'

His voice has already betrayed his disappointment at the attendance. An older man at the front glances around. The dozen members of the bored-looking audience are dotted about the forty or so chairs. The atmosphere is distinctly despondent.

'I know,' Stone says apologetically, 'it isn't much of an attendance this evening.' He is about to continue in the same vein when Creed interrupts and takes the reins of the meeting.

'I beg to disagree, Mr Chairman,' he begins. 'Personally, I don't look at a glass and say it's half empty.'

'Not unless it's a pint of best bitter,' one of the audience calls out.

Creed smiles indulgently, wondering what cave that Neanderthal crawled out of, then continues, 'I would rather say it is half full.'

The confidence with which he delivers the line and the certainty his listeners hear in his voice change the course of the meeting.

'So when I look at you, I don't see all the empty chairs and wonder about the missing people.' He makes eye contact with every one of his audience in turn, making them feel special.

'Rather I see the commitment of those who are here. You are the skeleton on which we can put muscle and flesh. I think it was Archimedes who said that if you have a lever you can lift the world. My friends, you are that lever.'

This earns him a ripple of applause, even if few in the room have even heard of Archimedes and at least one of them thinks he's Kylie Minogue's new boyfriend.

'We have a great cause,' he says, 'but we face a formid-able challenge.'

He proceeds to outline the threat of militant Islam to the British way of life. He talks of terror in the skies and the destruction of the twin towers.

'But our enemy doesn't just use the bomb,' Creed thunders. 'Oh no, militant Islam takes over quietly. Shops that once bore the name Jones are now called Iqbal's. British boys and girls are made to celebrate Ramadan at school. I tell you, our children will soon know more about Saladin than Richard the Lionheart.'

This has Stone clapping until his palms hurt.

'Imagine if they were forced to celebrate Christmas,' Creed snarls, earning a ripple of applause. 'What next?' he asks. 'Before you know it, they'll have us *all* fasting.'

As he piles up the grievances the members of the audience start to murmur their approval. With every repetition of the word *British* they become more animated, led on by Stone's example. Before long they are cheering him to the echo and stamping their feet. When Creed says defiantly that he, for one, won't be foregoing *his* turkey and sprouts this Yuletide, there is a roar of approval. In their minds there is a thin red line guarding the Christmas lunch. As Creed sits down to a standing ovation, Daz and Jason walk in.

'And what's more,' he says, looking right at them, 'the moment our young men learn a little self-discipline we few will become many. We happy few who won on the field of Agincourt can win again on the streets of Oakfield.'

'Agincourt?' Daz whispers. 'Is that the old people's bungalows?'

Jason shushes him. John Creed is drawing to a close.

'The bigger the lever,' he says, 'the greater the force we will exert.'

The words are met by an even stronger round of applause.

'Then,' says Creed, his voice rising over the noise, 'we will start to change the world!'

When Tahir pops his head round the living-room door to say he is going out later, Diane and Rabia are laughing again.

'What's the matter with you two now?' he asks.

'Don't worry, love,' Diane says. 'It isn't you this time.'

Tahir's face clouds. 'What do you mean, *this time*?'

Diane and Rabia exchange amused glances.

'Don't worry about it,' said Rabia, barely able to suppress the laughter that is again bubbling up inside her.

Tahir gives them another long, hard look then glances at the TV screen. The video of *Meet the Parents* is running and Ben Stiller has just accidentally strewn the ashes of Robert de Niro's mother over the carpet. Tahir stares disapprovingly then retreats from the room, shaking his head. The first time he saw it he laughed himself sore. Now he asks how they can watch Hollywood movies when America is bombing Muslims.

Diane sighs. 'I do wish Tahir would get over this phase,' she says. 'Maybe he thinks *laughter* is immodest now.'

Liam arrives home just as Mike is finishing washing the dishes.

'You're home early,' says Mike.

'I know.'

'Something wrong?'

Liam shrugs. 'It's Jason and Daz. They've gone to the Lion again.'

'Why? What's at the Lion?'

'A meeting,' says Liam.

'Don't tell me,' says Mike, 'they've taken up stamp-collecting. Philately for the intellectually challenged.'

'No,' says Liam, not seeing the joke. 'It's some outfit called the Patriotic League.'

Mike stiffens.

'You've heard of them then?' says Liam.

'Aren't they a bunch of raving Nazis?' Mike says. 'Liam, you've got to stay away from them. They're nothing but trouble.'

'Done,' says Liam. 'They're boring.'

Boring? Mike can think of better words to describe the Patriotic League.

'So how long have Jason and Daz been going to these meetings?' he asks.

'Dunno,' says Liam, searching the fridge for something to eat. 'A few weeks.'

'They don't know what they're getting into.'

'They do, you know,' says Liam. 'They know all about it. Daz says the League's going to clean up Oakfield.'

'Clean up?' says Mike. 'What does he mean by that?'

'Put it back the way it was,' says Liam. 'Before it started going downhill.'

He knows he is making Mike uneasy and he is enjoying his big brother's discomfort. Making Mike squirm like this is a way of paying him back, just a little, for all the years he has had to live in his shadow. Honestly, Mum thinks the sun shines out of him.

'Do you want to know what got Daz involved?' Liam asks, keen to annoy his brother even more.

'Go on,' says Mike. 'Enlighten me.'

'There was this gang of Asians hanging round North Park. That's where Daz's grandad plays bowls. They dug up the bowling green. Now they've ruined it for everybody.'

Mike takes the bait. 'How does he know it was Asians?'

'Who else would it be?'

Mike shakes his head. Liam is sounding just like the old man. They could found a limited company: Knuckle-draggers Incorporated.

'I bet they're just blaming it on those Asian lads. That's

the way it goes in this town. If there weren't any Asians to blame we'd have to invent them.'

Liam has started taking notice. This isn't so boring after all. All these years Mike has been so superior, now he is definitely rattled. This Patriotic League stuff is a good way of winding up his older, more successful brother.

'Daz says his grandad saw them do it. Why would he say that if it wasn't true?'

'Because he's a racist,' says Mike, 'just like your stupid mates.'

He knows right away that he has said the wrong thing. Liam's no angel, but he's never mouthed off in quite this way before. What's needed is patience, but Mike is all out. The quarrel escalates rapidly. By the time Mary walks in from her cleaning job at the dentist's the brothers are going at it hammer and tongs.

'Only somebody who's really thick would swallow that load of rubbish,' says Mike.

'Are you calling me thick?'

'You said it, Liam.'

Instantly he wishes he could retract the comment. Liam gets extra reading support in the school library first thing every morning. He hates it, especially when Mum keeps suggesting he borrow some of Mike's books.

'I'm going back out,' says Liam, smarting from Mike's insult. At the door he hits back the only way he can. *'Paki-lover!'*

Mike wants to kick himself. Way to go, Michael! he thinks. If Liam wasn't interested in the League to start with he certainly is now.

John Creed is standing outside the Lion chatting to Jason and Daz when Liam arrives. Creed smiles and makes a point of drawing him into the conversation. He can smell a possible recruit and he likes the lean, hungry look of this young Cassius.

'Are you interested in what we've got to say, Liam?' he asks.

'Could be,' says Liam, flattered by the interest. Wouldn't Mr High and Mighty Mike Kelly love that!

'You should come along to the next meeting,' says Creed.

'I can't. I'm too young to go in the pub.'

'Only if you're drinking,' says Creed. 'I'll have a word with the landlord. I'm sure Jack won't mind. After all, you'll be upstairs, not in the bar. So do you want to come along?'

Liam sees Jason and Daz looking at him. At least he will be with his mates, not trailing round on his own. Plus it will be out of the rain and the cold. He remembers the buzz he got evading the coppers.

'Sure, why not? Count me in.'

'Good man,' says Creed.

Jason and Daz slap Liam on the back. 'Another recruit to the cause,' they crow.

Liam grins broadly. Suddenly he feels part of something.

Tahir has gone down to The Gulam with his friends. So long as the restaurant is quiet the owner Rashid lets them sit around a table talking. That means they usually have somewhere warm to hang out until about nine when it starts to fill up.

'Did you hear what Tahir said to Freddie today?' says Nasir. 'Freddie' is Peter Starr, their PE teacher.

'No,' says Khalid, 'but I'm sure you're going to tell me.'

'Well,' says Nasir, 'it's like this. We're in the gym and Freddie tells Tahir to get up the rope. You know what Tahir says?'

Khalid shakes his head.

' "Ask nicely," that's what he says. You should have seen Freddie's face! So he *orders* Tahir up the rope.'

Khalid turns to Tahir. 'Did you go?'

Tahir grins. 'What do you think?'

'Anyway,' says Nasir, annoyed at being interrupted in mid-flow, 'Freddie tells Tahir to get up the rope or he'll be suspended. You know what Tahir does? He looks up at the top of the rope and says: "Surely if I climb up there I'll be suspended anyway?" Get it? Rope. Suspended. Sharp as a blade, our Tahir.'

'So were you?' asks Khalid.

'Was I what?'

'Suspended.'

'No. Freddie's all hot air. He's always threatening detentions and stuff. Never does anything about it. He's a prat.'

They exchange more school stories. The volume rises with each tale.

'Hey, tone it down,' says Nasir. 'Rashid's giving us the stare.'

There are a few people in the restaurant now. Three

noisy teenagers are bad for business. All they ever buy is a few soft drinks. Rashid is willing them to leave with his eyes.

'It's all right,' says Tahir. 'We get the message. We're going.'

They spill on to the pavement, laughing and joking. Two white lads their own age are coming from the opposite direction. They are starting to look edgy. Tahir can't resist taking a rise out of them. He approaches the more nervous of the two boys and blocks his way.

'Look, I don't want any trouble,' says the boy.

'You think this is trouble?' says Tahir. 'I'll show you trouble.'

The boy flinches in advance of the anticipated aggro. Tahir responds by stamping his foot and shouting: 'Boo!'

The white boys take to their heels. Tahir and his friends roar with laughter.

Daz is outraged.

'Is Mike calling my grandad a liar?' he demands. 'Because if he is, he'd better come and say it to my face.'

'He makes me puke,' says Liam, still angry at Mike. 'The pigsty we have to live in, and he wants all these foreigners coming over here taking our houses.'

He's heard his dad come out with stuff like this a thousand times before – how all the money goes to the Triangle – but he hasn't really paid much attention, at least not until now. Suddenly it's all starting to make sense. His lousy school, his lousy life – now he's got someone to blame.

'I know he's your brother and all,' says Jason, 'but I hate people like your Mike worse than the Asians. I mean, they're just doing the best for their own kind, aren't they? Your Mike, he's got no excuse. He's just a lousy traitor.'

Liam looks down Ravensmoor Road. His eyes come to rest on the Triangle. Jason's right.

'It's time you started telling Mike what's what,' says Daz. 'There's a war coming and he's going to have to take sides.'

'War?' says Liam, an alarm going off in his head. 'What sort of war?'

'Don't you listen to anything we tell you?' says Jason. 'The Asians have been taking this town over bit by bit. Now that John Creed's here we're going to start taking it back off them.'

Liam frowns. Since the quarrel with Mike he has been happy to talk the talk. But a war? Nobody mentioned anything about a war.

Colin Stone is the man responsible for the talk of war. But as he listens to John Creed he realises he is going to have to start singing a different tune, in public at least.

'There are local elections in May,' Creed is saying. 'We ought to put up a candidate, maybe two.'

'What about you?' says Stone. Elections aren't his style.

He prefers marching through a crowd of hostile demonstrators or fighting running battles to licking envelopes.

'No,' says Creed. 'I think it should be an Oakfield man – somebody like yourself, Colin.'

'Me?'

Stone didn't expect to be put forward as the *candidate*. He is flattered, even a bit excited. Nobody has ever listened to him before, not really. He has always been a loner, an oddball, good only to be used as a heavy. This is his chance to get noticed, to be somebody.

'But if you do stand,' Creed tells him, 'you've got to remember what I've been telling you. There can't be any of this street-fighting stuff. On our platforms we've got to be seen as the little man's party, defenders of the underdog. We've got to have an issue, a grievance. The programme boils down to this: the enemy is Muslim fundamentalism.'

'That's true though, isn't it?' says Stone. 'Look at the council. All the money gets spent on the Triangle. They never put anything into the Moorside.'

Creed looks interested. 'Have you got any proof of that?'

'Proof?'

'Yes, a few good examples we can campaign around.'

Colin stares down at the living-room carpet. Creed shakes his head. The man's elevator obviously doesn't go all the way to the top floor.

'This is *exactly* why the League's so weak here, Colin. You make the right sort of noises, but you've no evidence to back it up. Without facts it's just a load of hot air. We need something we can show people. "Look at this," we've got to be able to say, "proof that the Asians are getting everything and you're getting nothing." Think, man!'

Colin is wearing a pained expression. Just when he was starting to feel good about himself, too.

'Make your mind up, Colin. You've got a nice little town

here. British still means something. Do you know what it's like in London where I live? Coffee-coloured people – that's what I see every day. The Tube is full of them. Down there the multi-racial society has already arrived. Half the people are like overmixed cocktails. They've got so many races in them they've forgotten what their real origins are. Is that what you want here in Oakfield?'

Stone shakes his head. 'Of course not.'

'Then what we need is a grievance, Colin – a grievance.'

Rabia is on her way to bed when Tahir comes through the front door. Without any warning she turns to confront him.

'What do you think you're doing?'

Tahir is taken by surprise. 'I don't know what you mean.'

'No? What if I jog your memory a little? What were you up to outside The Gulam tonight?'

Tahir continues to frown, unsure what she is getting at.

'Those boys you were pushing around.'

'How do you know about that?'

'Nasreen phoned me. She was on the other side of the road with her parents. She'd just told them she knew you, then you started kicking off. She was so embarrassed.'

'I don't see what it's got to do with her.'

'She's a friend. She obviously thinks I ought to know my brother's acting like an idiot.'

'Who are you calling an idiot?'

Rabia rolls her eyes. 'You. Imagine if it was the other way round.'

'Meaning?'

'White boys pushing *you* around.'

Tahir sets his face hard. 'That doesn't take much imagination. It usually is.'

'Oh, I get it. Some of the local lads get jumped by racist thugs, so it's fair game for you and your mates to act exactly the same way.'

Tahir scowls. 'It isn't the same.'

'No? So how's it different? Tell me that.'

'Whites come down Clive Road all the time and there's no bother. How many Asians could say the same if they went up the Moorside?'

'But those boys came down Clive Road and *you* gave them bother, Tahir.'

Suddenly Tahir just wants to be left alone. 'It was only a bit of fun, Rabia. We didn't mean them any harm.'

'Is that the way they'll see it?'

Another scowl. 'What were they doing there anyway?' says Tahir.

Rabia throws up her hands. 'How do I know? Since when did they need a passport, Tahir? Maybe they were going for a meal – I don't know. Half the people you get in The Gulam are white. Maybe you want Mum to keep off the streets as well. Tell you what, let's declare a curfew on all the pink and beige people.'

'Don't be stupid.'

'No, Tahir,' Rabia snaps, 'I'm not the one who's being stupid. You're the one who's putting on an act to make your mates forget you're half-white.'

'Act!' cries Tahir. 'What do you mean, act? If I go up the Moorside estate, do you think they'll see somebody with a Muslim dad and a white mum? No, they'll see *a Paki*.'

'They're not all like that.'

'Mum's family is.'

For the first time Tahir has succeeded in getting under his sister's guard. As a little girl she was desperate to earn her grandma's whole-hearted affection but never quite managed it.

'Yes,' says Rabia, putting the painful memories out of her mind. 'And in spite of everything Mum fell in love with Dad and stayed in love with him. Nothing that anyone said made any difference. Not all white people are racist.'

She is about to go but Tahir steps in front of her.

'Listen,' he says. 'Maybe what you say is true, but do you know how many times I've been picked on or insulted by white boys? Remember last year when I had that new jacket? I went to town and somebody spat all down the back. Can you imagine how that feels?'

'Of course I do,' says Rabia, insulted that he even has to ask the question. 'There are some disgusting people about, Tahir. I get hostility too, you know. But that doesn't mean you can go taking it out on some poor kids on the street who probably haven't got a racist bone in their body.'

'You don't know what you're talking about,' says Tahir, starting to go. 'Try finding many whites in this town who aren't racist. They might enjoy the odd curry but that doesn't mean much. They still don't want us living next door, do they?'

'Oh, you're just picking a fight for the sake of it,' says Rabia. 'The reason you haven't met any non-racist whites is you go to Oakfield High. We don't get white kids at our school, just like Moorside doesn't get Asians. This town's hardly the melting pot, is it?'

'Anyway,' says Tahir, unimpressed by his sister's arguments, 'you're a girl. You've never had to put up with the kind of crap I have.'

'Shows just how wrong you can be,' Rabia retorts angrily.

Tahir whips round. 'What's that supposed to mean?'

Nice one, thinks Rabia, wishing she could reach out and

pop the words back in her mouth. And I was the one telling Dad not to give the game away about the other night. Oh well, confession time.

'If you must know, I got roughed up on Ravensmoor Road.'

'When?'

'The night of the Book Award meeting.'

Drawn by the raised voices, Diane arrives.

'What's going on here?'

'Rabia was attacked,' says Tahir, outraged.

'It wasn't exactly an attack,' says Diane.

Tahir stares in disbelief. 'So you know about it?'

'Yes,' says Diane. 'I know.'

'And Dad?'

Diane nods. 'Him too.'

'So I'm the only one to be kept in the dark about this?'

'Is it any wonder?' cries Rabia. 'Who'd want to say anything to Mr Angry? You'll only go blowing a blood vessel. You can be really embarrassing, Tahir.'

'You're crazy,' says Tahir. 'You're all completely crazy.'

Diane watches him. First those boys on Ravensmoor Road, now this furious row. Suddenly she feels as if there are invisible hands tugging at her family, trying to pull it apart.

Sean Kelly is staggering along Ravensmoor Road, muttering to himself. He has just been barred from the Stag's Head.

'What did I do? I mean *what* did I do? Funny sort of a country where a man can't drink in his own boozer any more.'

What Sean did was to hit a student so hard in the stomach he doubled up on the floor, but somehow that fact has got lost in the drink-haze. The student won't forget the night a pub crawl took him into Sean Kelly's local. Sean has spent the last twenty-five years hauling animal carcasses around the abattoir and he is powerfully and compactly built.

'Well,' says Sean, having a conversation with what's left of his own conscience, 'he asked for it. Shouting the odds about things he doesn't know anything about!'

Sean is feeling sorry for himself. He reels along Ravensmoor until he sees a gang of lads outside the Lion. The Lion? Doesn't Liam hang round here?

'And there's the lad himself. Liam! Hey, Liam!'

For a moment he thinks he sees a look of dismay on Liam's face. No, it couldn't be. He's read it wrong. Mike's the stuck-up one. No, thank goodness for Liam, a lad's lad, the apple of his old dad's eye.

'Liam!'

Great! Liam thinks to himself. Now the old beggar has to show me up right in front of Creed.

'Somebody you know?' Creed asks, an amused look spreading across his face.

Daz is laughing himself silly. 'That's his dad. Proper old alchy, isn't he, Liam?'

'Just look at that nose,' says Jason. 'More holes than a pincushion.'

Half the Moorside has seen Sean Kelly reeling up his path and swaying in front of his door, trying to get the key in the lock. But for his fists, he would be a figure of fun.

Liam ignores Daz and walks towards his father.

'Keep it down, Dad, will you?'

Sean puts a finger to his lips and starts to chuckle.

'Don't wake the kids,' he slurs.

'Kids?' says Liam, willing him to shut up. 'What kids?'

Sean throws an arm round Liam's shoulder. 'Introduce me to your friends, son.'

Liam can feel his insides crawling.

'Promise you won't show me up, Dad.'

Sean jumps back, unsteady on his feet.

'What did you say?'

His face has turned angry. Liam flinches.

'You tell me what you just said.'

'Dad, knock it off, will you?'

'Are you listening to this?' Sean yells. 'My own son's ashamed of me! What's the matter, Liam? Getting as stuck-up as your high and mighty brother, are you?'

Liam wants the ground to open up beneath him.

Suhail pulls up in front of the house.

'Your shift isn't over yet, is it?' Diane asks when he walks in.

'A drunk threw up on the back seat,' he says. 'I'll have to clean the cab before I can go out again.'

He starts filling a bucket with hot soapy water.

'Where are the kids?'

He notices Diane hesitate.

'Go on,' he says. 'What is it?'

'Tahir knows about the other night, when Rabia was followed.'

'How?'

'They had a bit of a barney. She got angry and blurted it out.'

'Don't tell me,' says Suhail with a sigh. 'He wants to get up a posse and go looking for them. I wish he'd put as much effort into his school work as he does into putting the world to rights.'

A couple of weeks ago Tahir wanted to go on a demonstration about the war in Afghanistan. Suhail and Diane said no. They were worried about trouble.

'Has he calmed down yet?'

'I don't know,' says Diane. 'He's been shut up in his room ever since.'

The thump of Tahir's CD player can be heard from upstairs.

'So I hear,' says Suhail.

'Anyway,' says Diane, 'you'd better get that cab cleaned if you want to take any more fares tonight.'

Suhail sighs. 'I don't feel like going out again. What I'd give to be back working in the mill!'

'I know, love,' says Diane, 'but those days are gone. If the taxi is all we've got then you've got to get back out there, Tiger.'

Suhail nods. He picks up the bucket, gives a low growl and makes a claw with his right hand.

'Here I go, tiger on the prowl.'

Outside the Lion John Creed has worked his charms on Sean Kelly, who is out of his belligerent phase and sinking into self-pity.

'Have you got any kids, Mr Creed?'

'Two,' says Creed. 'Both girls.'

'You're lucky,' says Sean. 'Don't have lads. They give you nothing but grief.'

The little crowd outside the Lion has broken up. Creed and the Kellys are there, so are Daz and Jason.

'Sorry about this, Mr Creed,' Liam whispers. 'He's had a skinful.'

Creed winks. While Sean sags drunkenly against the wall, Creed takes Liam into his confidence.

'My father was an embarrassment to me,' he whispers. 'I know exactly how you must be feeling.'

Liam is amazed. Creed has been on TV and in the papers and here he is taking an interest in a teenage lad. Creed squeezes Liam's arm sympathetically and turns to Sean.

'Come on, Mr Kelly. Let's get you home.'

He looks around. 'Where's Colin? Has he gone?'

Liam nods. 'He said he'd see you back at the house.'

'It'll have to be a taxi then,' says Creed. He sounds annoyed that Stone has left. 'Run in and tell Jack, Liam. He'll ring a cab for us.'

Five minutes later Suhail is pulling up outside the Lion. He isn't too happy about the fare. The pub is a notorious watering hole for racists. A couple of drivers have been assaulted after picking up there. Some refuse to go, but beggars can't be choosers. Rabia is doing well at school. If she goes on to university the family will need all the money they can get. Suhail winds down his window and speaks to the three men on the pavement.

'Did you ring for a taxi?'

Creed and Liam exchange glances.

'Yes,' says Creed after a moment's hesitation. 'We're the ones who called.'

'Do you need a hand with your friend?' asks Suhail.

'That's all right,' says Creed coldly. 'We can manage.'

Something in Creed's voice makes Suhail want to get this group to their destination as soon as possible. He is already thinking about what Imran on control said the other night: call for help and I'll have the other drivers on the way to give assistance in a couple of minutes.

'OK, driver,' says Creed, once he and Liam have man-oeuvred the snoring Sean into the back seat. 'We're ready.'

'What's the address?' asks Suhail.

'Fifteen, Saxon Avenue,' says Liam. 'What about you, Mr Creed?'

'That's all right, Liam,' says Creed. 'I can walk from your house. It isn't far, is it?'

'No,' says Liam. 'Less than five minutes. I'll show you.'

Suhail indicates and pulls away from the kerb.

'The evening paper is in the side pocket,' Suhail says. 'Help yourself. There's a light switch to your left.'

Creed leans across to Liam. 'Now we're reduced to taking charity from our Muslim friends,' he says, just loud enough for Suhail to hear.

Mike hears the commotion at the front door. Mum is struggling with Dad, trying to get him inside.

'Do you want a hand?' he asks.

'Thanks, love,' says Mum. 'Our Liam brought him home.'

'So where's Liam now?'

'He's giving some fellow directions.'

Mike wonders who Liam knows that can't find his way round Oakfield.

'Fellow? What fellow?'

Mum shakes her head. 'I didn't get a proper look at him. He was well spoken though, a real gentleman.'

'A gentleman?' says Mike. 'Round here?'

'I know,' says Mum. 'I was surprised.'

Mike frowns. Gentleman? It doesn't add up.

Suhail doesn't know it yet, but Creed has taken the evening paper from the cab. Creed leaves Liam at the top of Stone's street and hurries towards the double-glazed door. He runs the details of the front page story over in his mind: *Unfair! Local councillor's protest.* He has already committed most of the story to memory. This is the gist of it:

Independent councillor Martin Roberts is launching a campaign against the council's decision to fund the forthcoming

Eid celebrations. Councillor Roberts, who represents the Moorside ward, told the Chronicle, *'It's outrageous. We're going to have the Pakistani flag flying over the town hall at a time when the youth club in my ward is threatened with closure. Oakfield council needs to get its priorities right. It's time people stood up and were counted.'*

Creed reaches the front door and rings the bell. When Stone doesn't appear he starts hammering on the door and ringing the bell repeatedly. Stone answers. He is wrapped in a dressing gown, his thinning hair slicked back.

'Sorry, John, I was having a shower.'

Creed thrusts the copy of the *Chronicle* into his hands. 'Read that.'

'I don't–'

Creed is impatient. Stone hasn't got the wits he was born with. Not like young Liam. Creed likes the lad. If he was a bit brighter he could be a young John Creed.

'I said, read it!'

Stone snaps to attention and runs his eyes over the article.

'Well?' says Creed.

'Yes, it's wrong, but that's the way it is round here.'

'Don't you get it, man?' cries Creed. 'This is it!'

Stone looks out of his depth.

'This is it, Colin – firm proof that our Muslim friends are running the show in this town. This is what we've been waiting for. We've got our grievance.'

3
Among Friends

Two days after Creed read the newspaper report Liam, Daz and Jason are at the youth club. Normally they wouldn't be seen dead there, but Creed virtually ordered them to go.

'Full of nerds' is Jason's considered verdict.

But their personal feelings aren't important. John Creed says Moorside youth club is important so here they are, making sacrifices for the cause. He seems to have appointed Liam leader of the expedition.

'We could always have a game of snooker,' Liam says.

Jason nods. No way can snooker be considered even remotely nerdy.

'Is it OK if we have a table?' Liam asks the youth worker, a man in his early thirties called Bobby McAllister.

'Sure,' says Bobby, obviously glad to see some new faces at the club. 'Help yourself.'

'I hear you're getting closed down,' says Liam.

'We read about it in the *Chronicle*,' says Daz.

'Nothing's certain,' says Bobby, 'but closure is a possibility.'

'How come?'

'We had an inspection. The building's below standard. The council says the repairs will cost too much so they want to demolish the building.'

The building is Moorside Community Centre, a flat-roofed Sixties construction. It stands in waste ground at the back of the estate overlooked by the dark ridge of the Pennines. The rain from the hills has been spilling down over the faulty guttering for years, leaving long streaks of green mould down its white walls. The windows are covered with wire mesh and the glass panels in the doors have long since been replaced by thick boards after repeated vandalism.

'I bet you're all hopping mad,' says Liam.

'Well, we're not happy,' says Bobby, a softly-spoken Scot. 'I stand to lose my job, so do the other two members of staff.'

'You should get up a petition,' says Daz.

'Better still,' says Liam, 'have a demo at the Town Hall.'

'I'll think about it,' says Bobby, his tone of voice making it pretty clear he won't, at least not on the urging of a handful of teenagers. 'Anyway, why don't you get on with your game? Leave me to worry about the council.'

As he walks into the adjoining kitchen to make himself a coffee he gives the newcomers a quick glance. For three lads who have just walked in off the street they are asking a lot of questions.

———

Later that evening Rabia is up in her room, talking to her best friend Sofia. Sofia has claimed the bed while Rabia is squatting on a beanbag.

'Khalid's dead keen on you, you know,' says Sofia.

Rabia looks shocked. She nearly rolls off her beanbag with surprise.

'You've got to be kidding! I thought he was into the passive type, somebody who would hang off his every word.'

She mimics an imaginary girlfriend, doe-eyed and submissive. 'Oh Khalid, you're so *manly*!'

Sofia rolls her eyes. 'I don't care what you say, Rabia. He really likes you. Haven't you seen the way he looks at you?'

She puts on a mournful expression. 'Those big puppy-dog eyes.'

'Behave yourself,' says Rabia. 'You're just winding me up. The only one Khalid's in love with stares back at him every morning from the bathroom mirror.'

'I'm not making it up, you know. Just ask Tahir.'

Rabia sighs. 'I'm not sure we're talking.'

'Why?'

Rabia tells Sofia about the quarrel.

'He'll get over it,' says Sofia. 'So what about Khalid?'

'What about him?'

'Don't you fancy him, just a little?'

'No,' says Rabia. 'Not one bit. I don't go for the street look. He's all show. Mr Macho Guy.'

'Oh, I don't know,' says Sofia. 'You can tell he works out. He certainly fills a T-shirt.'

Rabia puts her fingers down her throat in a gesture of disgust. 'Anyway,' she says, 'I'm surprised at you, Sofia. Imagine if your dad heard you. He'd be horrified.'

'But he isn't here, is he?' says Sofia. 'I'll tell you who else works out – Tahir.'

'You *are* joking, I hope,' says Rabia. 'You can't like Tahir.'

'Give me one good reason why not.'

'My best friend and my brother? No, that would be just too weird.'

'Stranger things have happened,' says Sofia.

'Well, I sincerely hope they don't happen this time,' says Rabia.

She wonders what her newly traditionalist brother would make of this conversation. 'Anyway, can we talk about something else, please?'

There is a note of finality in her voice. They change the subject to talk of auditions for a dance festival in the spring.

Suhail has just dropped off a fare. On his way back to the rank he stops for a moment at Quarry Mill. It's a furniture outlet now. Once it employed hundreds. Now it has a staff of about a dozen. He closes his eyes and remembers the way it was: the workers streaming through the cast iron gates, the kiosk that sold sweets, drinks and newspapers to overalled men and women on their way into work, the clattering machinery that could be heard all the way out on the pavement.

Though the work was hard Suhail had enjoyed the mill. There was companionship there, somebody to talk to during breaks and in the canteen. He had met some of his closest friends there. Suhail didn't really think about it at the time, but it was amazing how the barriers came down at the Mill. When you work cheek by jowl with somebody for ten years it's pretty difficult not to make friends or at least be on nodding terms.

It was at the mill that he got to know Diane. She was a

wages clerk in the office. There was the odd murmur when they started getting serious, but that was all. Bigots got short shrift at Quarry Mill. Most people were only too glad to wish the couple well. There was a turnout of several dozen from the mill at the wedding.

Suhail opens his eyes. He wonders how he would get to meet Diane now. She might get in his cab, but how do you chat up a fare? No, when Quarry Mill shut down, Oakfield lost more than a few hundred jobs – it lost a way of life, a meeting place for the town's communities.

He notices a security guard looking his way. No sense drawing attention to myself, he thinks. A man in uniform doesn't understand nostalgia. Suhail turns the key in the ignition. Pointing the car towards town, he starts thinking about the night ahead, another reason for regretting the passing of Quarry Mill. You don't meet anybody doing this job. Not the sort you'd want to get to know, anyway. Hour after hour you run around town, maybe exchanging a few pleasantries and hoping you don't pick up any trouble-makers, or drunks.

Mike has just got in from the library. The Ravensmoor branch stays open until eight o'clock two nights a week and lets you use the computers for homework. Mike's own PC has been in the workshop for the best part of a fortnight. The part is on order. He has just finished his latest piece of English coursework and is feeling pretty pleased with himself. Not that coursework was the only thing on his mind on his way to the library. All the time he was typing away he was looking around, hoping his dark-eyed girl would pop in. She didn't, but you can't help hoping.

'You've got it bad, Michael,' he says to himself. 'Let's face it, you don't even know her name.'

The house seems unusually quiet. 'Anybody in?' he calls.

There is no answer.

'Mum! Liam!'

He doesn't mention Dad. He can't bring himself to utter the word. He hears a sound from upstairs.

'Mum? Liam? Is that you?' He can hear something, a scraping noise. He jogs upstairs.

'Who's there?'

By now he is thinking burglars. If I announce my presence loudly enough, he thinks, they're bound to scarper.

'Anybody?'

Finally Mum answers. 'It's me.'

'Mum! Why didn't you answer?'

'I'm just cleaning something up.'

Mike pushes at the bedroom door.

'No, don't come in.'

But he already is. Mum is on her hands and knees with a brush and dustpan, sweeping up small shards of glass.

'What happened?'

'Our wedding photo. It fell off the dressing table.'

'Fell?' asks Mike, instantly suspicious. 'Are you sure? Mum, look at me.'

'No, Mike.'

'Please, Mum.'

Slowly she turns. There is a small cut and a red mark over her right eye. It doesn't take Sherlock Holmes to work out that the old man has thrown their wedding photograph at her.

'Oh Mum, not again!'

A few days later Suhail and Tahir are carrying out their ablution. They wash their hands up to the wrists three times. They rinse out their mouths with water three times. They cleanse their nostrils by sniffing water into them, again three times. They wash their whole face, with both hands. After that they wash their right arms three times up to the far end of the elbow. They repeat the process with their left arms. They then wipe their whole heads, with a wet hand. They wipe the inner sides of their ears with their forefingers and the outer sides with their thumbs. Finally, they wash their feet up to the ankles three times, beginning with the right foot. They are ready to start their prayers.

Across town a very different ritual is taking place. A small group of men and youths has gathered outside Moorside Community Centre. Bobby is watching them from the kitchen window. He notices Liam, Daz and Jason. They are with two older men. Bobby has a bad feeling about this.

'Seen that lot?' he says to Kate, his co-worker.

'Yes, I was wondering about them,' she says, her voice betraying unease. 'I don't like the look of the guy with the British bulldog tattoos.'

'Me neither. I wonder what they're after.'

His suspicions are sharpened a couple of minutes later when a white minibus pulls up. The passengers get a warm welcome from the huddle in front of the community centre. Soon after, a couple of cars pull up. Creed and the missing link start handing leaflets to the now thirty-strong crowd.

'I'm going to get one of those flyers,' says Bobby.

He walks to the door and calls Liam over. He doesn't want to get too near some of the new arrivals. He can imagine their favourite meal: pit-bull on a bun.

'Can I have a look at one?' says Bobby.

Liam willingly obliges.

Fair play, it reads. Bobby is still scanning it when he is joined by Kate.

'So,' she says, 'what's it about?'

'Rights for whites,' says Bobby.

Ripples of shock eddy across Kate's face.

'What?'

'It says the council's putting all its money into the Muslim community and nothing into Moorside.'

'But that's ridiculous,' says Kate. 'There's precious little for anybody in this year's budget.'

'*I* know that,' says Bobby. 'Try telling that to people round here. The estate's falling apart: cutbacks, under-investment, crime, unemployment. There's a lot of anger. Now they've got somebody to blame it on.'

He looks down the hill at the Triangle. 'Whoever these characters are, they've found their scapegoat.'

Suhail and Tahir meet Rabia at the front door of the mosque. Sofia is hovering a few metres away.

'I hope you two are talking again,' says Suhail as they set off for home.

'That's up to Tahir,' says Rabia, giving him a meaningful look.

'I'm cool,' says Tahir.

'You?' laughs Rabia. '*You* cool? That's a laugh.'

'Now, now,' says Suhail. 'I thought a truce was supposed to have been declared.'

Rabia smiles. 'Sure. Why not?'

Suhail spots an old workmate from the mill and goes on ahead.

'What do you think of Sofia?' she asks her brother. Sofia is still hovering.

'Sofia?' says Tahir. 'Why?'

'Oh, just wondering.'

Rabia joins her friend, leaving Tahir to carry on wondering.

The leafleters fan out across the Moorside.

'Where are all these people from?' says Liam.

'The minibus is from Leeds,' says Daz. 'Dunno about the cars.'

'Manchester, I think,' says Jason. 'I don't see as it matters much, so long as we're all working for the same thing.'

Liam nods but he has the strangest feeling. It's like the moment in a movie when the train driver has a heart attack and slumps forward over the instrument panel. The train starts going faster and faster, nothing too dramatic at first, but everybody knows that it will soon be careering wildly out of control.

'Isn't this a bit over the top?' he asks. 'It's only a stupid youth club. Do we need all these people?'

Daz calls Colin Stone over. 'Tell him, Colin.'

'This isn't just about the youth club,' says Stone. 'Who cares about their poxy club anyway? This is about the Asians taking over the whole country. Well, that'll happen over my dead body.' He winks before moving away. 'Or theirs.'

Liam feels torn. He has no love for the Asians. He's his daddy's boy, after all – a British bulldog. But he still can't see what it's got to do with a bunch of people from Leeds and Manchester. As for Colin Stone, he gives Liam the creeps. Stone would give the Mafia a bad name.

Liam starts to feel better when they get to the top of the first street they canvas. An elderly man calls down the street.

'Is it you lads who're giving out these brochures?' he asks, beckoning to them.

'Yes,' says Daz, 'they're ours.'

The man holds out his hand. 'Put it there, boys,' he says. 'This little piece of paper says exactly what I've been telling folk for years.'

He is pumping the boys' hands. 'If we don't watch it we won't know this country in twenty years. There'll be a mosque on every street corner. They won't call it Oakfield any more – it'll be Karachi or Islamabad or some such thing.'

'You've got that right,' says Jason, delighted to have found a convert. 'Do you want to give a few out with us?'

'I'm too old for that malarkey,' their new friend tells

them, 'but you've got my vote any day. Old Enoch Powell, he told us what would happen. Rivers of blood, boys – rivers of blood. Anybody who stands up to our Muslim friends is a hero in my eyes – a real hero.'

He claps Liam on the back. 'It's good to see you young lads taking an interest in the world instead of hanging round on a street corner getting up to mischief.'

Liam smiles. It's all going to be OK if he's a hero.

Suhail watches Tahir talking to his friends. Something is happening to his son. Suhail remembers his own childhood. To his father Pakistan was always home; England was just a place where the work was. For the young Suhail, things were very different. He was born here. He had English friends. He grew up considering himself British-Pakistani – that's if he gave the matter much thought at all.

There were bigots around then, of course. There always are. Suhail had to fight his way out of trouble more than once as he grew up. But nothing shook his conviction that he belonged, not even the beating that put him in hospital. Oakfield was his home. He went to work and moved even further away from his parents' world. He wore flared jeans and tank tops and knocked around with his mates from work. They enjoyed Springsteen and soul. Suhail would even sink the odd pint of lager and give the mosque a miss. They used to joke about it – their own little multi-racial Britain. They were every racist's worst nightmare. When

Suhail met Diane and they had kids, he thought that was it. The melting pot had arrived.

But watching Tahir, Suhail knows that things are changing. Everything has come full circle. Disappointed by the divided Oakfield around them, frustrated by the lack of job opportunities and repulsed by the hostility of places like Ravensmoor Road and the Moorside, young Muslim boys have started to look in the direction of a country few of them know, or have ever visited. Suhail is doing his best to understand his son's generation. They seem to be saying two things: they have a right to live in this country, but they don't owe it a thing. Suhail sees their point. Just look how it has treated them so far!

Mike hears the door go.

'Liam?' he calls.

But, judging from the heavy tread on the floorboards in the hall, he knows it's Dad.

'No, it's me.'

Mike feels nervous, but he's got to challenge the old man.

'Can I have a word?'

Sean is hanging his coat up. Mike can smell the booze on his breath.

'You can have as many as you want,' he tells his son, 'just as long as you're not asking for money.'

'No,' says Mike, wondering how to put it. 'It's about Mum.'

'What about her?' Sean's voice is harsh and confrontational.

'I want to know how she got that mark on her eye.'

Sean spins round. Mike tries to get out of his way but Sean is too quick. He shoves Mike roughly against the wall.

'You want!' he roars. 'Since when do you tell me what you *want*?'

Mike is struggling, but to no avail. His father is as strong as an ox.

'Get off me!'

Sean forces his face into Mike's. 'Make me. Go on, you jumped-up little swine – make me!'

Mike knows he is on to a loser. Sean Kelly was a useful boxer in his day and all the sides of beef he has hauled have made him as tough as a mule. His muscles are still hard and his reactions quick despite the drink.

'Stop it!' The new voice belongs to Mum.

'Stop it, the pair of you!'

Mike feels like screaming. What does she mean *the pair of you*? Since when did I do anything to hurt you, Mum? What are you doing treating us the same?

Mike feels the injustice like a deep hurt. It burns into him like a brand.

'I'm going to bed,' says Sean.

He shoves Mike aside and climbs the stairs. Mike meets his mother's eyes for a second then walks away ignoring her pleas to come back. He feels betrayed.

As John Creed walks around the Moorside the morning after the leafleting he can feel a change in the atmosphere. In the newsagents two middle-aged women are discussing the issues.

'About time somebody had the guts to say something,' says one.

'They get everything, them Islamics,' says the other. 'Grants, hand-outs, all sorts. I bet half the National Lottery goes on them.'

'Yes, and meanwhile we're left to rot. Whose country is it anyway? What have they ever done for Oakfield?'

'I tell you,' the first woman says, 'if you're white you've got to go abroad to get any rights these days.'

Creed smiles. He can sense the sea change on this one estate. Things left unsaid for years are now being spoken out loud. Then he sees another reason to be cheerful. The newsagent has actually posted one of the leaflets up in his window. The message is spreading.

'It's all going to plan,' Creed informs Stone on his return. 'Our leaflets are the talk of the estate.'

'So what next?' asks Stone.

'Petitions,' says Creed. 'We'll get some run off today and start going door to door. I think we're ready to advertise our first public meeting.'

'You sound like you're starting to enjoy yourself,' says Stone.

'I am,' says Creed. 'It's not like the area where I live in London. It's fifty-seven varieties down there. Sometimes I think it's so far gone, there's no way back. Oakfield's still got a chance, though. We can make this a town where ordinary English people can live in peace.'

'So how much longer are you staying?' asks Stone.

'Maybe until the end of the week,' says Creed. 'I'll see how the meeting goes then pop home for a few days. We're building our influence and winning recruits. I like young Liam. He's one for the future.'

Creed misses Stone's scowl of disapproval.

'Colin, my friend,' he says, 'the times they are a-changing.'

The times continue to change for the rest of that week. Liam Kelly is out every night petitioning over the youth club, reminding people on the Moorside that *they* get everything while *we* get nothing. Almost half the people who are approached sign their names. Most of the ones who refuse say they that all they want is a quiet life. Only a handful say that the campaign is wrong. The ball is rolling. Daz and Jason don't leave their friend wondering where they have gone any more. John Creed is watching Liam's progress, pencilling in his name as a future leader of the League's youth wing. Liam is fast becoming part of the League's inner circle, a hard worker for the cause. What he lacks in brains he makes up for in energy and enthusiasm.

'Hey, Liam!' Creed calls. 'I've got a job for you.'

The rest of the branch watch the pair drawing up plans.

'John's taken quite a shine to Liam,' says Daz.

'I know,' says Stone dully. 'Thick as thieves, aren't they?'

'What's the matter, Col?' says Jason. 'Jealous?'

Stone silences him with a menacing stare.

Liam is coming out of the Lion that Friday evening when he sees an elderly Muslim man making his way home.

When Daz and Jason start to tease the old man, pulling his beard and shoving him around, Liam joins in, throwing his cap over a wall. He is a foot soldier now – a fighter in that war he used to question. He has come a long way in a short time. John Creed would be proud of him.

Next evening Tahir is up in arms.

'Did you hear about Khalid's grandfather?' he asks.

'No,' says Rabia. 'What about him?'

'He got picked on by a bunch of thugs on Ravensmoor Road last night. They knocked him down.'

'Is he all right?' asks Diane.

'He got cut over the right eye,' says Tahir. 'He's got a dressing on it. He's a bit shaken up. Otherwise, he's OK. That's not the point. It's out of order. Something should be done.'

'Like what?' asks Rabia.

'I don't know. Something.'

Suhail speaks for the first time. 'Just so long as you don't go taking matters into your own hands, Tahir,' he says.

'So it doesn't matter if our elders get harrassed?'

Suhail's eyes narrow. 'That's not what I said, Tahir. You're twisting my words.'

'He means,' Diane says, 'we don't want you going out making things worse.'

'That's easy for you to say,' says Tahir.

'Meaning?'

Tahir shrugs but Diane isn't about to let the matter drop. 'Look at me, Tahir,' she says. 'I want to know what you meant.'

'You know.'

'Speak properly to your mother,' orders Suhail. 'Show her some respect.'

'What I mean, *Mother*,' Tahir snarls, 'is you can walk up Ravensmoor Road without even being noticed. Khalid's grandad can't.'

Suhail looks as if he is going to react angrily, but Diane closes her fingers round his wrist.

'Rabia can't either,' Tahir adds.

'Don't drag me into this,' says Rabia. 'You're not using me as an excuse for setting up some vigilante group or whatever it is you're planning.'

Diane is still staring in disbelief at Tahir, wondering where the rage has come from.

'You're *ashamed* of me!' she says. 'You're actually ashamed of me, your own mother.'

Tahir lowers his eyes so they don't meet hers.

'Tahir, speak to me.'

He hovers for a moment, then explodes from the room.

'Leave me alone!' he cries, slamming the door behind him.

At the meeting of the town council two days later, John Creed is in the gallery watching Independent Councillor Roberts turning up the heat. Roberts is opening the door for the Patriotic League, but he is also a potential rival.

'We're not asking for much,' Councillor Roberts says. 'All we want is a fair deal. Funds are being ploughed into the Triangle like nobody's business. Look at this programme for the Eid festival.' He reels off a list of events from the official brochure.

'Where is the money coming from? Tell me that. At the same time as the Moorside estate's only social centre is threatened with closure, we are paying for the Triangle to have a big party at our expense.'

Councillor Mohammed Saddique represents the Triangle. He is on his feet, protesting loudly.

'Councillor Roberts is being deliberately misleading,' he shouts. 'The Moorside community centre is beyond repair. The money spent on the Eid celebrations is a fraction of what a new centre would cost to build. Alternative premises are being sought for the youth club, but Councillor Roberts isn't interested in the truth. He just wants to whip up prejudice. Would Councillor Roberts criticise the money spent on *Christmas* lights? Of course not.'

'I say again,' Councillor Roberts says, 'while money is squandered on these celebrations, our people lose their only local resource. That, ladies and gentlemen, is a scandal.'

'No,' says Councillor Saddique. 'What is a scandal is the bigoted ranting of Councillor Roberts.'

John Creed sees the *Chronicle* reporter writing furiously. The spat will be on the front page of the paper this week.

Creed leans across to Stone. 'You're in charge from tomorrow. The ball's rolling. I think I can give myself a well-deserved break.'

Stone nods. 'I won't let you down, John,' he says.

'I know you won't, big man,' says Creed.

By ten o'clock he is speeding down the motorway. *Lohengrin* is belting out of the speakers. Creed watches the Valkyries riding across the inky northern sky and smiles. He didn't dare dream that it would be so easy.

'Like taking candy from a baby,' he says as the stirring strains of Wagner sweep over him.

But he is not content simply to savour his achievements so far. He is a competitor, a winner. He has seen patriots come and go, hard men like Colin Stone. It is easy to see why they fail. Stone is short-sighted and inflexible too. His kind want the world all in one go. They want to see the swastika flying over the palace of Westminster without even trying to persuade the little man in places like Oak-field. They lay their policies out in front of the public, their whole programme red in tooth and claw, and wonder why they are treated as little more than a joke in bad taste. Stone will have to do for the time being, but only until young Liam is ready.

'If I let you have your way, Colin,' Creed says, 'you'd ruin everything. Not me. I won't let the mask slip. I'll give the common herd exactly what they want.' He eases back in his seat.

'The future belongs to me.'

4

The Dogs of War

Councillor Mohammed Saddique is woken about three o'clock in the morning. He frowns and reaches for his glasses. He picks up the *History of the Middle East* he was reading when he fell asleep, slips a bookmark into it, and puts it on the bedside cabinet. He listens again, wondering just what he heard. Strange, he thinks, shaking off the last cobwebby veil of sleep – it sounded like the postman but it is too early for deliveries. There was a definite thump, like a parcel being delivered. Maybe a drunk on the way home from one of the town's nightclubs stumbling against the front door. Councillor Saddique can think of better ways of enjoying yourself. His wife stirs and asks what's wrong.

'No need to worry,' he says. 'I heard a noise, that's all. Nothing to worry about. You go back to sleep.'

No more than half-awake, she rolls over. Satisfied that she has gone back off, Saddique walks to the top of the stairs. He has told his wife not to worry but he can't help but feel a twinge of anxiety himself. You hear such things! He notices his eldest son's cricket bat poking out of a cupboard on the landing and picks it up. He has read about a spate of burglaries on the Triangle. Gripping the handle of the bat, he listens for movement downstairs. You can't be too careful these days. Some of these young boys will resort to violence at the drop of a hat.

Halfway downstairs he sees something lying on the hall carpet. It is a brown envelope, shredded along one edge, probably from being shoved through the letter box. Saddique is wide awake now. He has heard about suspicious packages in the news but didn't expect to receive one himself. Warily he feels the brown envelope. He is not quite sure what he is looking for – a wire maybe. There is nothing suspicious.

'Let's see what this is all about,' he murmurs.

He opens the envelope gingerly. Inside there is a roughly-folded copy of this week's *Chronicle*. The front page features his row with Councillor Roberts. Saddique's reported words have all been highlighted in yellow ink. He is still wondering about the curious delivery when a sheet of paper falls from the folds of the *Chronicle*. He picks it up.

'Sick,' he says.

There is a cartoon portrait, unpleasantly caricatured, showing him with a noose round his neck and the scrawled warning: '*Keep your views to yourself, or else. Happy Ramadan, Councillor!*'

Councillor Saddique thinks about burning the offending piece of paper. Reconsidering, he decides to phone the police in the morning. Before going to bed he puts a bucket under the letter box. You never know what else might pop through.

M ike Kelly challenges Liam.
'Where did you go last night?'

Liam starts pouring milk over his cornflakes, and does it as nonchalantly as possible.

'I don't know what you mean.'

'Don't lie to me, Liam. It won't wash. I saw you go out. Whose car was that picking you up?'

Liam breaks off from shovelling spoonfuls of cornflakes in his mouth just long enough to say: 'None of your business.'

'I'm making it my business. Who gets up and goes out at half-past one in the morning?'

He thinks about adding *especially when you're only fifteen* but that would only get Liam's back up. It would sound too much like an adult talking. Liam's favourite phrase lately is: *Don't patronise me.*

'Dunno,' says Liam. 'Who does get up at half-past one? Is it the milkman? No, I've got it – an apprentice cockerel. What's this then – *Who Wants To Be A Millionaire?* Can I phone a friend?'

Mike knows he can't win. 'I ought to tell Mum.'

'Yes?' says Liam, adding his cereal bowl to the pile of washing-up in the sink. 'And what's she going to do, ground me? If you hadn't noticed, Mikey, I'm a big boy now.'

'Not too big to get burned. You're playing with fire, Liam.'

Liam shakes his head. 'No, I'm sticking up for my own kind. You should try it some time.'

The words strike through Mike like a pickaxe. He can feel Liam pulling away.

'Just try thinking for yourself, Liam,' says Mike. 'You've got a brain, even if you're determined to hide the fact. Stop listening to Dad and the Patriotic League for a minute and find out the facts.'

'I know the facts, Mike. The Moorside's a dump and getting worse, but there's the Triangle getting all smartened up for Eid.'

'And what's wrong with that? There'll soon be Christmas lights in town. Live and let live, Liam.'

'Just listen to Mr Multicultural!' sneers Liam. 'And what if I don't want to live and let live? People have been saying that all my life and what's it got us? Curry houses the length of Clive Road and boarded-up homes all round Moorside.'

Mike tries to interrupt but Liam isn't having it. 'Live and let live, you say? That's the trouble with Britain, Mike. We lie down and turn ourselves into welcome mats for anybody who wants a free ride. You know what happens to welcome mats? People wipe their feet all over them. It isn't our country any more.'

Mike snorts. 'Don't be ridiculous. Sure, we've got nothing, but neither have the people in the Triangle. Do you know the unemployment figures round there? You want to know where the money is, Liam? Take a walk round Shevington, and I'll tell you what – except for the odd doctor you won't find many black faces up there.'

'The Triangle does all right,' says Liam. 'When's the last time you saw an empty restaurant?'

Mike ignores his younger brother. When was the last time either of them went to a restaurant?

'Look, Liam, you can't make out the Triangle's some kind of Beverly Hills of the north. That's ridiculous. I seem to remember a youth club getting shut down there too.'

'You're joking, aren't you?' Liam retorts. 'The Asians are getting money thrown at them by our politically correct council.'

Politically correct? thinks Mike. This doesn't sound like you, Liam. None of it does. So who's been feeding you your lines?

Liam isn't finished. 'It used to be just the corner shops and the buses they had,' he says. 'Now it's everything.'

He holds out his palms as if cradling an invisible globe. 'Everything!'

Mike feels like screaming. He knows Liam is talking dangerous nonsense – but how to convince him? That's the question. Every argument he uses seems to backfire. Liam couldn't care less about reason. He's a disciple and he wants faith. He isn't interested in Mike's arguments.

'They're everywhere, Mike,' he says. 'They're even taking over the telly. Look at all the newsreaders.'

'Now you're being stupid.'

Liam pulls on his school blazer and walks to the door. 'It always comes down to that, doesn't it, big brother? Poor Liam, too thick to think for himself. Well, I *am* thinking for myself, only I'm not thinking the way you want. You don't like it? Well, tough. You don't own me, Mike, and you don't own my mind. I'm different from you. I'm not ashamed to be British. I don't want to change my colour. Unlike you, I believe in my country. Live with it.'

Mike watches Liam walk out of the door. You're getting in way over your head, he thinks, and there isn't a thing I can do about it.

'Seen this?' says Tahir.

It is Saturday afternoon and he is walking through the town centre with Khalid and Nasir. They've been playing on the consoles in the Games Centre. Tahir points out the leaflet pasted to a hoarding. It is advertising the first meeting of Councillor Roberts' campaign.

'Fair play?' says Khalid. 'What's that about?'

'Read it,' says Tahir. 'You'll soon get the idea.'

'The scum!' says Khalid, scanning the bullet-pointed campaign demands. 'The dirty rotten scum! This is all directed against the Triangle. I bet it's the same outfit that knocked my grandad about.'

'Got it in one,' says Tahir.

'We should do something about it,' says Khalid.

'Hang on a minute,' says Nasir. 'Have you seen where the meeting is? Moorside Primary. Surely you're not asking us to go up there? It's smack in the middle of the estate. We'll get our heads kicked in.'

'Not if we wait until everyone's safely inside,' says Tahir.

Nasir looks doubtful. Suddenly Khalid is wavering. 'I don't know . . .'

'Well, I do,' says Tahir. 'First Rabia gets shoved around, then your grandad. If we don't act they'll start thinking they can get away with anything.'

'What have you got in mind?' asks Nasir.

Tahir looks at the bustling crowds. 'Not here.'

Stone gets a knock on the door early Sunday evening. It's John Creed.

'John? I didn't expect you until later.'

'You should know me, Colin. We've work to do. Are you ready to get down to it?'

Stone can't help giving a little grimace. He feels stupid having to be coached like this. It's only a ten-minute speech. There will probably be nobody there anyway.

'How's the family, John?'

'Fine. Now let's get down to work.'

Stone has noticed this about Creed. Once he is focused on something there are no niceties. His private life is just that – private.

'I know you think you can speak off the cuff, Colin,' says Creed, 'but this is too important to take chances. Get the tone right and we move into the mainstream – the spokesmen for white Oakfield. Get it wrong and we come across as nutters.'

He gives Stone a meaningful look.

'And we don't want that, do we, Colin?'

'No,' says Stone. 'Of course not. We've got to keep this . . .' He searches for a word which will meet Creed's requirements. '. . . professional.'

'That's the ticket,' says Creed approvingly. 'Professional.'

Tahir is at the door of the motor parts store.

'Got the money?' he asks.

Khalid and Nasir hand over their share.

'Are you sure about this?' Nasir asks nervously.

'Do you want our women and old people to be able to walk the streets without being harassed?' Tahir asks.

'Of course I do,' says Nasir. 'But–'

'But nothing,' says Khalid. 'Tahir's right. My grandad's

still afraid to go out of the door since he got set upon. You should have heard some of the things they said to him! Disgusting.'

'All right,' says Nasir. 'I'm in.'

Tahir smiles. 'Right, I'll get the stuff.'

Half an hour into the coaching, Creed is glad he came back early. Stone is just like his name – dense and lifeless. He has all the charisma of a bowl of cold rice pudding.

'Let's go through it again, Colin,' says Creed. 'The speech has to be short and sweet. First you talk about the kids on the Moorside, the way they have nowhere to go and nothing to do. They end up hanging round the streets getting up to no good. Then what?'

Stone gives his next line: 'Sixty years ago they would have been fighting in defence of their country.'

'With passion, Colin. With *passion*.'

Stone repeats the line, even though he would probably have preferred to fight on the other side if he had had a chance.

'Better,' says Creed, listening to the speech. 'Now your big finale.'

Stone finds this bit easier. Every word, every joke is directed at the Muslims. He starts to warm to the task. He even adds some spontaneous stuff of his own.

'Excellent,' says Creed. 'Now, one more time.'

Stone sighs.

'No slacking, Colin,' says Creed. 'You're our main man in Oakfield.'

Stone knows this is pure flattery. He knows Creed is grooming Liam. He smiles anyway. Sometimes it's good to be flattered.

'This,' says Creed, 'is our crusade!'

He relishes the word, knowing how much it is hated by some inhabitants of the Triangle. It conjures images of the sack of Jerusalem. He likes the idea of a white man's jihad so much, he repeats it.

'Our *crusade*.' He makes a note.

'In fact, we'll put that in your speech. Anything that upsets our Muslim friends deserves lots of repetition. Let's hear it, Colin.'

'Fair play for all,' says Colin, rehearsing the closing remarks of his speech. 'Rights for the neglected people of the Moorside as well as for the Triangle. It's time to launch our *crusade* for justice!'

'Very good,' says Creed. 'That should have them stamping and cheering you to the echo. We're on our way, Colin. We're on our way.'

Just after tea Rabia sees Tahir rummaging in a cupboard. He catches sight of her out of the corner of his eye and straightens up quickly. It doesn't take a genius to work out that he is hiding something.

'What have you got there?' Rabia asks.

'Nothing.'

'What are you up to?'

Again, the same reply. 'Nothing.'

Rabia sighs. 'Tahir, I can read you like a book. I was covering for you when we were both still in nappies. You're not going to do something silly, are you?'

'What do you mean?'

'Look, I'm the one who got shoved around. You've no right to go taking the law into your own hands on my behalf. I can take care of myself.'

'Yes,' says Tahir. 'Sure you can. So why were you so glad to see Dad that night?'

'What I mean,' Rabia tells him, annoyed that he is being so patronising, 'is that I don't want you getting yourself in trouble over this. If I can put it to the back of my mind, you should too. It's not your problem, Tahir.'

'No,' says Tahir, 'it's my *responsibility*. Maybe it's the elders' way, to bow their heads and take it. It's not mine. There's a new generation growing up, Rabia. We've taken more than enough crap from this country.'

'You *are* going to do something, aren't you?'

Tahir brushes past her.

'Tahir, speak to me.'

He jogs downstairs.

'Tahir!'

Stone is standing in front of Creed, dressed in his best suit.

'Too much,' says Creed. 'The good councillor will be

wearing his suit. You need to look respectable but not too sharp. The audience will be suspicious of politicians. It wouldn't do any harm if a few of the members mentioned that Councillor Roberts lives in Old Moor. Too good for the Moorside, they could mutter – that sort of thing. Anyway, the point is, we've got to ditch the suit.'

'So what do I put on instead?'

'Trousers, open-necked shirt, jacket. Nothing too showy. You've got to be a man of the people, the guy next door.'

Stone grimaces. 'I *am* the guy next door.'

'So look the part, man.'

Stone trudges upstairs and changes his clothes. When he reappears, Creed voices his satisfaction.

'That's much better. Look at you, Col. You're the solid citizen, one of the common herd.'

Stone grimaces. If Creed wasn't the Leader he would wipe that stupid grin off his posh face. Oblivious to Stone's thoughts, Creed pulls out a notebook.

'Now, let's run through your speech once more.'

Stone gives a long sigh, but still manages to deliver his speech according to Creed's strict instructions. Creed smiles.

'You're ready, my friend. Let's go.'

At Moorside Primary, the site manager Ronnie Kellett has just opened up. He counts sixty chairs.

'Should be enough,' he grunts.

In fact they should be more than enough. What few meetings take place on the Moorside estate tend to be sparsely attended. Ronnie has to go back ten years to think of a meeting that mustered more than a couple of dozen.

'Maybe I should put a few away. Less work at the end.'

He is removing chairs from the ends of the rows when he hears something. He stares into the evening murk for a few minutes before returning to his task.

'I'm getting paranoid in my old age,' he mutters. 'Now I'm imagining things.'

An hour later Ronnie is having to put out more chairs.

'Good turnout,' he says to Councillor Roberts.

'Yes, very good,' Councillor Roberts replies.

The foot soldiers have been busy all right. There are over eighty people in the school hall and more are walking across the playground.

'I didn't think there would be this many,' Stone says to Creed.

'Nervous?' asks Creed.

Stone would rather face three Asians down a dark alley than stand up in front of this lot. 'A bit.'

'Well, that's not a bad thing. You don't want to be too polished. Go for the common touch. What we need is passion, Colin. Even if you make a mistake or two, don't worry. Everybody in this hall will be rooting for you. You're the local man, one of them.'

'So is Roberts. Old Moor is only half a mile down the road.'

'Yes, but to the locals it's posh. Besides, he's been on the council for years. He's become part of the system. He's never done anything for them. You're the one they will identify with.'

Stone nods. He sees Councillor Roberts walking towards the stage.

'You'd best take your seat,' says Creed. 'Good luck.'

Colin gives a thin smile. 'I'll need it.'

The audience has now swelled to well over a hundred.

Suhail is about to go out on his shift.

'Is Tahir in?' he asks.

'I don't think so,' says Diane. 'I'm sure I heard the door go earlier. Rabia, have you seen Tahir?'

Rabia is doing her homework at the kitchen table. She looks up from her science assignment. 'He went out with Nasir and Khalid.'

'I hope he did his homework first,' says Suhail. 'There was a note from the teacher in his Planner again. It's three weeks since he's given in any homework.'

'Maybe we should put a limit on the number of nights he's allowed to go out with his friends,' says Diane. 'The exams aren't that far off.'

'Good idea,' says Suhail, slipping on his jacket. 'Try having a word with him tonight.'

Diane's face falls. 'I think you're better doing that.'

'How can I when I'm out at work?'

'OK,' says Diane, 'I'll try, but he doesn't seem to take much notice of me lately.'

'Tell you what,' says Suhail, 'you have a word with him about his homework and I'll speak to him tomorrow about the way he's behaving towards you.'

He glances at his watch. 'Anyway, I've got to go.'

'Bye,' says Diane.

'Bye, Dad,' says Rabia.

She looks out of the window as if trying to imagine Tahir out there in the night. What are you up to? she wonders.

At the end of the meeting it is Colin Stone who is the centre of attention. He is surrounded by a crowd of Moorside residents, all keen to tell him how well he spoke. A disgruntled Councillor Roberts is still sitting on stage, virtually ignored.

'What did you think of Colin's speech?' John Creed asks Liam.

'Great,' says Liam, flattered to be spoken to by the great man. 'He said what everybody round here thinks.'

'Didn't he just!'

'And imagine speaking without notes! I didn't know Colin was that clever.'

Creed smiles. 'Neither did I. Neither did he for that matter.'

Creed laughs out loud. Liam frowns for a moment then

joins in the laughter, though he is not quite sure what he's laughing at.

'You could be up on that platform some day,' says Creed. 'What do you think about that?'

Liam shrugs. 'Sounds a bit scary.'

He pauses then adds: 'Did you hear that stupid Bobby fellow? Fancy him sticking up for the Asians in front of everybody! I thought the Jocks had more sense.'

'I know, but he got his comeuppance, didn't he?'

The moment Bobby McAllister had tried to argue against scapegoating the people on the Triangle and proposed a joint campaign by both communities for better funding, he was shouted down and told to clear off back across the border.

'Oh, brilliant!' Bobby had retorted. 'Now you're after deporting the Scots as well.'

Liam follows John Creed out of the hall. Councillor Roberts is just in front of them.

'What the–?'

The exclamation comes from the lips of Councillor Roberts. His car and half a dozen others in the school carpark have been spraycanned with the same slogan: *Racist scum.*

Tahir falls back against the privet hedge of one of the houses at the bottom of the Ravensmoor Road. He has never run so hard in his life. His chest feels as if it is about to burst, but he is exhilarated. He is laughing with triumph.

As he struggles to recover his breath, Nasir and Khalid catch him up.

'Do you think anyone followed us?' pants Nasir.

'No,' says Tahir. 'We got clear well before the end of the meeting. They'll be admiring our artwork just about now.' His face is glowing with pride. He is elated at the success of their mission.

'Are you sure that was the right thing to do?' asks Nasir.

'Oh, stop worrying,' says Tahir. 'You're not telling me you feel sorry for a bunch of white racists?'

'No, I just–'

'Oh, shut up!' says Khalid. 'You'd be singing a different tune if it was one of your family who'd been done over.'

Nasir falls silent.

'Let's get back on to the Triangle,' says Tahir, 'just in case they do come looking for us.'

Nasir is the first into Clive Road.

———

As he follows Creed into the Lion, Colin Stone is a man possessed.

'If I catch the ones who did it,' he snarls, 'I'll have their skins, for a tablecloth!'

Creed shakes his head. 'Tone it down a bit, Colin. You don't know who might be listening.'

'And what if all those car owners blame us for the damage?' Stone moans. By *us* he means *me*.

'They won't,' says Creed. 'They'll lay the blame exactly where it belongs – at the door of our Muslim friends.'

'I was the one up there on that stage,' Stone grumbles. 'It's me they'll come looking for.'

Creed chuckles. 'Colin, Colin, Colin,' he says. 'Is this really the man who brought the residents to their feet with his eloquence tonight?'

'It was your speech,' says Stone.

The euphoria of the meeting has long since evaporated. All that is left is an odd mixture of rage and resignation.

Creed buys a round of drinks. 'Get us a table in the corner,' he says.

He pays for the drinks and carries them over.

'Now, Colin,' he says, 'I take it you think the vandalism tonight was a setback.'

'Don't you?'

'Of course not. If there had been a big crowd opposing us, then maybe that would have been a setback. If the turnout had been poor, then that would definitely have been a setback. But Colin, think about it. One hundred and twenty people cheered you to the echo. Not Councillor Roberts but *you*, the Patriotic League's man.'

'But what about the cars? They won't feel so chuffed when they get the bill for a respray.'

'Do you know what tonight means to the good people of the Moorside estate?' says Creed. 'That one act of vandalism proved that everything you said was *true*. Just think about everything you warned them about – militant Islam climbing up the hill from the Triangle. It's come true, Colin. It's written on their cars in foot-high letters. Before the meeting they were suspicious of the Asians. Now they *hate* them. Before I left I got Councillor Roberts to phone the local rag. Even as I speak they'll have a photographer up there making a record of the latest instance of Islamic terrorism.'

Even Stone wonders whether 'terrorism' isn't a bit strong. 'People will still blame me,' he says. 'It's all right for you. If it goes pear-shaped, you can clear off back to London.'

'I'm not going anywhere,' says Creed. 'This is perfect. The whole thing will be on the front page of the *Chronicle*. Whoever it was that spray-canned the cars deserves our gratitude.'

Colin takes a sip of his pint. 'You think so?'

Creed's face crinkles with a triumphant smile. 'Colin, my friend, I *know* so.'

———

Daz is at the head of half a dozen youths. At the corner of Foulshurst Avenue his gang meets another group of the same size, led by Jason. Liam has been taking the lead in everything, but not in this.

'Anything?' Daz asks.

Jason and Liam shake their heads. 'No, they're well gone, back into their own territory.'

Daz stares with hatred at the Asian restaurants and shops on Clive Road. 'You know what?' he says. 'I'm thinking an eye for an eye, a tooth for a tooth.'

'Meaning?'

'Meaning we should give as good as we get.'

Liam looks unsure. 'Maybe we should ask John first,' he says.

'Come on,' says Daz. 'What are you, a man or a mouse? They came on to our patch. They're the ones who started this war, but believe me, we'll be the ones to finish it.'

Suhail Khan has just dropped off a fare at The Gulam when he sees a dozen white youths starting to gather at the top of Clive Road. He reverses round the corner and radios through to control.

'Phone the police,' he says. 'Something's going on in Clive Road. A gang of white boys. They're tooled up.'

Imran in the office tells him to sit tight. 'I'll have half a dozen cabs down there in five minutes. You may need some help.'

'But don't forget the police,' says Suhail.

'I won't,' says Imran, 'but I'm not going to hold my breath waiting for them to arrive.'

Suhail knows Imran is right. The people of the Triangle have learned the hard way that they can only rely on themselves.

In The Gulam Rashid has just served a group of students. They are noisy but good-natured, celebrating the birthday of a petite blonde girl.

'Enjoy your meal,' says Rashid.

'I'm sure we will,' says a young man in his early twenties. He is wearing an anti-war badge.

Rashid is on his way back to the kitchen when he hears raised voices. Turning, he sees the party of students on their feet, shouting and waving their arms at something. Rashid follows the direction in which they are looking.

Outside, a dozen white youths are brandishing sticks and half-bricks.

The glass explodes as a half-brick is thrown. Two of the youths run in from the street and lay about the student wearing the anti-war badge.

Suhail hears the window smash. He looks up the street. The other cabs haven't arrived. He punches the dashboard in frustration. Five minutes, Imran said. Where are they? He hears screams coming from The Gulam. There is nothing for it. He grabs a wheel-brace from the boot and races down the street. He smashes a makeshift club from the hand of one white youth and puts him and two others to flight. As the rest of the group turn on him he hears the sound of two, maybe three cars screeching to a halt behind him. The first of his fellow taxi drivers have arrived.

'Come on, you cowards!' Suhail roars, brandishing the wheel-brace.

He remembers a night of fear and shame when he lay at the feet of men like this. This time he will not go down without a fight. As he advances on one boy he thinks: *This is for Rabia.* Who knows, her attackers could be among these lads. The white youths start to back off, but they're not done yet. One hurls a half-brick. It misses Suhail's head and goes through the windscreen of one of the cabs. It's a signal to the rest of the youths to throw theirs. The windows of two shops are smashed. Suhail and his fellow drivers respond by chasing the boys back down the street on to Ravensmoor Road.

'That's it,' yells Suhail. 'Run!'

He is still standing with the wheel-brace in his hand when the police arrive.

'Put the weapon down please, sir,' says the first officer out of the car.

'You should be going after those boys,' says Suhail, using the wheel-brace to point out the way they went. 'They're the ones who attacked innocent people.'

'I have asked you to put the weapon on the ground,' the officer repeats coldly.

'But we were only defending ourselves.'

'I will give you one more chance,' says the policeman.

Suhail looks at the other drivers. They empty their hands.

Daz is addressing his group outside the Lion.
'We've got to split up,' he says. 'You never know, the police might come looking for us. They always take the Asians' side.'

There are nods all round. Coppers, the Asians' friends. The youths are elated. They took the war to the Triangle and wasted the place. What's more, they came away without any casualties.

'You did well for your first time, Liam,' says Jason. 'I didn't know you had it in you.'

Nor did Liam. In the heat of the moment he'd knocked

one of the students to the floor, but as he looked round the scene at The Gulam he didn't feel joy, he felt revulsion. He had been pumped up over what happened at the school, but the sight of that girl with her bloodied face . . . He felt sick.

'You were brilliant,' says Daz. 'That student will have a sore jaw in the morning.'

Inside The Gulam Rashid is helping the students. The petite blonde girl is in a bad way. Blood is streaming down her face from several deep cuts to her head. The student with the anti-war badge is holding his side. It looks like he has broken a rib. An ambulance has arrived and two paramedics are picking their way over the broken glass. A policeman is looking the place over.

'Did anyone see what happened?' he asks.

'Are you kidding?' cries the student with the anti-war badge. 'We were attacked by racist skinheads. They just stormed in and laid into us.'

The policeman clocks the badge.

'And that was it?' he says. 'You didn't say anything back? You didn't offer them any provocation?'

The student groans.

'This young man is telling the truth,' says Rashid. 'One of those boys threw a brick through the window. Then two more came in and started beating people.'

'Are you willing to make a statement, sir?'

Rashid nods.

'And you?'

There is no *sir* this time. The student gets to his feet. 'Yes, I'll give you your statement.'

T‍ahir and his friends hear the mayhem from Cardigan Street.

'What's that?' says Nasir.

Tahir shrugs. 'Let's find out.'

They arrive in Clive Road just in time to see the police talking to Suhail.

'That's my dad!' Tahir rushes to his father's side.

'What have you stopped my dad for?' he demands.

'Go away, sonny,' says the policeman.

'I'm not your son,' says Tahir, 'and I won't go away. Why are you arresting my dad?'

'It's all right, Tahir,' says Suhail. 'I'm not under arrest.'

He turns to the policeman. 'I'm not, am I, officer?'

The policeman shakes his head. 'No, sir, you're not. But next time, please leave the keeping of public order to the police. Vigilantism really doesn't help.'

'Maybe if you arrived more quickly, we wouldn't need to defend ourselves,' says Suhail.

The policeman's eyes narrow. 'Put the wheel-brace back in the car, sir. Keep it for its proper use.'

With that the policeman joins his colleagues at The Gulam.

'What happened, Dad?'

'White boys attacked The Gulam.'

Tahir starts to walk towards the restaurant.

'No, don't, Tahir. I want you to go straight home. There's been enough trouble tonight.'

'You're not going back to work after all this, are you?'

'No, I'm going to help Rashid clean up. But you must do as I say. Go home, Tahir.'

The three friends are halfway down Clive Road when Tahir stops. 'See what happens when the racists start holding meetings?' he says. 'Words lead to actions. We've got to be ready for them next time.'

He clenches his fist. 'This is war.'

5
Two Tribes

Tahir is walking up the road from the school with Khalid and Nasir. Rabia and Sofia walk past them. They catch the boys' eyes and start giggling.

'What's the matter with them?' asks Khalid, disappointed by the reaction.

He doesn't like being laughed at, especially by Rabia. Ever since she started to turn into a beautiful young woman he has been unable to take his eyes off her.

'I wish I knew,' says Tahir.

They cut down Clive Road and stop outside The Gulam.

'Much damage?' they ask Rashid. He is supervising the glazier puttying in a new window.

'I'll be able to reopen tomorrow night,' says Rashid.

'You know what these gangs from the Moorside need?' says Tahir. 'A taste of their own medicine.'

Rashid scowls. 'That's enough of that kind of talk,' he says. 'There's been too much trouble already. I just want to get back to normal.'

'What if the racists won't let you?' asks Tahir. 'Have you thought of that?'

As the boys walk away Tahir shakes his head. 'See what I mean about the elders?' he says. 'They just want to roll over and die.'

Khalid nods while Nasir just looks straight ahead, wanting to talk about something else.

'But we won't, will we, Tahir?' says Khalid.

Tahir's eyes are hard as stones. 'Never!'

John Creed and Colin Stone are waiting for Liam outside Moorside High.

'There he is,' says Creed.

Stone winds down the car window. 'Get in, Liam.'

Liam feels a tug in his heart. 'What's this about?' he asks.

'Just get in,' says Stone, stretching to open the back door.

It isn't a request. Liam does as he is told. They drive to a car park on an industrial estate and pull up. Liam is scared.

'I hear the boys had a bit of fun last night and you were part of it,' says Creed, looking at Liam's face in the rear-view mirror.

'Who says?'

'We've just left Daz and Jason,' says Creed, his tone of voice making Liam's skin slide. 'They were pretty tight-lipped, but I've got a good idea what happened. You went on a rampage down Clive Road without my permission.'

Stone tosses Liam a copy of the *Chronicle*. TWO TRIBES, screams the headline. The front page is divided in two, one photograph showing the damage to cars on the Moorside, the other depicting the scene on Clive Road.

'Looks like you've all been getting up to a bit of extra-curricular to me,' says Stone. He is enjoying Liam's discomfort.

'Sorry,' says Liam. 'We were just angry about what they'd done . . .'

'I know,' says Creed. 'You're young and headstrong, Liam. You were acting according to your patriotic instincts and I understand that. What red-blooded Englishman wouldn't be angry about what our Muslim friends did last night?'

Liam hears something verging on admiration creeping into Creed's voice. Stone looks disappointed.

'So you're not angry?'

'Not angry, no,' says Creed. 'As it happens, no harm is done. The battle lines have been drawn and no blame can be laid at the door of the Patriotic League. No, unintentionally our campaign has been taken to the next level.'

Liam is starting to fill with pride, but before he can get too swell-headed, Creed turns round. The look in his eyes strikes terror into Liam. There is a darkness in Creed's stare. It penetrates Liam's brain. Unease flutters in his head like the wingbeats of a trapped bird.

'But you listen to me, son. The next time you undertake an unauthorised operation you'll have to answer to me. Not Daz, not Jason, me. Do you understand what that means?'

Liam nods. To his relief, a smile spreads across Creed's face.

Mike is worried. He has seen Liam getting into a strange car. He recognises one of the men. It was John Creed.

'You idiot!' Mike breathes.

'Talking to yourself?' asks one of Mike's classmates.

By way of reply, Mike gives a half-smile.

'I'll see you tomorrow, Ady,' he says. 'Stuff to do.'

Ady waves and sets off in the opposite direction. Mike hurries after Liam. He comes across him a couple of minutes later, crossing Moorside Avenue.

'Liam! Hey, Liam!'

Liam turns. 'What are you after?'

Mike jogs towards him. 'What did those men want?'

For a brief split-second Liam wants to confide in Mike, but the moment passes. He knows what Mike would say: I told you so. So Liam pulls up the drawbridge. 'Nothing,' he says.

'So when did you start getting in a car with the likes of John Creed?'

It's the wrong question. It reminds Liam that he is nothing without the League, just Mike's thicko brother.

'Since I joined the movement.'

'Oh, you haven't! You didn't actually join that bunch of lunatics?'

Liam pulls out his membership card and waves it under Mike's nose. 'What do you think?'

'Look, Liam, these people are way beyond scary. They don't just give out leaflets, they beat people up. They were probably involved in that business last night.'

Liam's face changes. Mike sees the shadow of guilt stealing across his brother's features.

'You weren't there! Liam, I don't believe you.'

'I'm not telling you anything.'

Liam tries to walk away, but Mike blocks his path.

'Two people needed hospital treatment after the violence,' he cries. 'One was a woman. They say she could be scarred for life. Is that what you're into now, hurting women?'

'You don't mention what the Pakis did at the school,' says Liam.

'Stop using that word,' snaps Mike.

'OK then, the *Asians*.'

'Vandalising the cars was wrong as well,' says Mike, 'but at least nobody got hurt there.'

'There you go again,' says Liam. 'Always taking their side.'

'There are no sides,' Mike protests.

'That's where you're wrong,' says Liam. 'There's a war coming. It's time you made your mind up, Mike. Whose side are you on?'

'Oh, for crying out loud!' snorts Mike. 'You want to know whose side I'm on, Liam? Mine. It's about getting on with your own life and respecting the way other people live. I'll tell you whose side I'm on – the side of somebody who's going to get an education and hightail it out of this scabby little town.'

'In your dreams!' says Liam. 'You know what happens to people like you, Mike? They get hit in the crossfire.'

Tahir has his hand on the kitchen door handle when Diane intercepts him.

'Oh no you don't, mister.'

'I'm going out with Khalid and Nasir. I told you.'

'No, Tahir, you didn't. Besides, you don't *tell* me what you're planning to do, you *ask* me. I'm your mother, remember.'

'So I can't go out?'

'I'm not stopping you doing anything,' says Diane. 'I just want you to do your homework first.'

'I haven't got any,' says Tahir.

'That's not what your Planner says.'

Tahir is outraged. 'Have you been in my bag?'

'Your dad has.'

'Then I'll talk to Dad about it.'

'No, you'll talk to me. Your dad's getting the cab serviced.'

'Look,' says Tahir, 'I was late with the homework, that's all.'

'The teacher says in here that you didn't do it at all.'

'Then he's lying!'

'Oh Tahir, do we have to go through this every time? Just find the worksheets and get them done.'

Tahir pulls out his mobile. 'Fine. I'll phone the others and tell them I'm going to be late.'

He slams the bag down on the table and pulls out the worksheets.

'Happy now?' he says as he starts writing.

'Yes,' says Diane, but she is anything but.

At about the same time John Creed is on the phone. He is working his way through a press list.

'*Chronicle*? Roger Gray in Features, please.'

There is a brief pause. 'Hello Roger, this is John Creed. That's right, National Organiser of the Patriotic League.'

He chuckles at the eagerness in the journalist's voice. 'I thought you'd want to hear from me.'

Roger Gray fires a question at him.

'Clive Road? No, we didn't have anything to do with that. We're a disciplined organisation. We don't go in for mindless hooliganism.'

On the other side of the room Colin Stone barely suppresses a guffaw.

'But I am concerned about race relations in Oakfield.'

Stone leaves the room. Creed hears hacking laughter from the upstairs bathroom.

'The Patriotic League is holding a press conference tomorrow. We're calling for a Peace Wall between the warring communities. Good. I'll look forward to your attendance.'

He hangs up and calls to Stone. 'You're going to have to get a grip on yourself, Colin. This is a serious business.'

But when Stone walks into the living room Creed can't help joining him in ringing laughter.

'Now can I go out?' asks Tahir.

'After I've seen your homework,' says Diane, holding out her hand.

She runs her eyes over it. 'See, that's only taken you ten minutes. You're a bright lad, Tahir, when you put your mind to it. Why can't you just buckle down to your work?'

'What for?' demands Tahir. 'There are no jobs round here anyway, not if you've got an OK9 postcode.'

Diane knows he is right but she is not about to give him an excuse for his current attitude to school.

'Islam values education, Tahir. You should know that.'

Tahir shakes his head. 'Since when were you an expert on what Islam is about, Mum? I don't remember seeing you at the mosque.'

He sees the hurt look in her eyes but makes no attempt at an apology. 'I'm going out.'

Diane lets him go. She has got him to do his homework but she knows she hasn't even started to win him over.

Rabia walks into the kitchen. She has been listening to the conversation from the hall.

'You OK, Mum?' she asks.

Diane nods half-heartedly.

Rabia reads her letter from the Oakfield Book Award. The next meeting is on Monday, 7 January at four o'clock. Rabia fills in her reply slip, puts it into an envelope and addresses it to Ravensmoor Road library. Once she has stuck on a stamp she walks over and rests a sympathetic hand on Diane's shoulder.

'I think somebody needs a cup of coffee,' she says.

'Rabia, you're a gem.'

Rabia smiles. 'I know.'

The Patriotic League's press conference is at the Lion at twelve noon the following day. The upstairs room is packed. The call for a Peace Wall has even attracted the attention of a few of the nationals. The conference is being chaired by Colin Stone.

Five minutes into proceedings Councillor Martin Roberts slips in at the back.

'So you see, ladies and gentlemen,' Creed is saying, 'the reason why the two communities are at each other's throats is because they are as different as chalk and cheese – different religions, different cultures. I am not saying one is better than the other, just different.'

He eyes his audience and drops a second, more loaded word, into the discussion: 'Separate.'

He is careful to avoid using the word *race*.

'All we are saying is this: Catholic and Protestant had to be kept apart in Northern Ireland. Why not Christian and Muslim here in Oakfield?'

A journalist is on his feet. 'Are you really suggesting that a wall be built between the Oakfield Triangle and the Ravensmoor Road?' he asks.

'Yes,' says Creed. 'I am suggesting precisely that.'

'But surely this is nothing like Northern Ireland!'

Creed holds up a copy of the *Chronicle*. 'I refer you to the front page of your own newspaper,' he says. 'To me it looks exactly like Northern Ireland.'

A few minutes later the *Daily Mirror*'s northern correspondent poses a question: 'Do you intend to stand candidates in the forthcoming council elections, Mr Creed?'

Creed smiles. 'This has not yet been fully discussed by our local branches,' he says.

Stone shifts in his chair. Branches? Since when was there more than one?

'I can tell you, however,' says Creed, glancing pointedly at Councillor Roberts, 'wherever the people's local representatives are letting them down the Patriotic League will put forward its own candidates. And when the time comes, Colin Stone here will be coordinating our election campaign.'

At half-past four that afternoon Mike Kelly is walking back from the library. He has walked down to Ravensmoor Road library to post his reply in person. His thoughts are full of the dark-eyed girl. January 7 can't come too soon. He is about to turn for home when he notices Daz and Jason hanging round the community centre.

'Is our Liam with you?' he asks.

'Can you see him?' Jason says.

Mike walks away slowly. They seem to be waiting for someone, but it isn't Liam by the sound of it. They seem edgy too, as if they're up to something. By the time Mike gets home he has other things on his mind, however. He runs his eyes over the letter from the library again. The whole judging process should take three or four meetings, it says.

Three or four meetings.

That's how long Mike has to get to know the dark-eyed girl.

Bobby McAllister leaves work at eight o'clock. The youth club was particularly badly attended tonight – just five kids. Bobby alarms the building and locks up. He told Kate she could leave at seven o'clock so he is on his own.

'No sense us both wasting our time here,' he said.

He turns round and finds himself facing Daz and Jason. They both agreed it would be better not to tell Liam what they had in mind. He wants to check everything with Creed.

'What do you want?' Bobby asks.

'An apology would be nice,' says Daz.

'Yes,' says Bobby. 'It would also be a miracle.'

He brushes past the youths and starts walking to his car. He is just pressing the key fob when a blinding pain rocks him. He has been punched on the side of the head. He turns, raising his fists, but kicks and blows are raining in on him from all directions. There is no way he can defend himself against them all.

'Get off me!'

As he shouts at his attackers, Bobby can taste the blood filling his mouth. 'Get off!'

They don't get off. A jarring kick to his left knee sends Bobby sprawling. Now the boots are thudding into his ribs. Bobby curls up the best he can, defending himself with his arms. After another blow to the head he is losing consciousness.

The following afternoon Suhail Khan is sitting at the railway station taxi rank, listening to John Creed on local radio. Creed is promising a demonstration of the Moorside's feelings.

After a few moments Suhail changes channel. He remembers past Eid celebrations: early baths and new clothes, prayers and presents of sweets and dried fruit. This year will be no different but there are shadows around the festivities. There are men with hatred and anger in their hearts. There is talk of peace lines and tit-for-tat attacks.

He gets a call from the office. He has a pick-up at the hospital.

'Where to?' he asks when the fare gets in.

'Sixty-six, New Hall Avenue,' says the man in a Scots burr.

'What happened to you?' asks Suhail.

'I got jumped by youths,' says Bobby. 'They caught me by surprise. I've been in overnight for observation.'

'It's terrible when you can't even walk the streets without being assaulted,' says Suhail. 'What was it, a mugging?'

'No,' says Bobby. 'This was political, the work of professional thugs.'

'Are you talking about the Patriotic League by any chance?' asks Suhail.

'That's them.'

'What did you do to upset them?' asks Suhail.

'I stood up at a meeting and said the Asian community wasn't to blame for the Moorside's problems. I must be a bit of a masochist.'

'Maybe it's just that you can tell right from wrong,' says Suhail.

He pulls up in front of 66, New Hall Avenue. Bobby reaches out, offering a ten-pound note.

'That's all right,' says Suhail. 'There's no charge.'

'Nice gesture,' says Bobby, 'but I'll pay my way.'

Suhail gives him his change. 'Take care, sir.'

'Yes,' says Bobby. 'You too.'

As Bobby reaches his front door he shakes his head. He had good reason for turning down Suhail's generosity. He doesn't deserve it. He has decided not to report the beating to the police in case it means more of the same. He is too scared to tell the truth.

That evening Rabia is reading the cards with their traditional greeting: Eid Mubarak. She hears the door go.

'Tahir?'

'No, it's me.'

'Oh, hi, Dad.'

'Is Mum in?'

'No, she's gone late-night shopping.'

'So you're on your own, then?'

Rabia nods.

'What have you been doing with yourself?'

'I'm reading my way through the long list for the Book Award,' Rabia tells him.

'Any good ones?'

'I've chosen three that I think are pretty special.'

'You're enjoying this, aren't you?'

Rabia nods. 'So what are you doing in at this time?'

'I just called in to tell your mum about something that

happened tonight.' He tells Rabia about the fare he took home from the hospital.

'You ought to tell Tahir about him,' says Rabia.

Suhail nods. 'I know what you mean. Anyway, I'd better get back to work.'

Just under twenty-four hours later, in the night of the new moon, the Eid celebrations are under way. The houses on the Triangle are decorated with brightly coloured lights. The greeting of Eid Mubarak can be heard along Clive Road.

But it is not the scene on Clive Road that will be in the news tomorrow. Less than a hundred metres further on the press and the TV are focusing their cameras on the Patriotic League. As yet it is not clear what the thirty or so demonstrators are doing. The only clue is the pile of plywood sheets they are guarding.

'So what have you got for us, Mr Creed?' asks the *Chronicle* reporter.

'You'll see,' says Creed, enjoying being the centre of attention. He nods in the direction of Colin Stone.

'Right, lads,' says Stone.

Willing hands snap up the plywood sheets. On Colin Stone's command, the demonstrators turn and raise the line of sheets. Each one is painted with artificial brickwork. The slogan printed on the mock wall is: *Moorside residents say: rights for local people. Build a peace wall now.*

The crowd at the bottom of Ravensmoor Road has attracted the attention of some of the Triangle's young men.

'Just look at them,' says Tahir. 'They're rubbing our noses in it. Next thing you know they'll be on our turf.'

'They already have been,' says Khalid.

Eyes turn instinctively in the direction of The Gulam. The crowd at the northern apex of the Triangle is growing. Word has got around that there is some kind of protest on Ravensmoor Road. The police are there.

'Move back, please ,' says a uniformed policeman.

'Typical,' says Tahir. 'You let those racists demonstrate but you move us on.'

'This is a legitimate peaceful protest,' the policeman says, indicating the Patriotic League and their Peace Wall. 'An application to demonstrate was filed several days ago.'

'But they attacked Clive Road!' Khalid cries.

'Yes,' says Tahir. 'And they roughed his grandad up.'

'Just move back, please,' says the policeman. He takes hold of Tahir's arm and starts to guide him towards Clive Road. Tahir pulls his arm away.

'You let go of me!'

Two more officers close in.

'Just move back, please.'

'What if I don't?'

'Then we will have no choice but to arrest you, sir.'

The officer is aware of the TV cameras. He is being studiously polite. As the police move in, Tahir still refuses to budge.

'I will ask you once more,' the policeman repeats. 'Step back, please.'

By now Tahir is determined to stand his ground. 'Why

should I? I haven't done anything wrong. I live here. They're the ones who should move. I bet half of them are from out of town.'

'That's it,' says the senior policeman. 'Take him away.'

The officers seize Tahir by the arms and drag him towards a police van.

'This is ridiculous,' Nasir protests. 'What's he done wrong?'

'Let him go,' cries Khalid.

The cry is taken up by about fifty onlookers. 'Let him go! Let him go!'

Furious at the arrest, the crowd have started to throw stones. Some are directed at the police, others at the Patriotic League. When a few of the League's supporters go to pick up missiles to return them, Creed quickly intervenes.

'No, this is working in our favour. Don't throw them back. That's it, put them down.'

He whispers something into Stone's ear. Stone nods and starts leading the chants of: 'Peace now! Build the wall! Peace now! Build the wall!'

The TV cameras are running. To Creed's delight the news bulletins will show young Asians throwing stones while the Oakfield branch of the Patriotic League chants about peace.

The phone rings at the Khans' house. Rabia takes the call. Her eyes widen.

'Mum,' she says, 'you'd better take this. It's Tahir. He's at the police station.

'Police!' Diane takes the phone.

'Is he all right? It's not an accident, is it?'

'No, Mrs Khan,' says the officer at the other end of the line. 'It's nothing like that. Your son is fine. He is being held for a public order offence.'

'Public order? How do you mean, public order? I don't understand.'

'Could you come down to the station please, Mrs Khan?'

'But what's he done?'

'If you come down to the station we can explain everything to you.'

Diane puts down the phone. 'I'm going to the police station, Rabia,' she says, pulling on her coat. 'Ring your dad for me. I'll meet him down there.'

Rabia starts punching out Suhail's mobile number.

'Did you see that young fool's face when the police arrested him?' says Creed mockingly.

He mimics Tahir in a whining voice. ' "I haven't done anything wrong. I live here." '

The Lion is packed with League supporters. The Leeds

and Manchester crews are much in evidence again. Stone nods to Creed.

'Settle down, lads,' says Creed, noting that the League's membership has at least doubled since he arrived. 'We're on the news.'

The regional bulletin has just started. A hush descends over the bar as everyone looks up at the television.

'Trouble flared in Oakfield this evening. During the town's Eid celebrations groups of young Asian men started throwing missiles at a largely peaceful protest by residents of the Moorside estate.'

Creed savours the words. *Asians . . . missiles. Moorside . . . peaceful.* John, he thinks, you couldn't have scripted it better yourself.

'Look!' shouts Daz. 'There's you, Liam.'

Everyone is straining to pick themselves out in the crowd. The report cuts to John Creed. He is speaking directly to the camera. *'Tonight's events prove what we have been saying all along,'* he says. *'These people refuse to observe normal democratic channels. They don't want to accept the customs of this country. Special measures are necessary to control them.'*

The TV camera homes in on the slogan: *Build a peace wall now.*

M ike looks up from his book.

'Mum,' he says, turning up the sound on the TV, 'you should see this.'

Mary Kelly comes in from the kitchen. 'That's our Liam! What's he doing?'

'It's a demonstration. He's at Ravensmoor Road by the look of it.'

Mary shakes her husband awake. 'Sean, our Liam's just been on the telly.'

It takes a moment for Sean to focus on the screen. 'Where?'

'He was on a moment ago. There he is now.'

There is another shot of Liam chanting '*Peace now*'.

'He's not doing any harm, is he?' says Sean.

'Isn't he?' Mike retorts.

'Why?' says Sean. 'What's it about?'

'Those morons want to build a wall between the Triangle and the Moorside.'

Sean grunts. 'Sounds a good idea to me.'

―――――――

'I hope you're proud of yourself,' says Suhail as he ushers Tahir inside the house. 'My son picked up by the police! I could see the way they were looking at me. I was so embarrassed.'

'I was trying to defend my community,' Tahir protests, not for the first time that night.

'You picked a fine way to do it,' says Diane. 'Throwing stones at the police! Very clever.'

'I didn't throw any stones,' says Tahir.

'No,' says Suhail, 'but your hot-headed young friends did.'

'How can you condemn us?' cries Tahir. 'You were there

when they attacked The Gulam. You saw them in action with your own eyes.'

'That doesn't mean I've got to go out and get myself arrested,' says Suhail.

'You could have been,' Tahir yells. 'I seem to remember you with a wheel-brace in your hand, Dad.'

'That's different,' says Suhail.

'Is it? How?'

'It was self-defence.'

'And what about tonight? What do you think that demonstration was about? They're the same people who came down Clive Road smashing windows. The same people, Dad.'

Suhail squeezes the bridge of his nose between his thumb and forefinger. 'Go to your room, Tahir.'

'Why won't you listen to me?'

Suhail raises his voice for the first time. 'Go to your room!'

Rabia passes Tahir on the landing. 'Are you all right?'

Tahir shakes his head. He looks close to tears. Rabia has almost forgotten how sensitive Tahir can be. All his life he has wanted Dad's approval.

'I'll try to talk to Dad,' she says.

Tahir squeezes her arm and walks past. Rabia goes into the living room. She sees the anxious, defeated looks on her parents' faces and hesitates for a moment, wondering how to play this.

'What did the police say?' she asks.

'They've given Tahir a juvenile reprimand,' Diane tells her.

'What does that mean?'

'It's a formal warning. So long as he doesn't do anything else wrong it won't appear as a conviction.'

'He's really upset,' Rabia says quietly.

No matter how they quarrel, Rabia can't forget how much her twin brother means to her. However rash and unthinking he can be, he is her brave other half.

'So he should be,' Suhail says. 'He's disgraced this family.'

'Don't be too hard on him, Dad,' says Rabia. 'He was provoked. I've been watching the evening news. Those people are Nazis.'

'We know what the demonstrators stand for,' says Diane, 'but Tahir can't go taking the law into his own hands. He's been very stupid.'

Rabia looks out into the night.

The following evening John Creed is packing a holdall. He's off home for Christmas.

'I'm going to spend some quality time with the family,' he says.

Colin watches the meticulous way Creed folds his clothes. 'You deserve a break, John,' he says. 'You can pride yourself on a job well done.'

'Thank you,' says Creed. 'But I must correct you. The job's only half done. We'll continue our efforts in the New Year.'

He zips the holdall. 'How are you going to spend the holiday, Colin?'

'Dunno. I'll probably go round my mum's as usual.'

'So there's no special lady in your life?' Stone shakes his head.

'Ah well,' says Creed. 'Have a good Christmas break. I'll see you on January 7th.'

Stone watches Creed walk to his car and follows its rear lights as Creed drives to the end of the road. He sits down and channel-surfs for a few minutes. By the time he finally switches off the TV his eyes are as cold and desolate as a fish's. He feels so lonely he could scream.

Mike is keeping out of the old man's way. He finds Liam in the kitchen making some toast.

'Do you want anything?' asks Liam.

Mike is taken aback. It's the first civil word they have exchanged in days. He shakes his head. Liam is aware of his brother watching him.

'OK, what's the problem?'

'No problem,' says Mike. 'Well, unless you think your younger brother being a filthy Nazi is a problem.'

'I'm not a Nazi,' says Liam. 'I'm a patriot.'

'Surely you don't believe that,' Mike says. 'Are you telling me nobody in this Patriotic League of yours has let the mask slip yet? They're Hitler-worshippers, Liam. You can't be that naïve.'

Liam half-remembers a German song the Leeds and Manchester boys sang in the Lion. He remembers the look in Creed's eyes that time down the industrial estate. He knows there is more to the League than a campaign for justice, but it is making him somebody. For the first time in his life people are taking notice of him.

'Mike, you don't know what you're talking about.'

Mike watches him go and closes his eyes. 'That's the trouble, Liam. I do.'

*

The night wind is soughing in the eaves as Mike Kelly wonders where he and his younger brother are going with their lives. The wind whips down the hill past the community centre with its reinforced windows, past Colin Stone's house where its occupant is watching Leni Riefenstahl's film of Hitler's Nuremburg rally, past Ravensmoor Road library and along Clive Road with its curry houses and halal butchers. By the time it rattles the window panes at the Khans' small terrace it has travelled a little over a mile, but it has crossed a vast chasm of loathing and mistrust.

PART TWO
HISTORY'S CHILDREN

1
Hitting a Wall

'What time do you expect to be finished?' Suhail asks, as he drops Rabia and her best friend Sofia off at Ravensmoor Library. It is January 7th and it is bitterly cold.

'Half-past five,' says Rabia. 'Six o'clock at the latest.'

'Any change at all, you must call me on your mobile,' Suhail says in his sternest fatherly voice.

Rabia holds up a silver Nokia. 'All charged up,' she says. 'I promise I won't budge from the meeting room until you're parked outside.'

Satisfied, Suhail waves and drives off.

'Doesn't your dad go on?' says Sofia. 'He ought to lighten up a bit.'

'That's what I used to think,' Rabia answers. 'But you should have been here that night. You and that stupid 'flu! I was completely helpless. I've never felt that way before. It was . . . disturbing.'

Sofia smiles sympathetically. 'I can imagine.'

It is doubtful whether she can. For all her outward confidence Sofia is a home girl, reluctant to take the kind of chance Rabia did that November night. If it had been the other way round, and Rabia had been ill, Sofia would definitely have given the meeting a miss. As the two girls climb the stone steps to the front door of the library, a white boy their own age is coming up the street.

That's her!

Mike's heart misses a beat. The dark-eyed girl! That was her getting out of a taxi and going inside. Pity she's got a friend with her though. It's always harder to get talking to a girl when she brings a friend along. Cramps your style. Oh, who do I think I'm kidding, Mike asks himself – talking like I know this stuff from experience!

Unlike some of the other lads in his year, Ady for instance, Mike has only been out with two girls and one of those was a one-date thing, OK until he opened his mouth and put his foot in it. That's my trouble, Mike has decided. I've got a mouth with a mind of its own. He can't remember the number of times it has got him in trouble. He has a brain that imagines magical chat-up lines and a mouth that comes out with the most wince-making nonsense ever.

Still, she's here and that's a start. Mike walks into the meeting room. Puccini is playing low, the 'Vissi d'Arte' from *Tosca*. Mike likes the sound of it and wonders what it is. One thing's for certain – nobody back on the Moorside would have a clue.

There are ten of them present, including the Book Award coordinator. She's the one responsible for the music. Mike scans those present: seven girls and only two boys.

He examines the competition. Nothing to worry about there, he tells himself. The lad is a classic nerd – be-

122

spectacled, slightly chubby, painfully shy. But Mike has spoken too soon. Just as the meeting is about to start, the door swings open and in walks a tall, blond-haired lad. He looks like a refugee from a boy band. Mike scowls. Just his luck, he's up against Ronan Keating's younger brother, Adonis.

'Thank you ever so much for coming,' the Award coordinator says breezily. 'It's good to see that the attendance has held up. It's so disappointing when people have to drop out of the judging process midway.'

She smiles and everyone smiles with her. She's that sort of person. Her enthusiasm is infectious.

'Now, if I could explain the purpose of this evening. We will draw up a shortlist of between fifteen and twenty books. These will go out to the town's schools. Shadowing groups in each school will read the books and send in their comments. In a month's time we will meet again and draw up the final shortlist, which will be published in a special feature in the *Chronicle*. They've promised to include a photograph of the judging panel. I'm told it will be in colour.'

Mike is looking across the table at Rabia. When Sofia catches his eye and frowns, he looks away. But not for long.

'There will be two meetings after that, one to choose the eventual winner and a celebration event to which the winning author will be invited.'

Three meetings after tonight, thinks Mike, stealing a second glance at Rabia. I can't afford to mess up.

Suhail drives home along Ravensmoor Road and up Clive Road. The Gulam is back in business and is already filling up. The attack doesn't seem to have frightened any customers away, but something has changed. The atmosphere around the Triangle is edgy. Strangers are inspected as they walk up the road. The knots of young lads on street corners pay just a little more attention to the people coming and going.

Suhail pulls up outside the house and goes inside. Tahir is flicking through the TV channels. He has been grounded since the arrest. He has two more days before he can go out again. 'Then,' he says, in that surly way of his, 'I've done my time.'

'Don't you have any homework to do?' Suhail asks.

'You are joking, aren't you?' says Tahir. 'We've only just started back after the break.'

Suhail grins. 'Just asking,' he says.

Tahir gives an almost imperceptible shake of the head. Almost.

'You ought to get yourself an interest,' says Suhail, 'like Rabia.'

'I'm not taking part in some stupid book prize,' says Tahir.

Suhail decides to leave well alone and finds Diane in the kitchen.

'His mood doesn't improve much,' Suhail observes.

'He's not been that bad,' says Diane. 'I thought he'd kick up more than he has. Two weeks is a long time to be grounded.'

Suhail snorts. 'I don't agree. I wanted to make it a month, if you remember.'

'Yes,' says Diane. 'And we agreed that Tahir had been provoked. A fortnight has been quite enough.'

Suhail rubs his chin. 'Maybe.'

At Ravensmoor Road library, the judges are discussing the longlist. Rabia is taking Blond Boy to task.

'Oh, I don't agree,' she says. 'The characters are so one-dimensional.'

'One-dimensional!' retorts Blond Boy. 'What about the way things turn out? When did you get the ending?'

'*I* got it early on,' says Mike, diving in on Rabia's side. 'I thought it was really obvious from the beginning.'

'Come again?' says Blond Boy, treating Mike the way he would a moth that has started flying round the lightbulb. 'None of the important things are mentioned at the start. Two of the key characters don't even appear until halfway through. Have you even read this book?'

Mike is sure he is blushing. His intervention has backfired big time. Wonderful! he thinks. Now I look like a prize wombat. My runaway mouth has done it again. You wait, Mouth – when I get you home I'll give you such a slap! Mike doesn't actually know which book they are discussing. He noticed his dark-eyed girl arguing with Blond Boy and decided to earn some brownie points by supporting her.

'Of course I have.'

Mike cranes his neck to see the book Blond Boy is holding. It's one of his favourites. Blond Boy is right. The sting in the tail is brilliant.

'Oh, sorry,' Mike says. 'I thought you were talking about a different one.'

'Which one would that be?' Blond Boy demands.

There you go again, Mouth! Did I say one slap? Make that three. Mike picks up the nearest book. It is one of the short, early junior titles. Rabia and Blond Boy shake their heads. Even better, Mike thinks. I've brought them together over this.

'Rabia,' says the girl she came in with, 'what's that other dead cert you wrote down for the longlist?'

Rabia. Her name is Rabia.

Great, thinks Mike. I'm on my way. I know her name, now I've got to get to know *her*. But before Mike can take advantage of the precious information, he is interrupted by Chubby Nerdy Guy.

'Can we get back to the longlisting?' he asks impatiently.

Mike returns reluctantly to his own group.

A mile away, on the Moorside estate, the Patriotic League are leafleting. Colin Stone has arranged it to impress John Creed. Creed is due back in Oakfield later that evening and Stone wants to present him with a job well done. Halfway through the leafleting Stone is telling his troops which streets to do next. He is interrupted by Councillor Roberts, who has just stopped his car next to them.

'What do you call this?' Councillor Roberts demands.

'I don't know what you mean,' Stone says coldly.

Councillor Roberts waves the leaflet. 'This is a direct attack on me,' he says angrily. 'You say I've done nothing to save the youth club.'

Stone grins at Daz, Jason and Liam. 'You haven't.'

'No? So how come the youth club has got a temporary home in the primary school? They're moving into one of the spare classrooms next month.'

Stone's eyes widen.

'That's right,' says Councillor Roberts. 'I've won it a reprieve. I've just got it through the council sub-committee. Maybe you ought to get your facts right before you start mouthing off.'

Stone looks stunned.

'I was at the Youth Club just giving them the news when I was handed this rubbish. Are you totally stupid, man? You can't even spell *Councillor* correctly.'

Still lost for words, Stone lowers his eyes like a guilty schoolboy.

'If this is the quality of your organisation,' Councillor Roberts says, 'then I've nothing to worry about in the May elections. I'm holding a surgery tomorrow night. I'll be telling everyody who turns up just how much faith they can put in you and your Patriotic League.'

He gets in his car and drives away, leaving a humiliated Colin Stone to face his foot soldiers.

————

'Is there a toilet here?' Mike asks.

'Out of the door and up the stairs,' someone tells him.

Mike jogs up the stairs and walks along the corridor. He is feeling good. The girl is every bit as attractive as he remembered. What's more, she is poised, confident and intelligent. His sort of woman. Oh, there I go again! Any girl that gorgeous is my sort of woman.

On his way back Mike is humming a tune from *West Side Story*. He's watched the movie half a dozen times on one of the satellite movie channels. Before he reaches the top of the stairs he starts to sing softly to himself: 'Rab-i-a! I've just met a girl called Rab-i-a!'

That's when he hears footsteps behind him. He freezes. He feels a heat rash sweeping up his spine and the hairs on the back of his neck stand up. Not her! Please don't let it be her. He half-turns. It isn't her, but it is just as bad. It is Rabia's friend. What was her name? Yes, Sofia, that's it.

So-fi-a! I've been caught red-handed by So-fi-a!

Mike sees the smile playing on her lips. There you go again, Mouth. You don't deserve to be connected to a brain like mine. Now you've really blown it.

When Mike goes back to his place he can see Sofia whispering in Rabia's ear.

No! he groans inwardly. Don't. Don't do it.

But judging by Rabia's reaction, Sofia's already done it.

Rabia looks across the table. For a moment her eyes meet his. Sorry, he is saying, using his eyes to plead for forgiveness. No deal. The eyes can do their worst, the Mouth has already sunk him. Rabia dismisses him with a flick of her hair.

John Creed arrives right on time. Isn't he ever late? wonders Stone. He isn't a man, he's a robot. Stone is wondering how to own up over the misjudged leaflet.

'So how was your Christmas, Colin?' Creed asks, as if he didn't know. 'You really went to town on the decorations, didn't you?

There is a thirty-centimetre fibre optic tree in one corner. Every ten seconds it changes from red to blue, then from blue to silver. Other than that one concession to the festive season, there is nothing. Still, what's the point of Christmas crackers when you've nobody to pull them with?

'Doesn't seem much point making a fuss when you don't have kids,' says Stone.

'Don't talk to me about kids!' says Creed, unable to resist rubbing it in. 'Mine ran me ragged all Christmas. I'm glad to get back up north so I can have a bit of peace. Any news over the holiday?'

Stone hesitates, then takes a deep breath. 'There is one thing.'

Mike decides to come right out with it. OK, he's going to say, I acted like a complete wally, but I'd really like to get to know you. Oh God, how sad is that? But what *do* I say, and how do I stop Mouth fouling it up? In the event, he doesn't get to say anything. All the time the meeting is breaking up Sofia sticks to Rabia's side like her bodyguard.

'Oh, come on!' he murmurs under his breath. 'Give me a break.'

Mike sees Rabia pick up her shoulder bag.

'Great.'

But as he is about to fling himself on her mercy Chubby Nerdy Guy steps in the way. 'Which way are you going, Mike?'

What timing! Don't you understand? She's going.

'Not your way,' Mike says, trying to shove past.

'You don't even know where I live.'

Mike realises how rude he has just been. Desperate as he is to talk to Rabia, he doesn't like hurting anyone's feelings.

'I'm going up the hill to the Moorside.'

Chubby Nerdy Guy looks shocked, as if he didn't know people up there *could* read. 'You live on the Moorside!'

'That's right. Somebody has to. You?'

Rabia is heading for the door.

'I live in Shevington.' Shevington is Oakfield's attempt at a leafy suburb.

'Then we're going in opposite directions. See you next time, er . . .' Mike has been in Chubby Nerdy Guy's group all night and he doesn't remember his name.

'I'm Simon.'

'Right, see you next time then, Simon.'

Mike rushes after Rabia, only to see her getting into a cab – the one he saw her arrive in. It pulls away before he has a chance to attract her attention.

C olin Stone is in his shed. It is large with a net-curtained window, more a den than a shed. This is his private retreat. Even Creed has not been admitted into this private sanctum. Here, in his Third Reich time capsule, Stone doesn't have to take orders, not even from His Highness John Creed. There are posters and news clippings on the wall, all devoted to the activities of the far right. In pride of place on the end wall is a large flag, brought back from a rally in Germany, bearing the Iron Cross insignia.

Stone is smarting from the roasting Creed has given him

over the leaflet. How he would love to wipe the smile off that smarmy upper-class face! No matter what Creed says, Stone knows the real battles will be fought where it matters – on the streets. But Creed's the boss. There is no way round that simple fact.

Stone finds consolation in his collection of badges. Most feature the same few symbols: eagles, swastikas, black German crosses. He fingers each one carefully, then puts them away. Suddenly it is as if these images of primal white power are showing him the way forward. If Creed won't do the necessary, Stone thinks, then I'll have to do it on the quiet. With a smile he takes out his toolbox.

There is a job to be done.

Rabia and Sofia are in Rabia's room, listening to music. It's the piece they plan to use when Miss Jamil starts auditioning for the dance festival. They are trying to put together a sequence of movements and burst out laughing at each new mix-up.

'Are you sure it was my name he was saying?' Rabia asks.

'He wasn't just *saying* it,' says Sofia, 'he was *singing* it.'

'How do you mean, singing it?'

Sofia gives an exaggerated rendition of Mike's Rab-i-a song.

'That's from *West Side Story*,' says Rabia, instantly warming to this unknown boy.

'Come again?'

'*West Side Story*. You must have heard of it. It's a famous American movie from the Sixties, a retelling of *Romeo and Juliet*.'

Sofia is none the wiser. She doesn't share Rabia's fondness for Hollywood's backlist.

'Sounds like you've got another admirer,' she says.

'Don't be silly. How would he know my name? No, you've got the wrong end of the stick.'

'I don't think so,' says Sofia. 'I caught him looking at you a few times.'

'Now you're definitely being silly,' says Rabia.

'Am I?'

There is a knock at the door.

'Sofia,' says Diane, 'your father's here.'

'Dad?'

'He thinks it's late. He's come to walk you home.'

Sofia opens the door.

'Don't worry,' says Diane. 'You're not in any trouble. I think your father's a little worried. You know, with all the things that have happened lately, he doesn't want you walking home alone.'

'Oh, for goodness' sake!' says Sofia. 'I'm sixteen, not ten.'

'I wouldn't say that to your dad,' Diane says. 'There *have* been incidents. He's genuinely concerned.'

Sofia nods. 'I suppose. I'll see you tomorrow, *Rab-i-a*.'

Diane gives Rabia a questioning look.

'Forget it, Mum. It's nothing.'

The following evening Councillor Roberts is holding a surgery at Moorside Primary school. He listens to the usual complaints and tales of woe, and promises to take up each and every one of them. After the third mention of the Patriotic League leaflet, he is wondering whether he wouldn't be better handing the job over to Colin Stone, after all. But it's over by nine o'clock and he walks to his car. He runs his hand along the new paintwork and scowls when he remembers the cost. He is getting into the driver's seat when he hears something. He lowers the window and looks across the car park and playground.

'Must be imagining things,' he mutters.

He is tired and looking forward to an hour or two's telly, then a warm Horlicks and bed. He gives the school grounds another look then fastens his seat belt and turns on the radio. They're playing gangsta rap. Councillor Roberts listens for a few moments then shakes his head and changes channels.

If he had checked his mirror just one more time he might have spotted Colin Stone standing in the shadows.

Mike is wearing a defeated look when he walks into the kitchen.

'I'm an idiot,' he has been repeating all the way home. 'A prize idiot.'

He runs the tap and splashes his face with cold water. An

evening which began with *Tosca* and high expectations has ended in humiliation.

'Fancy singing her name! What's she going to think of me now?'

He looks out of the kitchen window at the patchy lawn and the broken down fence.

'I'm an id-i-ot.'

He even starts to sing that: 'Id-i-ot! She's just met a lad called Id-i-ot,

And suddenly I know exactly what a dope can be.

Id-i-ot, id-i-ot, id-i-ot, ID-I-OT!'

Sean walks in.

'Were you singing?' he asks.

'No.'

Sean gives Mike a questioning look then swigs down half a carton of milk. Some of it runs down his chin and on to his checked shirt. 'You're a funny one, Michael,' he says.

Mike sighs. Yes, just a barrel of laughs, that's me. For once, Dad, he thinks, you're dead right.

———

The following evening the Oakfield branch of the Patriotic League are holding their first meeting of the New Year. It is sparsely attended, a far cry from the heights they reached during December. Even John Creed looks disappointed.

'Thank you for turning up,' Colin Stone is saying to the sixteen people present. 'It looks like some of the membership are still recovering from their Christmas hangovers.'

It is meant as a joke but nobody so much as smiles. John Creed rises to address the meeting.

'No,' says Creed. 'No excuses, Colin. I'm afraid the members are not showing the right attitude at all if they want to make a difference in this town.'

He glances at Stone. 'It doesn't help when we give out inaccurate leaflets, either.'

Stone squirms in his seat.

'Still,' says Creed, 'what's done is done. What we need now is seriousness, real application to the task in hand.'

Liam exchanges glances with Daz and Jason.

'Turning up to demand a peace wall is one thing,' Creed continues, 'to translate our dreams for Oakfield into reality is quite another. The next step is to stand a slate of candidates in the council elections. We have made something of a name for ourselves but stunts are useless. They are soon forgotten.'

He has the audience's interest.

'What is needed,' he concludes, 'is representation. We have to turn the support we earned at the campaign meeting into votes and eventually into bums on seats in the council chamber.'

Daz raises his hand.

'Yes, Darren?' says Stone.

'Does this mean we're definitely going to stand against Roberts?'

'I'll answer that,' says Creed. 'Darren, we needed Councillor Roberts to get the bandwagon rolling. He has served his purpose. Now he is an obstacle to our further progress. At the meeting people weren't interested in him. They wanted Colin.'

He slams his fist down on the table and Stone jumps. He is clearly on edge. A few members of the audience laugh.

'We can't trust the old, discredited politicians. All they have given us is a town that could be part of the Indian subcontinent.'

There are murmurs of *Hear hear*.

'Yes, Darren, we are going to stand our own candidate against Roberts.'

'Who?' Jason asks.

'Why, our branch secretary here, your very own Colin Stone.'

Colin receives the applause with a thin smile. He knows he has blotted his copybook with the leaflet. One more mistake and Creed will drop him like a hot potato. He has something to do before he can become the councillor for the Moorside ward, and it involves Councillor Roberts.

That night Mike finds it hard to sleep. How did I manage it? he wonders. How could I actually blow my chances before I've even spoken to her? Classic! He can hear Sean snoring noisily down the hall and the loose window frames rattling. He can hear the pub-goers walking past, shouting and laughing. Every sound seems to be amplified four or five times, just like the humiliation he is feeling. After an hour of tossing and turning he sits up in bed, feeling the chill of the January night on his skin.

'I wonder if I've got some kind of death wish,' he says with only the damp, badly-decorated bedroom to hear him.

He had a month to prepare for the meeting. That's right – a whole month. So did he have a good chat-up line ready? Did he have any sort of line at all? Of course not. What he had was the Mouth from Hell. He just jumped in feet first and came out with the dumbest thing any human being has ever said or done. Mike groans and looks forward to a sleepless night. He wishes he could stop thinking about Rabia. It would make him feel better. Worrying about a girl is like banging your head against a wall: good when you stop.

On the other side of town Rabia Khan is unlikely to have much problem sleeping. For one thing, by going back to Ravensmoor Road she has laid her fears to rest. It is not a no-go area. There are no demons in the shadows. It's just a perfectly ordinary road where something unpleasant once happened to her. Rabia has worries, of course. Who doesn't? There is the prospect of her forthcoming GCSEs, but she is doing well at school. She can look forward to good, maybe even outstanding results. Miss Jamil has told her that if she doesn't make it to university then nobody will. Then there is Tahir. She worries about him. He always has to stick his neck out, always has to be first on the scene when there is any trouble. But he has got away with a caution. It could have been worse.

Rabia brushes her hair before going to bed. For some reason the boy from the library pops into her mind – the one who sang her name. What is he, some sort of weirdo? Somehow that doesn't seem right. He wasn't leering, he didn't seem terribly sexist, he wasn't trying to come on to her or anything. He was just there, very earnest, taking an obvious interest in her. Rabia pauses between strokes. So where does an obvious interest end and a sexist leer begin?

Answer me that. She leaves the puzzle hanging in the air. Then, with a brief smile she gets into bed and switches off her bedside lamp.

By the time Colin Stone checks that John Creed is asleep and slips out of the house, Rabia has been asleep for a couple of hours. Even Mike, tortured by his gaffe at the library, has dozed off. Oakfield is quiet. Stone walks along the darkened streets. In his pocket he has the tools he picked out last night. There are times when being a mechanic comes in handy. This is one of them.

Colin is crossing Boundary Road when he sees a police car in the distance. He slips down an entry and watches the car go by. Giving it plenty of time to disappear into the night, Colin walks on past the Baptist church on Norman Road and turns into Southern Avenue. He's arrived. Time for action. His skin starts prickling. He is still seething with the humiliation he suffered on Monday. Checking that the coast is clear, he sets to work.

Mike eats breakfast alone. Liam must still be in bed. There's Mum now, knocking on the door, trying to rouse him. Sean has just set off for work. For once the old man isn't nursing a hangover.

All the while Mike is munching his way through his toast, he is thinking of Rabia. He creates a number of scenarios. In one he waits for her outside Oakfield High. He rushes across the road and rattles off his carefully-scripted explanation of events at the library. In another version his fevered mind actually has him putting a finger to her protesting lips. Oh behave, Michael, as if you'd be able to get away with that! That's assuming he would get as far as Rabia without one of the Asian lads asking what he is doing on their patch. Then he is conjuring up all sorts of happy accidents. Coincidence really would be a beautiful thing. But it isn't going to happen, is it? He went a month without bumping into her the last time, and a whole lifetime prior to that. So it's hardly likely to change, is it?

'Is he up yet?' Mike asks.

Mary shakes her head.

'Do you want me to have a go?'

'There's no point,' says Mary. 'His bed hasn't been slept in. Some time after we went to bed last night he must have sneaked out of the house. You don't have any idea what he's getting up to, do you?'

'No, Mum.'

But that's not true. Mike's got a very good idea what Liam is getting himself into.

Councillor Roberts finishes the *Daily Mail*, wipes his plate with a round of bread and slips on his jacket.

'Good grub,' he tells Yvonne, his wife of thirty-five years. 'I always say there's nothing like a fried breakfast inside you.'

Yvonne smiles. She has read about stuff like cholesterol in her magazine but decides not to mention it. Why spoil it? Martin does enjoy his food.

'Right, see you about seven o'clock,' he says.

He gives her a peck on the cheek, collects his packed lunch and walks to the car. He has to turn on the engine and the rear windscreen heater. There is a layer of frost on all the windows. He scrapes the windows then slides into the driver's seat. He glances at his watch.

'I should have checked the weather earlier,' he grumbles. 'Now I'm running late.'

He revs the engine hard and pulls away. If he had seen the pool of brake fluid under the car he might not have been in quite such a hurry to get going.

Colin Stone is washing the dishes when John Creed laughs out loud. 'Seen this, Colin?' he says, holding up the newspaper.

'No, I haven't looked at the paper this morning.'

'The Home Secretary says our immigrant friends are to blame for their isolation from the mainstream. Don't you just love it when the government does your job for you?'

'Mm.'

'Is everything all right, Colin?' Creed asks.

'Yes. Why wouldn't it be?'

'I don't know. You seem a bit distracted. Got something on your mind?'

Colin notices the sports reports on the back page of Creed's newspaper.

'No, I'm a bit disappointed about the Oakies, that's all. They're at the bottom of the league and they've just sacked the manager.'

'Oh, football. I didn't have you down as a fan.'

'Oh yes, I'm a keen Oakies supporter. There was a time I didn't miss a single home match. I don't get down there much these days, what with branch business.'

'That's the problem with commitment,' says Creed. 'I'm a rugby man myself, but I had to stop playing when I started working full time for the League.'

Stone nods and gets on with the washing up. He is relieved when Creed turns back to his newspaper. He does have something on his mind and it isn't the fortunes of Oakfield Town Football Club.

Rabia and Sofia are crossing Clive Road on the way to school when they hear the ambulance sirens.

'I wonder what's going on there,' says Sofia. 'Do you think there's time to take a look?'

'Not really,' says Rabia. 'It's Maths first. I like Miss Jamil.'

Sofia looks disappointed. Then her expression changes.

'We're going to find out anyway,' she says. 'Here come the boys.'

'What is it?' Rabia asks.

'Car accident,' says Khalid, eager to be the first to answer. 'The driver's in a bad way. He must have lost control on the hill before ploughing into the wall. I don't know how he managed it.'

'The wall was big enough,' says Nasir.

'Guess who the driver is?' says Tahir.

Rabia and Sofia shake their heads.

'Only that lousy racist, Roberts.'

'The councillor?'

'That's him,' says Khalid. 'The one who started that campaign against the Eid celebrations.'

'Couldn't have happened to a nicer guy,' says Tahir.

'Tahir!' says Rabia. 'You don't mean that.'

'Why not?'

'If you don't know,' Rabia says, 'it's not worth me trying to tell you.'

When they set off again Rabia and Sofia walk on ahead.

'Given any more thought to lover boy?' Sofia asks.

'Who?'

'Oh, don't tell me you've forgotten. *Rab-i-a! I just met a girl called Rab-i-a!*'

'Stop it,' says Rabia. 'The boys will hear.'

'Oh, got something to hide, have you?'

'Don't be daft. I don't even know his name.'

'Does that mean you'd like to?'

'Sofia, I couldn't care less.'

But that isn't true. Rabia is feeling more than a twinge of curiosity about the boy who sings songs from *West Side Story*.

Liam Kelly wakes up in a sleeping bag on Darren Wright's floor. He can taste the bottles of Bud they downed last night before turning in. The first thing he notices when he opens his eyes is the red paint stain on his hand.

'You awake, Daz?'

There is a grunt from the bed.

'Got anything for breakfast?'

'Dunno,' says Daz. 'It all depends on the old lady.'

'Mum!' he shouts. 'Have we got anything in for breakfast?'

'There's a packet of Frosties and a loaf,' she shouts back, 'but go easy on the milk.'

'There you go,' says Daz. 'Feast fit for a king.'

'What time is it?' says Liam.

Daz squints at his watch. 'Half past nine.'

'I'm late for school.'

'You mean you were planning to go?'

Liam shrugs. 'Not really.'

'I wonder if the mosque's open yet,' says Jason.

Liam, Daz and Jason were up till two o'clock last night. They have covered the Clive Road mosque in graffiti.

'I'd love to see their faces,' Daz says.

Liam laughs. 'Yes, me too.'

But deep inside he feels a deep unease. Things are running out of control.

Councillor Roberts' injuries are not life-threatening. He has a broken leg, a broken collarbone and two broken ribs, plus lacerations to the face and whiplash. When Yvonne comes to see him she asks the obvious question.

'What happened? How could you run into a wall? You're usually such a safe driver, Martin.'

'It was the brakes,' says councillor Roberts, wincing. He is in a lot of discomfort.

'The brakes?'

'That's right. They failed.'

'But you only had the car MOT'd last week. I don't understand.'

'The police are looking at them.'

Yvonne's face drains of colour. 'You mean somebody tampered with them? Who would do such a thing?'

Councillor Roberts shakes his head. 'I don't know.'

But he has a good idea.

Mike intercepts Liam when he gets home at six o'clock that evening.

'Where've you been?' he demands.

'What's it to you?'

'Mum's been worried sick about you. You disappeared for over twenty-four hours, and you weren't in school.'

'Notice, did you?' Liam sneers.

'Yes, I noticed and so did the teachers. I don't like being grilled about my brother's whereabouts.'

'Feel ashamed of me, did you?' says Liam. 'As per rotten usual.'

'Oh, come off it!' says Mike. 'I care about you, that's all.'

'You!' Liam scoffs.

'Yes,' Mike says. 'Me. You've done some stupid things but you're still my brother.'

Mary Kelly appears in the doorway.

'Liam, where have you been?'

'I stayed at Daz's house. I told you I was going to.'

'I don't remember—'

'Of course you do. We had it planned for ages.'

Mary knows Liam is making it up but there is nothing she can do. 'Oh well,' she says, 'you're home now. Sit down in the living room, the pair of you, and I'll bring you in a sandwich.'

Liam sits next to Sean. Mike sits on his own in an armchair. The evening TV bulletin announces the news of Councillor Roberts' crash.

'The police are not ruling out foul play,' says the presenter.

'There you go, Mike,' says Sean. 'That's your fine Paki friends for you.'

'What do you mean?'

'Somebody fixed Roberts' brakes for him. Who else would do it?'

'You're jumping to conclusions,' says Mike.

'There you go again,' says Liam, 'sticking up for the Muslim brothers. It was Asians, Mike. It had to be. Why can't you admit it?'

'Because there's no proof,' Mike cries.

'Proof!' sneers Liam. 'How much proof do you need? I was on Ravensmoor Road when they started chucking bricks at us.'

'I know,' says Mike. 'Now say why they had a go at you

– because you were peddling the Patriotic League's poison.'

'Just admit it, Mike, they don't know how to behave in a civilised society.'

'Oh, and this is civilised, I suppose,' Mike retorts. 'Condemning a whole community without any evidence. Whatever happened to British justice? What happened to being innocent until proven guilty?'

He glares at his father and brother.

'You can give Liam my sandwich, Mum,' he says, storming out of the room. 'I'm not hungry.'

Rabia is on the Internet when Tahir walks past on the way to the fridge.

'You don't think the local boys had anything to do with that car crash, do you, Tahir?' she asks.

'How would I know?'

He takes a long drink of fruit juice. 'They'll blame it on us anyway. They always do.'

Rabia nods. 'I know.'

'The guy's in politics,' says Tahir. 'I bet he's made loads of enemies. Cutting his brakes though – I can't think of anybody round here who would do something like that. It's not our style, Rabia.'

'I certainly hope not.'

Tahir smiles. 'You can rely on it.'

Less than an hour later Councillor Martin Roberts is starting to doze off when he notices somebody standing over the bed.

'Who's that . . . ?'

His voice chokes off. He has recognised the figure of Colin Stone.

'What the hell are you doing here? I'm going to call the nurse.'

'I wouldn't do that if I were you, Martin. Have you seen *Misery*?'

'I don't have to listen to this,' says Councillor Roberts.

'I'm afraid you do,' Stone tells him. 'Anyway, about *Misery*. It's a really good film. You must have seen it, Martin. Let me refresh your memory.'

Stone is enjoying the way the tables have been turned. He wants to pay Councillor Roberts back for every moment of humiliation. 'Do you remember the scene where she breaks his legs for the second time? It goes through me every time I watch it, it really does.'

Councillor Roberts can feel the sweat running into his eyes. 'What do you want, Stone?'

'Nothing. I just wanted to tell you about *Misery*.'

'OK, Stone, you can knock it off now. I get the message. I won't tell the police who messed about with my car. Just stay away from me.'

'Oh, I don't mind you saying who sabotaged the car,' says Stone, 'so long as you get the details right. You do remember seeing those Asians hanging round, don't you?'

Councillor Roberts stares for a moment then gets Stone's drift. 'Yes,' he says.

'So tell me.'

'I saw an Asian . . .'

'*A couple* of Asians,' says Stone.

'OK, I saw a couple of Asians by the car. That must have been just before I got in.'

'That's the boy,' says Stone. 'It's good to see your memory's coming back.' He runs a hand over Councillor Roberts' plaster cast then walks towards the door.

'Just you make sure you get your story right, Councillor,' he says. 'I wouldn't want that leg of yours coming to any more harm.'

Mike Kelly finds himself walking along the canal towpath, surrounded by clinging, freezing fog. It is dark and cold and moonless down here among the bent and twisted pram wheels and the supermarket trolleys. It is ugly, so ugly. It is just like the things that go on around the Moorside, ugly as the sins of men.

Mike stares into the rainbow-coloured swirl of oil in the cloudy canal water and imagines the bruised, discoloured face of his mother; the twisted features of his brother and father. He tries to recall the tune he heard at the library, but it is swallowed up in raucous echoes of life on the Moorside. Ugly, so damned ugly! But the things you see day in, day out are not the boundaries of your imagination, and Mike Kelly has imagination to burn. The dreams he has open doors in his mind and behind one of the doors there is Rabia Khan.

'Rab-i-a!' he murmurs tunelessly. 'I just met a girl called Rab-i-a.'

Then it hardly seems to matter that he has made a fool of

himself. The fact that they live in the same town makes anything possible. The night traces a finger of cold down his cheek and he imagines her touch, her kiss. Even in Oakfield you can still dream.

2
A Diamond with no Sparkle

'There is a world beneath your feet,' says the tour guide. 'Whenever you walk to school or go to town this other Oakfield is here below. The tunnels you are about to enter extend for several hundred metres in each direction.'

It is the Wednesday after Mike stormed out of the house. He came home later that night, of course. There isn't much dignity in being sixteen. You are too dependent on other people for the food in your belly and the roof over your head.

Mike can't just walk away from the crumbling council house where he lives with his warring parents. Where else could he go? But he hates the house in Saxon Avenue even more than before. He hates the smell of sadness and defeat within its walls. He hates the divisions that are tearing it apart. In Rabia he has seen a promise of a different life, however unlikely it is that she would even give him a second glance. When you dream, the reality to which you return looks even worse than before you dreamt. Mike stares ahead into the darkness beyond the thin string of lights that illuminate the way into the tunnels. There is so little light in the darkness.

'Here you will discover another Oakfield,' the guide continues, breaking in on Mike's thoughts. 'Not the cosy little town where you go to school and watch your Sky TV, but an alternative Oakfield with its underground chambers and chapels – a place that really belongs to the annals of gothic fiction.'

Cosy? thinks Mike. Where have you been hiding? Mike Kelly's Oakfield isn't cosy. It is a raw, harsh place. Derelict houses blight the estates, providing druggies with shelter to ply their trade. Wild dogs and even wilder kids roam the glass-strewn roads. Every third or fourth woman has been knocked about by her husband or partner. Cosy! Suddenly it seems that there aren't just two Oakfields, there are many. From the tree-lined avenues of Shevington to the badlands of the Moorside, from the new malls in the centre of town to the Muslim ghetto of the Triangle, the place has more faces than a diamond. But it is a diamond with no shine.

'I wish he'd get on with it,' says Ady. 'As school visits go this isn't bad, but why do they have to treat us to all the hot air?'

'Because,' the unnoticed Mr Harris informs him, 'this is an *educational* visit. You're here to learn, Adrian.'

'Yes, sir,' says Ady, winking at Mike.

'The first tunnels were created by rainwater penetrating the limestone,' their guide is continuing. 'Over the years, however, most of the enlarging has been done by unknown human hands. Come with me and we'll see what those hands produced.'

At the same time as the Moorside school group is edging forward into the tunnels, Councillor Mohammed Saddique is putting his car in for repair. When he left for work this morning at seven o'clock he found both wing mirrors lying smashed in the road next to the vehicle. The windscreen wipers had been damaged too.

'It could just be vandals,' his wife says when he comes in to report the news to her. 'I've been told it happens quite a lot.'

Councillor Saddique shakes his head. 'No, I'm afraid this was the same bunch of cowards who sent me that threat.'

He produces the Patriotic League leaflet he found tucked under the damaged windscreen wiper. 'Their calling card,' he says. 'I will show this to the police.'

'Will it do any good?' says Aisha Saddique. 'The last time those racists came, the Patriotic League denied all knowledge. They will say anybody could have put one of their leaflets there.'

'I know,' says Councillor Saddique. 'But I have to tell the police if anything happens. Why should these people get away with such things?'

He folds the leaflet and puts it in his pocket. 'I'll book the car into the garage later. It means I will probably be about half an hour late this evening. I would love to talk to these thugs face to face, try to understand what makes them tick.'

He walks as far as the hall then pauses. 'Aisha,' he says, 'if you answer the door, make sure you put the chain on first.'

He sees her change of expression. In an attempt to reassure her he takes her arms and gives her a comforting squeeze. 'Don't worry,' he says quickly. 'I'm sure there's no need. It's just a precaution.'

But precautions are becoming necessary in this part of

Oakfield. Not that such things are reported in the *Chronicle*. An incident like the damage to Councillor Saddique's car is unremarkable. Nobody reads about it. Nobody notices.

'Above our heads,' the tunnel guide is saying, 'traffic jams are forming. People are working. Mothers are changing nappies. Operations are being performed at the hospital. But down here you would never imagine that a busy town of eighty thousand people is going about its business just a few metres away.'

Mike listens. The stark silence encircles him. He could live here away from the pounding music and the raised voices of domestic disputes, away from the hatred and the mistrust. He could sink into the still, voiceless dark and make it his home.

'Good, isn't it?' says Ady. 'Pity we're going to have to write about it in English tomorrow.'

Mike gives a noncommittal smile. He doesn't want to talk. Speech breaks the spell. He wants the subterranean quiet to go on and on. He wants it to transport him away, to swallow him up for ever and shelter him from the ugly world above.

'Now follow me,' says the guide. 'Around the next corner is the wonder of our town.'

The party follows and spills into an open space the size of a tennis court. Dug into one wall is a small chapel.

'This altar with its handful of stone pews was discovered

about sixty years ago but has only recently been opened to the public. Nobody knows who built it or why. It is doubtful whether these tunnels will ever give up this particular secret.'

Mike stands at the back of the small crowd, daring the darkness to take him. But the guided tour ends. When the party emerges back into the daylight Mike is still there.

Suhail is taking Diane to visit her parents. She has only seen them once over Christmas and wants at least to show her face. Suhail attracts a couple of stares as he drives down Boundary Road. He hates coming up here. On the Triangle or around the town centre he is a man, here he is *one of them Islamics*.

'You're sure you won't call in?' Diane asks.

'I'm positive,' Suhail tells her. 'You know how they feel about me.'

Diane sighs. 'And they know how *I* feel about you.'

Diane knows the statistics off by heart. She saw them in the *Chronicle*. In the United Kingdom maybe one in ten Pakistani men marries a white woman. In Oakfield it is probably less than that. But Suhail and Diane are not statistics. They are people. They have children, a life together. So when the car stops Diane leans across and kisses Suhail on the lips. She touches his face before she leaves the car.

'What time will you be home?' Suhail asks.

'That all depends on the mood they're in,' Diane tells

him, nodding in the direction of her parents' house. 'No later than seven. I'll probably be glad to leave by then. I made sure Rabia and Tahir had their keys before they left for school.'

'I'll see you later then,' says Suhail, pulling away.

Diane follows the car with her eyes until it turns right towards Ravensmoor Road. The smile is only gradually fading from her face when she comes face to face with two teenage girls. They have crossed the road on purpose. Diane wonders if they want directions. She is in for a surprise.

'White slag!' says one.

'Paki lover!' says the other. 'You should be ashamed of yourself.'

It hasn't happened to her in a while but it isn't entirely unexpected. It's the way people think on the Moorside. Diane is too upset to answer the girls back. She watches them walk away. One of them, who looks no older than sixteen, is pushing a baby in a buggy. The incident won't be reported in the *Chronicle*. Like the damage to Councillor Saddique's car, the insult is unremarkable. Nobody will read about it. Nobody will notice.

At Oakfield High Sumeara Jamil is auditioning some of the girls at the end of the school day. The cultural festival that once seemed so far away is only a few months off now. Sumeara is preparing a display of modern Asian dance. She already has an idea of who she will choose.

Rabia Khan is the most talented girl in her year, an academically gifted pupil as well as a graceful and eye-catching dancer. What's more, her best friend Sofia Akhtar would make such a good partner for Rabia. Sameara just hopes the pair will turn up.

'OK, girls,' she says to the half dozen who have turned up. 'When you're ready.'

She turns on the music. She is disappointed that Rabia and Sofia have not come, but not surprised. They are already committed to the Book Award. Maybe in this, their GCSE year, the dance festival is one thing too many. She is thinking straws, camels and backs.

'Pity though,' she murmurs.

She is watching the group in front of her going through their paces when she hears a knock on the door of the drama studio. It is Rabia and Sofia.

'We're not too late are we, Miss?' Rabia asks. 'Only we had to see Mr Jones about how the Book Award is going.'

'No,' says Sameara. 'You're just in time.'

Rabia has only been on stage for a minute when the other girls start exchanging glances. They know she is in a different league, and that Sofia will be chosen as well because there is such a chemistry between them. The audition is as good as over.

There are other unremarkable incidents in Oakfield that evening, other events that are not worth reporting in the *Chronicle*, that nobody notices. At about 7.45pm a colleague of Suhail's is dropping a fare outside Oakfield Town Football Club. The three youths jump out of the taxi and run off without paying. As they disappear into the football crowd one of them shouts an insult. It is 'towel-head'. Later Suhail will listen to the other driver's story and remark that, of all the insults that have come his way, that is the one he hates most.

'We don't even wear turbans!'

During the match a middle-aged man is spotted by stewards. The burly, red-faced man has homed in on one of the Oakies' few Asian fans and is treating him to a mouthful of abuse. The steward, new to the job and keen to put his training into action, alerts a police officer on duty and the man is ejected from the ground. He argues violently that he is a long-standing supporter but club policy has been enforced. The man the police escort from the ground is Sean Kelly.

'First the Stag's Head,' he grumbles as he heads for the nearest pub, 'now this! A man can't say his piece in this town any more.'

But at 9.25pm Sameara Jamil discovers a man who can still say his piece. She is waiting at traffic lights on the way home from the Year 8 parents' evening when a black Audi pulls up. There is a small stars and stripes flag displayed in the windscreen. The driver isn't a skinhead. He isn't poor or badly educated. He is a middle-aged businessman with a cellophane-wrapped suit hanging in the back. He winds down his window and spits at her. Fortunately her driver's side window is up. The spittle runs down the glass.

There is nothing unusual about these incidents. They happen regularly. Nobody reports them. Nobody notices. Nobody except the victims.

Later that night Mike Kelly is reading in bed when he hears the door slam. Liam rolled in half an hour ago so it has to be the old man. When Mike hears the slurred voice downstairs he winces inside. His father has had a skinful and he is shouting the odds over something. Mike strains to hear.

'They slung me out on my ear! That's right, some jumped-up copper who doesn't look old enough to shave has the gall to tell me to get out of my own club!'

Good on him, thinks Mike. All around Oakfield Town's ground there are notices warning that abusive and racist language will not be tolerated. It's about time they enforced them. So the old man's got his come-uppance. He's fallen foul of the new rules. Good, thinks Mike. I hope they take his season ticket off him.

'It's coming to something when you can't even say what you think,' Sean Kelly is shouting. 'Do you know how many years I've been following the Oakies? I was six when my dad took me to my first match. Our Muslim friend was probably still home in Pakistan at the time. So who gets chucked out? I do.'

Mike has heard his mother's voice for the first time. She is asking Sean to keep his voice down. It's a mistake.

'There you go again, you stupid cow! I'm your husband, not some stranger off the street. You should be listening to what I've got to say, not telling me to keep my voice down.'

Mike tenses.

'What did you say to me, woman? Making a fool of myself, am I? I'll show you who's making a fool of himself, you lousy bitch!'

Mike jumps out of bed and pulls on his tracksuit bottoms. By the time he reaches the top of the stairs Liam is already on his way down. Liam may think like Dad about the town's Asian community but he hates these fights as much as Mike. The brothers reach the living-room door just in time to see Mary being flung to the floor. She is crouching on all fours sobbing when Sean shapes up to kick her in the ribs.

'Dad, no!'

It is Liam's voice. Sean focuses on his younger son's face.

'What did you say?'

'Please Dad, don't. You've had a bad night. It isn't Mum's fault, is it? Just leave her alone, eh?'

Sean sways for a moment, uncertainty written across his face. If it had been Mike who had yelled the protest there would already be a fight in progress. But this is Liam, the favourite son, not the mummy's boy who has never shown an ounce of respect in his life. Finally, after thirty seconds, Sean staggers to the door. He leans on Liam for a moment then leaves the room snarling: 'She isn't worth the trouble.'

Mike is already at his mother's side, helping her up.

'One of these days I'm going to kill the old–'

'Don't, son,' says Mary, trying to cover his mouth with her fingers. 'Don't say something you'll regret later.'

'I mean it,' says Mike. 'I mean every word. He's a pig.'

'It's the drink,' says Mary. 'He'll be a different man in the morning.'

For a moment Mike meets Liam's gaze. Sure, he'll be a different man in the morning. He's a drunken pig now. In the morning he'll be a sober one.

The cause of Councillor Roberts' misery is also watching television. Creed is speaking in Bradford so Stone is alone. He is glad he sorted Roberts out. The man made him look a fool in front of the foot soldiers. Stone is old enough to be their father, but he is nobody's father. The only family Stone has is his mum, but even she doesn't seem to like him much. He is desperate to be somebody and only the League can do that for him. He looks forward to Creed's return. Then there will be planning meetings for the election campaign, discussions of tactics and briefings of key members. Then Stone will no longer be alone. He will be *somebody*.

On Saturday Mike takes the bus into town. He is on his mobile making arrangements to meet Ady at the Cyberspace Café.

'I don't see why we've got to drag all the way into town,' says Ady. 'It gets packed. Why can't we just play on your PC?'

'It's at the workshop,' Mike tells him.

'Still?'

'Yes, the part's got to come from the main factory.'

'So where's that?' says Ady. 'Outer Mongolia? They've had it weeks.'

Mike doesn't tell him the real reason his computer still hasn't come back. Over Christmas Mike looked in the jar where he kept the cash to pay for the repair. There was just a poorly spelt IOU. Dad had drunk away the money, the way he boozed away Mum's savings for a new coat and the fund to get a replacement microwave.

There's no point challenging the old man. All he ever says is: 'What are you whining about? Whose money is it anyway? Tell me this: who worked his guts out to get it in the first place?'

Mike gets off the bus. Ady should be about twenty minutes so he wanders round the shops, staring in the windows. Every time he sees a teenage Asian girl he finds himself looking twice, just in case it's Rabia. There is a lot of looking twice. In Oakfield on Saturday afternoon every eighth or ninth girl is Asian, but not one of them is Rabia. Eventually, after many false alarms, Mike makes his way to the Cyberspace Café where Ady is waiting.

Colin Stone is in his element. He is someone again. He has organised twenty League members to petition the crowds going into Oakfield Town's vital game with Tranmere Rovers. Imagine the brownie points this will earn him! He can just hear the approval in Creed's voice. The focus of the campaign is no longer the Moorside youth club but the funding of the Eid celebrations. There is a new example of 'reckless council spending' on the horizon – the Asian cultural festival which will occupy much of Rabia and Sofia's time in the next few weeks.

Stone watches Liam Kelly working the crowd and feels a

prickle of jealousy. The young upstart has a good way with people. That's what makes him Creed's blue-eyed boy. Where so many of the leading members – not least Stone himself – are prone to picking a fight at the drop of the hat, Liam talks to them, jokes, gets them laughing. He is not the typical foot soldier at all. Sometimes Stone wonders what he is doing in the movement.

'How's it going, Liam?' Stone asks.

'Great,' says Liam. 'We've got this lot filled in already.'

Stone leafs through the completed petitions. There is the odd signature of Mickey Mouse or Osama Bin Laden, but most are genuine.

'Good work,' says Stone. 'Keep it up.'

He says it grudgingly. He can just hear Creed going on and on about Liam and how he is one for the future.

'We're running short of petitions,' says Liam. 'I was going to go round the estate one day next week.'

'No problem,' says Colin. 'Call round at mine any evening. I've got plenty.'

With kick-off fast approaching Colin Stone gathers up the completed petitions and carries them to his car.

'I'll be round for more then,' Liam says.

Colin nods and leaves the young lads to their afternoon. Some of the other League members drift off to the pub or into town. Most head for the turnstiles. Daz and Jason are regular fixtures in the Centenary Stand. This week Liam has scraped together just enough money to join them. When the Oakies take the field they rise from their seats, arms raised, and sing the Town's anthem *Men of Oakfield* to the tune of *Men of Harlech*.

Rabia and Sofia are sitting in the coffee shop opposite the fountain in Market Square.

'I knew we'd pass that audition,' says Sofia. 'I just *knew* it.'

'Miss Jamil said we might even be going to Manchester for a day this summer,' says Rabia, 'to take part in the festival there.'

'We need some new outfits,' says Sofia. 'Something that *shimmers*.'

Rabia has a good idea who Sofia wants to shimmer *for*. It has to be Tahir. They have just started discussing what they will wear for the performance when Sofia's mobile rings.

'Hello? Oh it's you, Mum. Is she? OK, I'll be home soon.'

'Something wrong?' asks Rabia.

'Yes, it's my gran. She isn't very well. Mum wants me to baby-sit Shahnaz while she goes to Gran's.'

'I'd come with you,' says Rabia, 'but I've got to get a new print cartridge for the PC. If I don't get it today I can't get on with my coursework.'

'So are you coming up later?'

'Yes,' says Rabia. 'I'll only be half an hour.'

'I'll see you back at mine then,' says Sofia.

Mike is leaving the Cyberspace Café with Ady when he spots Rabia walking into the PC store.

'Hey, Ady,' he says, 'I'll see you later. There's something I've got to do.'

Ady frowns.

'Look, I know I'm being weird but trust me, there's somebody I have to see. I'll ring you later, OK?'

'Sure,' says Ady. 'Whatever.'

Mike sets off at a run.

'Oh Mike,' Ady shouts after him, 'this somebody – you're talking about a female, right?'

Mike grins. 'What do you think?'

Mike hurries through the sliding doors of the PC store. He has been up and down three aisles when he spots Rabia looking through the racks of print cartridges.

'Hi,' he says. 'It's Rabia, isn't it? I'm Mike, from the Book Award group.'

Rabia is starting to look uncomfortable.

'Look, don't walk away, please. I know you must think I'm a first-class wally and all that . . .'

He takes a breath. Come on now, Mouth, don't go letting me down here. This is your big chance to put things right. Mike beats his head with the palm of his hand just to prove how big a wally he is.

'I mean, Rab-i-a! What was I thinking of?'

'*West Side Story*, wasn't it?'

Mike's eyes widen in surprise. Somebody my generation knowing that, what are the chances?

'Oh, you recognised it.'

'Of course.'

'I thought–'

'What, that I only watched the Asian satellite channels? Maybe you're one of these well-meaning types who can't tell his Hindus from his Muslims.' She imitates a starlet from a Bollywood movie.

'No. I mean yes. I – I don't know what I meant.' Oh God! thinks Mike. I'm dying here.

'What is it this time?' Rabia asks before he has time to recover. 'Hugh Grant in *Four Weddings and a Funeral*?'

'I beg your pardon?'

'This little act of yours,' Rabia says. 'The hapless fop, confused but amiable. That *is* what you're doing, isn't it?'

'Am I?'

'Or are you really this confused?'

Mike tries to gather himself. How do I react? he wonders. What am I supposed to do, carry on burbling or pull myself together and come right out with it?

'Look, Rabia,' he says. 'I know this is crazy but the first time I saw you I was dying to come across and say hello.'

'So why didn't you?'

'You mean you wouldn't have minded?'

'I didn't say that, but if you don't ask you don't get.'

Mike is making a mental note. Scrub all that stuff about the passive Asian female.

'Can we start again?' he asks. 'I did a dumb thing–'

'Agreed,' says Rabia, interrupting him. 'You should only serenade a girl *after* you get to know her.'

'I did a dumb thing,' Mike continues, 'but maybe you could give me a second chance. Could I take you for a coffee or something?'

'I've just had a coffee,' Rabia tells him.

Mike says a disappointed *Oh*.

'But we could find somewhere to talk.'

'Oh.'

This *Oh* is a very different affair from the first. Suddenly Mike is walking on air.

Mike and Rabia finally find a couple of seats in a corner of Oakfield's new mall, the Market Centre.

'So what did you think when your friend told you I was singing your name?'

'I thought she was mistaken.'

'And after that?'

'I thought you were mad.'

'Do you still think I'm mad?' Mike asks.

'I don't know you well enough to comment on your sanity.'

'The question is,' Mike says, 'do you *want* to know me?'

Rabia is wondering how to answer this one when she hears her own voice.

'I might. It depends what you say to convince me that your intentions are honourable.'

'My intentions,' Mike assures her, 'are entirely honourable.'

That's when Rabia hears her voice again. 'Pity.'

Who said that? What am I doing? she thinks. Oh my God, where did that come from? She looks at Mike. He's quite good-looking. What's more, he seems to have a brain, which is more than she can say of some of the lads who have tried to chat her up. A few minutes ago it was Rabia who was in control, now she can feel herself turning all girly. This is crazy! she thinks. For Rabia, read confident. For Rabia, read empowered. For Rabia, read . . . late! She has just seen the time. Sofia will be wondering where she is.

'Listen, Mike,' she says, 'I've got to go in a minute. I promised to help my friend baby-sit.'

'I'll walk you to the bus stop,' says Mike.

'There's no need.'

'That's all right. I'd like to.'

In the Centenary Stand things are hotting up. Jason is mouthing off about the team, asking if they're *Pakis in disguise*. Somebody objects to his language.

'Haven't you seen the signs?' the man asks. 'Racism out of football.'

'Yes,' says Jason, 'I've seen them. More people telling me to be ashamed to be English.'

Liam wishes he could calm things down. The Oakies are 2–0 down and it isn't even half time. When their opponents get up to remonstrate, Jason and Daz jump forward and start throwing punches. Liam reluctantly joins in. Ten minutes later the second member of the Kelly family in a week is ejected from Oakfield Town's ground.

Mike and Rabia are standing at the bus station waiting for her bus.

'You're not what I expected,' Mike says.

'And what *did* you expect?' Rabia asks.

'I don't know. Not *you*. I didn't expect you to be so into the movies for a start.'

'Why not?'

'Well, there's an Asian cinema, isn't there?'

'Yes, but my mum's white. Besides, there's a world culture these days. One of my favourite movies is *The Seven Samurai* and that's Japanese.'

'World culture?' says Mike, thinking of the Moorside.

'Not in Oakfield there isn't. Not unless you mean the McDonald's opposite Tesco.'

Rabia nods. Mike's right. There are plenty of examples of people who have tried to break out of their territory. Mum and Dad are a case in point. But in the end they had to choose: get dog dirt through the letter box on the Moorside or go to live in the Triangle. It didn't take a whole lot of soul-searching to make their decision.

'I know,' says Rabia. 'But the problems of two little people–'

'Don't amount to a hill of beans in this crazy world,' says Mike, completing the quote. 'So you like *Casablanca*?'

'I love it,' says Rabia. 'I must have watched it six times.'

'Yes, me too. Don't you just love the last scene?'

As if in answer to Mike's question, Rabia's bus comes into view. Suddenly they are Bogart and Bergman looking in the direction of the aeroplane. Rabia is about to get on the bus when Mike remembers.

'Your mobile number,' he says. 'Give me your number.'

Rabia scribbles it on a piece of paper and hands it to him. As she takes her seat on the bus, she asks herself a question: 'Rabia, what do you think you're doing?'

Tahir is in town too. He, Nasir and Khalid are crossing the walkway which leads towards the Triangle. They would have taken the bus like Rabia but they are all skint. They don't have a bus fare between them.

'Can we go to your house for a bit?' Nasir asks. 'I'm freezing.'

'Yes, I suppose so,' says Tahir.

They are about to discuss what they are going to do with the rest of the afternoon when they hear a shout. They look to their left and see half a dozen Oakfield Town supporters walking along the pavement below. The one who shouted is Jason.

'Oh great!' says Khalid. 'I think we'd better move.'

The three friends race down the steps at the far side of the walkway. They've got to put some distance between themselves and the Oakie fans.

'Hurry up,' says Tahir. 'If we get stuck on the walkway we've had it.'

Nasir is the last off and almost gets caught. Fingers snag his jacket sleeve before losing their grip.

'Move!' yells Tahir.

It would be stupid to stand and fight. Two on to one is bad odds.

Liam Kelly is, however, encouraged by them. He is getting caught up in excitement of the pursuit. 'Get them!' he shouts.

His blood is up. First the Oakies go two down, then they get thrown out of the ground. And all because of some lefty traitor who doesn't know the colour of his own skin!

'Nasir!' bawls Tahir. 'Move yourself.'

Nasir is falling back. Two of the Oakies are nearly on him. Tahir stops and butts the leading Oakie.

'Now will you move?' he barks at a grateful Nasir.

Liam and Jason attend to Daz. His face is pouring blood.

'You stay with him,' Liam tells Jason. 'We're going to finish this.'

In the event they lose the three Asian lads on the edge of the Triangle.

'Give it up,' Liam tells his posse. 'We're on foreign soil.

The one who did that to Daz, though, I won't forget his face.'

Less than a hundred metres away Tahir is saying almost the same words.

'That weasel-faced kid,' he tells the other two, 'he was at that protest when I got arrested. I'll know him again. The next time we meet he'll wish he'd stayed home.'

3

How Big the Storm?
How Dark the Night?

It is another Saturday afternoon. Mike has phoned Rabia twice during the last week only to be disappointed by her replies. She made excuses for not seeing him and each time there seemed to be the ghost of something else hovering behind her words. Second thoughts? He isn't sure. First it was homework, the second time something to do with a dance routine.

Mike has managed to stop himself phoning her for the last forty-eight hours. He is determined not to come across as too needy, too *desperate*, even though he is. After all, he's got to hang on to some kind of pride, however cosmetic. Then again, he thinks, I would give up all the pride I've got just to see her again. He knows it isn't cool to feel this way. Irony is the flavour of the times. And yet . . . And yet . . . he can't help thinking she is the most beautiful creature he has ever seen. He remembers their conversation in the Market Centre and, though he cringes at all the cultural gaffes Mouth led him into, he aches to see her face.

Finally he decides to make a call. It's been a long two days. But just as he is about to switch on his mobile, he hears somebody coming into the living room. It's Liam.

'What are you looking so guilty about then, our Mike?'

'What are you on about?'

'You look as though you've got something to hide.'

Mike scowls. 'Clear off and leave me alone. I'm not in the mood for this.'

Liam drops on to the couch and puts his feet on the coffee table. 'Try and make me.'

Mike shakes his head and walks out of the room. He is halfway up the stairs when he meets Mary coming the other way. Talk about no hiding place!

'Is Liam still in?' Mary asks.

'Yes, he's in the living room.'

A moment later Mike can hear her asking Liam to put his clothes away.

'Later,' says Liam.

Mike flops on his bed and pulls out his mobile.

'Great!' he groans when the Menu comes up. 'Low battery.'

He puts his phone on charge and lies down on his bed, looking up at the ceiling. There is nothing else to do but dream.

Twenty minutes later Liam is standing at Colin Stone's front door. This is the third time he has called to get more petitions. Liam is fast turning into the branch's star member. He's the first to raise his hand for any activity. He rings the doorbell twice but there is no answer. After a couple of minutes he decides to pop round the back, just in case. Sure enough, halfway down the path he can hear music.

'Colin?'

There is no answer. Liam pushes open the gate at the end of the entry.

'Col?'

The shed door is open. Liam recognises the song that is playing. It's the one the Leeds and Manchester boys were singing that night at the Lion – the *Horst Wessel* something. Liam reaches the door. He is about to call Colin's name again when he sees him through the gap. He stares in disbelief. Stone is dressed from head to foot in a replica SS uniform. The moment he starts to turn round, Liam makes for the gate. By the time he has reached the street he is feeling physically sick. He's in way over his head.

Rabia is finding it hard to concentrate on her coursework. Maybe she should have found a way to see Mike. He's nice and it isn't often a lad makes up a song about you. That's 'not often' in terms of 'never'. But somehow Rabia doesn't feel good about bringing Mike home. You wuss! she tells herself. Why can't you just show some courage?

The trouble is, Oakfield is pulling apart. If you refuse to take sides and choose to stand in no-man's-land you're likely to be shot at. The commonest sight just lately is of heads disappearing below parapets. And here's me ducking with the best of them, thinks Rabia. Just imagine what will happen if Tahir finds out! He's been like a coiled spring since those white boys chased him through town.

'Sofia's at the door,' shouts Diane.

Rabia waves her friend inside and they sit at the kitchen table.

'Something wrong?' asks Sofia.

'No. Why?'

'I don't know. You look . . . preoccupied.'

'It's nothing.'

Sofia shrugs, then holds up a carrier bag.

'Take a look at this,' she says.

She pulls something from the bag and holds it up. It is modelled on the traditional salwar kameez and is in blue satin with glittering beadwork. Rabia can just see the patterns each bead will trace beneath the studio lights as she and Sofia whirl through their dance. The main thing Rabia notices is that the outfit is tucked and shaped so it will fit close to the dancer's figure.

'My mum ran it up last night,' says Sofia. 'What do you think?'

Rabia touches the fabric. 'Is this for the dance festival?'

Sofia nods. 'So will it do?'

'It's beautiful,' says Rabia. 'Though I don't think everybody would approve.'

'I thought you'd say that,' says Sofia. 'Who cares what people think? This is the twenty-first century. I've already asked Mum to make you one. We've got to match. Hey, we'll be like twins. Come over and she'll take your measurements.'

They are on their way out of the house when Rabia runs back inside.

'What was that about?' Sofia asks.

'My mobile,' Rabia tells her.

You never know. He might phone.

Across town Colin Stone answers the door. The SS uniform is now safely stowed away in the shed. It's John Creed. He is punctual as usual. Half-man, half-chronometer, that's the leader of the Patriotic League. Creed said he would be back at two o'clock. It is three minutes to.

'Any news, Colin?'

'No.'

'No?'

Stone frowns. What does Creed want from him?

'How's the petitioning going?'

Stone pulls a couple of cardboard boxes out from under his desk.

'Liam's got half of them filled all by himself,' he says.

Creed flicks through them. 'Is this some sort of joke?'

'No, I–'

'You what exactly, Colin? How many signatures do you reckon you've collected?'

'I don't know, a few thousand probably.'

'That's my point, Colin. You've collected a *few* thousand. Or should I say *Liam* has.' Creed throws the petitions in Stone's face.

'And a large number of the rest appear to have been filled in by such prominent local citizens as Robbie Williams and Kylie Minogue.'

He jabs Stone in the chest. 'We're not amateurs, Colin. How do you think these will go down with the council when we present them? Just in case you haven't noticed, we're trying to create a serious presence in this town. Now you get on the blower and organise some petitioning round the estates for tomorrow.'

'I'll never get anyone in,' Stone protests. 'Not on a Saturday.'

Creed shakes his head. 'You listen to me, Colin. Either

you get something sorted right here, right now or the Oakfield branch is going to have a new secretary.'

Stone nods disconsolately and starts dialling.

Mike rushes to answer the phone. You never know, Rabia might have looked up his home number. It's got to be her. But it isn't. Instead of Rabia, he hears a man's voice.

'Can I speak to Liam, please?'

'Who wants him?' Mike asks, suddenly suspicious.

The answer is abrupt. 'My name is Colin Stone. Now can I speak to Liam?'

Mike takes a deep breath. 'No,' he says. 'As a matter of fact, you can't.'

'I beg your pardon!'

'You heard,' Mike snarls. 'Just leave Liam alone.'

'Who the hell do you think you are?' Stone demands.

Suddenly Mike feels like laughing out loud. Here he is, this guy who thinks he is a big cheese on account of a couple of TV appearances standing next to John Creed, and I'm telling him to get stuffed!

'I'll tell you who I am, Mein Herr Stinkbrain,' Mike says. 'I'm the person who has just hung up on you.'

With that he bangs down the phone and walks away, the ghost of a smile playing on his lips.

Liam is confused. Daz and Jason have just arrived on the doorstep and asked him if he is petitioning the Moorside tomorrow morning.

'I don't know anything about it,' he says. 'How did you get to hear about it?'

'You mean Colin didn't phone you?' says Daz. 'Here, give him a ring on my mobile.'

Liam looks uncertain. In his mind's eye he can see Stone in the SS uniform.

'Is something the matter?' Daz asks.

'No.'

'Then give Colin a ring.'

Trying to put the image of Stone in the uniform out of his mind, Liam taps in the number.

'Colin,' he says, 'it's me, Liam. What's this about tomorrow?' He listens for a moment.

'He what? Don't you worry, Colin, I'll soon sort the ignorant toerag out.'

Liam storms inside, leaving a mystified Daz and Jason standing on the doorstep.

'Here,' says Liam, finding Mike sitting in the living room reading, 'I want a word with you.'

Mike lays his book face down on the arm of the chair and looks up expectantly.

'What do you think you're doing hanging up on somebody from the branch?' Liam demands.

'I think,' Mike says as patiently as he can, 'that I'm saving you from yourself.'

'You've no right to interfere,' Liam screams.

'I've every right,' Mike tells him.

'You're trying to make a fool of me in front of my mates.'

'Liam,' says Mike, 'these people aren't worth the dirt on your shoe and the sooner you realise that, the better it'll be for all of us.'

'Say you won't do it again,' Liam demands.

'No can do, Liam,' Mike says. 'Why can't you see I'm trying to help you?'

Liam stares at Mike for a moment then throws a punch. Mike dodges it and pushes Liam away. Moments later Liam cannons into his friends.

'What the–?'

Mike follows Liam outside. 'You want to be with these losers?' he says, giving Liam another push. 'So go. I can't get through to you, that's for sure.'

Liam has only answer for Mike. 'I hate you,' he says.

Tahir and his friends have returned to the town centre. This time it isn't just three of them – at one point their group numbers a dozen or more. They draw their fair share of anxious and suspicious glances from passers-by. Tahir isn't offended by all the interest – in fact he gets a kick out of it. There is an extra swagger in his step. When you have recently known fear it is sometimes good to be feared yourself. He is enjoying the security and power that strength in numbers can give.

'If we see those Oakies,' he tells the others, 'we'll see who does the running this time.'

Khalid nods. Nasir just digs his hands in his pockets and shuffles along beside them.

They have only been in Market Square for a few minutes when they attract the attention of a couple of policemen.

'Going anywhere in particular?' the officers ask.

'No,' says Tahir. 'Just hanging around with friends.'

He gives the officers a defiant stare. 'I bet you haven't asked any of the white lads where they're going.'

'As a matter of fact we have,' says one of the officers, a man with a thick black moustache. 'Groups of young men have this odd knack of attracting trouble.'

'We don't want any trouble,' says Nasir hurriedly.

'But if we get it we won't walk away,' says Khalid. 'Where were you when we got chased and almost beaten up last week?'

'We can't be everywhere,' says Black Moustache.

'We didn't say you could,' Tahir says, 'but it's funny how you're never there when Asians are attacked, but the moment we come into town we get pulled.'

'You're not being pulled,' says Black Moustache. 'We were only seeing what you were doing. There's no reason to be so defensive.'

Tahir snorts as the group moves away. 'There's *every* reason to be defensive.'

Rabia is on her way back from Sofia's house when her mobile trills.

'Hello? Mike, hi!'

She is smiling broadly, with relief as much as anything. She has been thinking that her less than welcoming replies to his calls have put him off.

'Yes, I'd love to see you again,' she says in answer to his next question. 'Where do you live, anyway?'

When he answers her face changes. 'No,' she says. 'I don't think it would be a good idea for me to come up *there*.'

She is not too keen on him coming to the Triangle either, not that whites get much aggravation – nothing like the hostility an Asian would face on the Moorside. She's more worried about running into Tahir. In his present frame of mind he wouldn't understand.

'What about town again?' she suggests. 'The shops are open all day Sunday.' She chuckles. 'You could call it neutral territory.'

When she hangs up she feels like laughing out loud. She really does like him, more than she has even admitted to herself until now.

Mike and Rabia go for a coffee. She is telling him about the dance routine she is doing with Sofia.

'I'd like to see that,' he says. There is a warmth in his voice that sends the butterflies fluttering inside her.

'I'll get you a ticket,' says Rabia.

'So we'll still be seeing each other in the spring?' says Mike.

'Funny,' says Rabia. 'I didn't think about it like that.'

She looks at him and laughs. 'Actually, I don't see why not. I feel comfortable with you.'

Then she laughs again.

'What?' asks Mike.

'No, it's nothing.'

'Go on,' he says. 'Tell me.'

'It's what Mum says about my dad,' Rabia explains. 'She says he's like a pair of old slippers – you know, comfortable. If he's even five minutes late he calls to tell her why. He's always there for his family, completely reliable and predictable. I bet you think that's stupid.'

'No,' says Mike. 'I think it's nice.'

'Really?'

'Sure. Why shouldn't I?'

'It doesn't quite fit the picture,' Rabia tells him.

'What picture?'

'The white boy from the council estate. I thought you were all supposed to hate commitment, only be after one thing – that's what my grandad says.'

Mike blushes. 'You're direct,' he says. 'I'll give you that.'

'Maybe too direct,' says Rabia. 'You don't like me talking this way, do you?'

'You know what my mum says?' Mike replies.

'No.'

'She says I'm made of glass, easily hurt.' He almost says *broken*. 'The old man says my bladder's too near my eyes. Quite a way with words, hasn't he?' Mike smiles. 'I even blush at the drop of a hat.'

'Well, if you do go singing a girl's name in public . . .' Rabia says, teasing him gently.

Mike grins.

'It's funny though,' Rabia adds. 'I can't quite see you living on the Moorside. I thought it was really rough up there.'

'It is.'

'So how do you survive? I mean, you don't seem tough enough. You're sensitive, you like books and old movies and . . .' She smiles. 'You won't be very popular with our racist friends.'

'I survive,' Mike explains, 'because I have to.'

Rabia nods. 'Mm, I don't suppose there is anything else you can do, really.'

Mike starts asking Rabia about her family.

'You're a Muslim, right?'

'Yes, I've been brought up in my father's faith.'

'But your mum didn't convert?'

Rabia shakes her head. 'There's a white woman in the next street who did. She married Mr Ali. She's changed her name and everything.'

'But not your mum?'

'No, I don't think Mum is that keen on *any* religion. Live and let live, that's her motto.'

Mike nods. 'Sounds a good idea to me. I doubt if it will ever work though.'

Rabia looks surprised. She didn't expect Mike to come out with such pessimism.

'What makes you say that?'

Mike sighs. 'My family. Take my Dad – repatriation's his middle name. He thinks you should all be sent home.'

'That wouldn't be difficult,' says Rabia. 'I was born at Oakfield General and I've lived all my life on the Triangle, same as my dad.'

'You know what I mean,' Mike replies.

'So he's a racist?'

'Is a lion carnivorous?'

'There's one thing I don't get: how do the two of you get on?'

Mike laughs. 'We don't! We're like a couple of cats in a bag. I call him a bigot. He calls me an ungrateful scumbag. That's pretty much it for our relationship.'

Rabia takes Mike's hand in hers. He starts as if with an electric shock.

'Sorry,' he says. 'I'm not used to this. I'm not exactly a babe magnet.'

'Good,' says Rabia. 'I don't want to be anybody's *babe*.'

She smiles. 'You know what you were saying about your dad, Mike?'

'Yes.'

'It would drive me mad. I couldn't stand it if I ever fell out with my parents.'

'You're lucky,' he says. 'You've got a real family.'

Then, with a note of fierceness he adds: 'Don't let anyone ever hurt it.'

'Don't worry,' says Rabia. 'I won't.'

Tahir and his friends are on their way home when Khalid asks a question.

'Who's that with Rabia?'

'Where?' asks Tahir.

'There, in the café.'

Tahir follows the direction of Khalid's gaze. The expression in his eyes changes. 'What's going on?' he says.

Leaving his friends standing on the pavement looking on, Tahir storms inside to confront Rabia.

'Who's he?'

Rabia turns to face him. 'Tahir!'

Tahir is beside himself, seized by the kind of eye-popping rage Mike usually expects from his dad. 'I said,' Tahir repeats, 'who's he?'

'This is Mike.'

'I don't want to know his name,' Tahir snaps, spitting his contempt. 'I want to know what you're doing with him.'

The staff are staring.

'Tahir,' says Rabia, 'keep your voice down, will you? You're making a fool of yourself.'

'*I'm* making a fool of myself! That's a bit rich coming from you.'

'Please don't!'

'Oh, this is just great,' says Tahir. 'I get chased through town by racists and now you're sitting drinking coffee with one.'

'Mike isn't a racist,' Rabia retorts, tears welling in her eyes.

'They all are,' snorts Tahir.

Rabia wipes away her tears, angry with herself that Tahir can get to her so easily, then hits back hard.

'All of them?' she asks. 'Even Mum?'

Tahir's face twitches as if he has just been slapped. 'We'll talk about this back home,' he says.

Rabia turns away. If she tries to talk she will dissolve into tears completely. Tahir leaves and walks away with his friends but Rabia knows it isn't over. He'll never let this drop.

'This isn't going to get you in trouble, is it?' Mike asks.

Rabia shakes her head. 'Just ignore Tahir,' she tells him. 'I do.'

'It looks like it,' Mike says, handing her a handkerchief. 'Your mum and dad, they won't mind, will they?'

'How could they?' says Rabia. 'I've told you about them, remember.'

Mike nods but somehow he isn't reassured. After Tahir's performance Rabia is feeling equally uneasy.

It is eleven o'clock on a frosty Sunday morning and John Creed is finding out that some of his 'poor white trash' lie in late.

'How are we doing, Colin?' he asks.

'OK,' says Stone. He is still smarting from yesterday's dressing-down. If you weren't the Leader, Stone thinks, I'd flatten you for talking to me like that.

'No, really,' says Creed. 'How are we doing?'

'All right when people are up. The trouble is, a lot of them aren't.'

'Which is why England needs a wake-up call,' says Creed. 'While our people are lying in their pits sleeping off their hangovers, all the Muslim worker-ants over on the Triangle are up and about taking over the local economy.'

'You're right,' says Daz.

Liam thinks that's a bit rich coming from Daz. Except for a few weeks' shelf-stacking at B&Q, he hasn't done a day's work in his life and doesn't particularly want to. But Liam doesn't say anything. You don't speak ill of a fellow foot soldier, especially when he's a mate.

'You know what we need?' Creed says. 'Another outbreak of vandalism by our Muslim friends. The only time Moorside people stir from their torpor is when something drastic happens. The trouble is, the Youth Club closure is old news. Besides, you never get more than half a dozen kids turning up. Let's face it, the place is a dump and people round here are more interested in their satellite TV, or their lottery tickets. No, we need a new grievance, something that will really stir up the natives.'

Liam exchanges glances with Daz and Jason.

Diane and Suhail have just cut short another quarrel between Tahir and Rabia.

'Tahir,' says Suhail, 'find something to do.'

'Promise you'll talk to her,' Tahir complains. 'She shouldn't be out on her own with that boy.'

'Oh, grow up, Tahir,' Rabia snaps. 'Who do you think you are, the Taliban? I can just see you in a black turban. You'll be issuing me with a *burkha* next. Yes, dressed from head to foot in a sheet. You'd like that, wouldn't you?'

'Don't be ridiculous!'

'And since when did you start giving out advice? I'm not the one who got himself arrested. You can't tell me what to do.'

'Somebody should!'

'That's enough,' says Diane.

'I'm going out anyway,' says Tahir.

'Can you believe him?' Rabia cries as Tahir's footsteps fade on the pavement outside.

'He might have a point,' says Suhail.

Rabia's eyes widen. 'You are joking! Oh Dad, tell me you didn't mean that.'

'What do you know about this boy?'

'He's got a name, you know. He's called Mike.'

'What your dad means,' Diane says, 'is that things are a bit difficult in Oakfield at the moment.'

Rabia folds her arms. Her face is set stubbornly. 'Go on.'

'All this trouble,' Diane continues, 'it makes things . . . difficult.'

'Yes,' Rabia says. 'You've said that, but what does it mean?'

'We don't want you to get hurt,' Suhail says.

'So who's going to hurt me?' Rabia demands. 'Mike?'

Suhail shakes his head. 'That's not what I mean.'

'Then tell me what you *do* mean,' Rabia cries. '*Exactly* what do you mean?'

When nobody speaks, Rabia throws up her hands. 'See? You don't even know yourselves. Why should I be any different from you?'

'You don't understand,' says Diane. 'It was hard enough for us, but times have changed, and not necessarily for the better. Now it's . . .' She looks at her daughter. 'You know.'

Rabia remembers the boys on Ravensmoor Road, the attack on Clive Road, Tahir's arrest and, behind it all, two aircraft that have changed the New York skyline for ever. Oakfield's communities are retreating behind the barricades in their minds.

'Of course I know, but we should be standing up to all this. It can't always be Muslims here and whites over there living parallel lives. Surely that's what your life together is all about? I just want to see Mike and have a bit of fun. I don't know how we'll get on. Who does? We might only go out a few times. I just want to be like any other girl meeting a boy. What's wrong with that?'

Diane smiles. 'Nothing.'

She glances at Suhail. 'And we won't stand in your way. How could we? Just – just be aware of the obstacles.'

'That's all,' says Suhail. 'Be careful where you go. People will be watching you and they won't always be friendly.'

'I'm not stupid, Dad,' says Rabia. 'I've got eyes. I know what's happening. I know the way people think.'

4
Betrayal

It is mid-February. There is a scattering of snow on the hills. In the dying light it glows in pale strips on the darkened slopes. This time when Mike sees the two teenage Asian girls getting out of Suhail Khan's taxi he doesn't just follow them into the library wishing and hoping for some way to break the ice with Rabia. He doesn't have to. He and Rabia are an item although, with schoolwork and Oakfield's self-imposed boundaries, only on an irregular basis. Mike hails her brightly.

'Hi, Rabia! That's what I call good timing.'

He glances at Sofia a little more warily. He knows that Rabia's closest friend has misgivings about their relationship. She isn't exactly hostile, more uneasy. It is as if she is taking her first uncertain steps into a challenging no-man's land. She has been hearing murmurings about her best friend and can't help being affected by them herself.

Don't talk too much, Mike tells himself, picking up the vibes. Don't give her a reason to dislike you. Hear that, Mouth? Control yourself!

'Are you all right, Sofia?' That's good – brief, neutral but friendly.

'Yes, I'm fine.'

Mike bends down and talks to Suhail through the

driver's window. He has an idea he might be trying just a bit too hard but, what the heck, he is trying and that's what matters.

'Hello there, Mr Khan.'

'Hello, Michael.'

Suhail likes this boy. His heart is good. Honesty and responsibility radiate from him. But he brings with him a lot of baggage. There is the father of course – a man who, by all accounts, is a racist and a bully, a man who treats his wife as little more than a slave or, even worse, a punchbag. As if that wasn't bad enough, Suhail feels there is more to this young man's story – something Mike has not dared reveal. All of Suhail's protective instincts are working overtime.

'I could walk Rabia and Sofia home, you know,' says Mike.

Suhail can see at least two problems with that: the gangs that might be hanging round the bottom of Ravensmoor and, maybe more pressingly, Tahir and his friends waiting on the Triangle. He hates the atmosphere round the house when Tahir and Rabia are arguing. No, it's not a good idea at all.

'Thank you, Michael,' Suhail tells him, 'but I prefer to give them a lift back if you don't mind.'

Mike nods. 'Sure, I understand.'

He watches Suhail's brake lights flare as he reaches the T-junction where Councillor Roberts crashed, then turns to Rabia and Sofia.

'Right,' he says, clapping his hands and leading the way inside. 'Selection time.'

Sofia turns and whispers in Rabia's ear. 'Is he always like this?'

'No, he's nervous, that's all,' says Rabia. 'It makes him a bit hyper.'

Mike turns round at the door. 'Are you talking about me?' he asks. *What have you been up to, Mouth?*

'Why?' asks Rabia. 'Are your ears burning?'

'They certainly are. Are you going to tell me what you were saying about me?'

'Of course not,' says Rabia. 'This is girls' talk.'

Mike leans his head on one side and stares into her eyes. His throat goes dry just looking at her.

'Are you going to tell me what you're thinking about now?' says Rabia, her eyes sparkling.

Mike glances at Sofia, blushes, then says: 'Later.'

On the Moorside Liam and his friends are going door to door. Liam has told Daz and Jason about Stone in his uniform, but the other two lads can't see what the fuss is about. Although he feels uneasy about it, Liam is still working hard for the branch.

Under the heading *Why we need a peace wall*, the latest leaflet from the Patriotic League leads with Councillor Roberts' crash.

As you may know, it begins, *a few weeks ago your representative for this ward, councillor Martin Roberts, suffered severe injuries after his car hit a wall.* **This was no accident!** *It was a deliberate act of sabotage. Two Asians were seen near the councillor's car just before the crash. Like yourselves, the Oakfield branch of the Patriot League wants answers to these two questions:*

* *Why are the guilty parties still walking free?*
* *Why does Oakfield council resist calls for a peace wall to*

protect our citizens? If you, like us, are sick of one section of the community holding the rest of us to ransom, join the Patriotic League.

'Strong stuff,' says Daz.

'Who wrote it,' asks Jason. 'Col?'

'John, of course,' says Stone.

Stone watches the leaflets disappearing into letter boxes and smiles with satisfaction. Councillor Roberts is laid up and most probably ready to resign his council seat. What's more, the Asians have got the blame for it. Colin, my lad, you're a genius!

Daz sees Stone smiling. 'What's up, Col?' he asks. 'Got a hot date tonight?'

Stone looks away, the smile fading from his face. Not tonight. Not any night.

Tahir is towelling down after the gym.

'Is this Mike character still on the scene?' asks Khalid, already knowing the answer to his question.

'Yes. I don't know what's got into Rabia. Mum and Dad don't seem to care, either. They're letting her do just what she wants.'

Khalid pulls on his trackie bottoms and starts slipping on his socks. 'Somebody ought to do something about it,' he says.

He means himself, but Tahir isn't on the same wavelength.

'Khalid,' Tahir replies, 'don't you think I've tried?' He slips on his trainers. 'I just wish there was something we could do. Rabia needs someone to make her see sense.'

Khalid looks interested. Nasir as usual thinks this sounds too much like trouble.

'Any ideas?' says Khalid excitedly.

Tahir shakes his head. 'No, but I'll keep thinking.'

Mike enters the library walking on air, but immediately comes down to earth with a bump. *Oh no!*, he groans inwardly. *I'd forgotten about Chubby Nerdy Guy – I mean, Simon.*

Simon has been sitting on his own and his face lights up when he sees Mike.

'Great!' Mike hisses.

'What's up?' Rabia asks.

'Simon there. I was hoping to sit next to you, but look at him! If I don't go over he'll be on his own for the whole meeting. I can't do that to the guy.'

Sofia sees Rabia looking at her.

'Don't worry,' Sofia says, with just the slightest hint of a sigh. 'I'll take care of it.'

She walks over to Simon and strikes up a conversation. Soon she has drawn him into a group of the other judges.

'She's all right, isn't she?' says Mike.

'Yes,' says Rabia. 'She's the best.'

Five minutes later the Award coordinator opens the meeting.

'Nice to see you again, everybody,' she begins. 'I've had the returns from the school shadowing group so now we can cut the list down to the final six books. I'd like you to take the recommendations into account, but you don't have to follow them to the letter. You're the judges. Your verdict is final.'

Mike and Rabia have soon picked five of their six. They have just got to choose the last book from three possibles.

'So what do you think?' Rabia asks.

'I think you've got lovely eyes,' Mike replies.

'About the books,' Rabia says. 'The books, Mike.'

He chuckles. '*You* pick one. I'll watch you.'

'No,' says Rabia, starting to tire of his corniness. 'We've got to keep this professional.'

Eventually they choose their final candidate.

'Do you want to come to my house?' Rabia asks. 'I'm sure Dad would drop you off after.'

'Will Tahir be there?' Mike asks. He remembers a couple of uncomfortable meetings with Tahir since he and Rabia started going out.

'I doubt it,' says Rabia. 'He's always out with his friends.'

'Then yes, that would be great.'

The leafleters all meet up at the Lion.

'How did it go tonight, boys?' Creed asks.

'Excellent,' says Daz. 'We got a really good response. Do you know who we saw?'

'Surprise me,' says Creed.

'Bobby McAllister.'

'The youth worker?'

'That's him. He was getting into a van. It seems he's got a new flat away from the Moorside. Things must be getting a bit too hot for him here.'

Liam isn't smiling. He knows who drove Bobby off the estate. It's one thing getting into the odd punch-up, but this is getting heavy. Then there's Stone, and the uniform.

'Why, Daz,' Creed says, pretending to be shocked. 'Whatever do you mean? Are you telling me McAllister didn't appreciate the welcome the Moorside gave him?'

He throws back his head and laughs loudly. Daz and Jason join in. Liam does too, just for form, but without their enthusiasm.

'Find out if he's staying on at the Youth Club,' Creed says.

'We already have,' says Jason. 'He's bottled it good style. He's got a new job over in Shevington.'

Creed nods and smiles. Another opponent bites the dust.

'I'd better be going,' says Sofia, 'before my dad comes to walk me home again.'

Mike and Rabia see her off then stand watching the full moon from the front step. There is nobody on the street so Mike steals a kiss. Rabia darts a glance at the front window, just in case her parents are watching.

'I wish we had more places where we could meet,' Mike says, noting the look. 'There are always people around. Your parents, Sofia . . .' He grimaces. '. . . Tahir.'

'Plus we go to different schools,' says Rabia.

'Yes, and live in different areas. There couldn't really be more obstacles, could there?'

Rabia shakes her head. 'It's a wonder we ever got together,' she says. 'Mum says it used to be easier than it is now. She and Dad met at the mill.'

'Yes, I know. You told me.'

Rabia looks up at the sky. It is one of those clear, frosty nights when the sky is studded with stars so bright they take your breath away.

'I wonder if there's an angel up there.'

'You're a dreamer,' Mike says. 'You know what they say about Hollywood in the Thirties? Things were so bad, what with the Depression and all, that people wanted dreams. The whole place was a dream factory. Right now nobody needs a dream factory more than I do.'

He looks at Rabia and sees her still staring up at the stars. 'If there *was* an angel up there,' he says, 'what would you wish for?'

'I'd wish he could get a great big bag,' Rabia answers. 'He could put all the people in Oakfield in it and shake them up.'

'Then what?'

'Then he could drop them down anywhere, all higgledy piggledy so there was no talk of ghettos or peace walls, then maybe they would have no alternative but to find a way to live together.'

'It sounds a nice idea,' Mike says. 'Do you think it will ever come true?'

'That's just it,' says Rabia with a fierce conviction. 'I *know* it will.'

'Really?'

'Yes. You know what I read the other day? Half of all

British-born black men have a white partner. That's one in the eye for the racists, isn't it? You never know, it might turn out the same way for a lot of young Asians. I bet in twenty or thirty years' time nobody will be able to understand how we could get ourselves in such a mess wondering where we belong or who we owe our loyalties to.'

'I hope you're right,' Mike says, edging closer so that his arm touches hers and her hair brushes his cheek. 'I really do.'

Later that evening Suhail is running Mike home.

'You'd better drop me here,' says Mike halfway up Ravensmoor Road.

'I can take you closer,' Suhail says, glancing back at Mike in his rear-view mirror. Mike is sitting on the back seat next to Rabia. She wanted to come along for the ride.

'No,' says Mike. 'Here is fine. You know what the Moorside is like.'

'Yes,' says Suhail. 'I'm afraid I do.'

But Mike isn't asking to be dropped off here for the sake of Suhail. He doesn't want anybody seeing him and Rabia together. He doesn't want anybody putting two and two together. He hasn't told anybody about the girl in his life, not even Mum. Apart from books and movies, Rabia is the only good thing in his life. He won't let the dirt and the ugliness of the Moorside touch her.

'I'll give you a call,' he says to Rabia.

'Bye, Mike,' she says.

With Suhail in the front seat Mike isn't going to kiss her. Instead he traces his fingers across the back of her hand as he gets out.

'Thanks for the lift, Mr Khan.'

'Take care,' says Suhail.

It is doubtful whether Suhail Khan has had a premonition but Mike would do well to take those two little words to heart. At the very moment when he is waving goodbye to the two people in the red Ford Sierra, his brother Liam is leaving the Lion not twenty metres away.

'Since when did your Mike have the money to run round town in taxis?' Daz asks.

Liam doesn't answer. It isn't the cost of taxi fares which is exercising his mind. There was an Asian girl in the back of the cab with Mike.

'Do you want to come back to mine?' says Daz. 'I've got a few bottles of cider stashed under the bed. I feel like getting hammered.'

'I'm in,' says Jason. 'What about you, Liam?'

'Not tonight,' says Liam. 'I've got things to do.'

At the top of the hill Daz, Jason and a couple of others turn right and set off in the direction of the cider. Liam turns left and follows Mike, maybe a hundred metres ahead. He thinks about Jason and Daz and what they did to Bobby McAllister. Then he thinks about Stone in that uniform. The League is just about the best thing that has ever happened to him and suddenly he is finding it hard to believe in it any more. Liam hates Mike for being so right about it.

'Right again, big brother,' Liam says. 'Well, don't feel so rotten smug, Mikey. This time I've got something on you too.'

Rabia is on her way home from school two days later when Sofia nudges her.

'Don't look now but here comes Khalid.'

'Can I have your autographs?' Khalid asks.

'What are you on about?' Sofia says.

'You haven't seen the *Chronicle* then?'

'No.'

Khalid holds up page five. Right in the middle there is a photograph of the Oakfield Book Award judging panel.

'Oh, look at me!' says Sofia. 'I've got my eyes closed. I must have blinked when he was taking it.'

'I didn't think they were going to use the photograph until the winner was announced,' Rabia says.

'Why?' asks Khalid. 'Does it make any difference?'

'No, not really,' says Rabia.

B ut it will make a difference – a big one. In the kitchen of the house on the Moorside Mary Kelly is passing the newspaper round.

'Have you seen yourself, Michael?' she says. 'It's a good photograph.'

Mike picks up the paper but he isn't interested in himself. He only has eyes for Rabia.

'Let's see,' says Sean.

Reluctantly Mike hands the paper to his father. Sean scowls.

'You didn't say that half the panel were Pakis,' he grumbles.

'You didn't ask,' Mike retorts. 'And when are you going to start saying Asian?'

'Never,' says Sean. 'I've talked this way all my life. I'm not changing now.'

Mike shakes his head and leaves the room. Liam picks up the paper and reads the names from left to right. He examines the faces of the two Asian girls.

'That's her,' he says to himself. 'Rabia Khan.'

Khan. That will probably be as common as Smith round the Triangle, but it's a start.

'See you soon, Rabia Khan,' Liam murmurs.

Half an hour later Councillor Roberts hears a knock. With the help of an NHS crutch he gets to the front door.

'You!'

John Creed is standing on the doorstep. Councillor Roberts looks round for Colin Stone.

'I'm on my own,' says Creed. 'I thought it was time we had a bit of a talk. Are you going to invite me in, Martin?'

'No,' says Councillor Roberts. 'Anything you've got to say to me, you can say right here.'

'Now that isn't very hospitable, is it, Councillor?'

'What do you expect?' Councillor Roberts retorts. 'Haven't I had enough trouble with you people?'

John Creed frowns. 'And what exactly do you mean by that, Martin?'

Councillor Roberts toys with the idea of telling Creed everything but he dismisses the idea immediately. 'Nothing.'

The chilling hammer scene from *Misery* keeps running through his mind. Stone actually seemed to enjoy putting the frighteners on him.

'Just tell me what you want,' Councillor Roberts says.

Creed is still mulling over the Councillor's outburst, wondering what to make of it. After a few moments he starts talking.

'This is a courtesy call really,' he says. 'I just wanted to confirm that Colin Stone will be the Patriotic League candidate for the Moorside ward in the May elections. I will be standing here in Old Moor and two other candidates will contest wards nearer the town centre.'

'OK,' says Councillor Roberts. 'So now you've told me. Goodnight, Mr Creed.'

'That isn't quite all,' Creed tells him. 'I was just wondering if you would be standing yourself.' He indicates the plaster cast on Councillor Roberts' leg. 'Considering the state of your health, I mean.'

Councillor Roberts wants to spit in Creed's face and shout his defiance, but he keeps seeing that leg contorted in an impossible position.

'No,' he says. 'I won't be standing.'

'I think you've made the right decision,' says Creed. 'Goodnight, Councillor Roberts.'

There is no answer.

Tahir sees Diane sitting at the kitchen table, cutting the photograph out of the paper.

'What are you doing?' he asks.

'I'm going to put it in the album,' Diane tells him. 'It isn't every day your daughter gets her picture in the paper.'

'You could at least take *his* face out,' says Tahir.

'I assume you mean Mike,' says Diane.

'That's right.'

'Now why would I do that, Tahir?'

'The sooner he's out of our lives the better,' snorts Tahir.

'He isn't in *your* life, Tahir. He is part of Rabia's, and if you don't like it then you'd better lump it.'

'She's going to be sorry.'

'Why?' Diane demands. 'Why, Tahir? Just answer me that.'

He frowns. 'Because, that's all.'

'Because different races shouldn't mix, is that it?'

Tahir looks down.

'No matter how hard you try, you can't make one of the central facts of your existence go away. I'm your mother, Tahir, and I'm white.'

Tahir looks uncomfortable.

'Look at me, Tahir. You can't wish me away.'

'I don't want to, Mum.'

'So what is it? What's the problem?'

'I don't know. It's easy for Khalid and Nasir. They've no doubts about who they are. But me – what's *my* culture?'

'You're lucky,' says Diane. 'You've got two cultures. You're richer, not poorer for it.'

Tahir isn't convinced. 'You just don't get it, Mum. Sometimes it feels like I just don't belong anywhere.'

'You belong *here*.'

'Mum, that's not what I'm talking about and you know it.'

Diane is about to say something when the phone rings. It is Suhail. He has a fare to Manchester and he will be late finishing his shift. Diane puts the phone down and hurries back to the kitchen to continue the conversation but Tahir has already gone out.

––––––––––

At the following week's meeting of the Oakfield branch of the Patriotic League, John Creed has an announcement.

'I propose,' he says to the twenty-five people present, 'that we leaflet the town centre this Saturday. I think it's time we raised our profile again.'

Liam, Daz and Jason look at each other. This sounds exciting, thinks Liam. Some action at last. Something to make the doubts go away.

'The subject,' Creed continues, 'will be the unfortunate injury to Councillor Roberts and the failure of the police to find the culprits.'

Colin Stone sits impassively beside Creed.

'Are there any questions?' Creed asks when Stone in the chair fails to throw the meeting open.

'I've got one,' says a new recruit. 'Won't it attract counter-demonstrators?'

'So what if it does?' Creed asks. 'That's never done us any harm in the past. Remember the peace wall demonstration: the Asians throwing stones and our people chanting for peace. It was excellent publicity.'

'What if there's trouble?' Liam asks.

'We leave public order to the police,' says Creed. 'We are, after all, a law-abiding organisation.'

There are one or two chuckles, especially from Daz and Jason, but Creed silences them with a stare. For some reason, Councillor Roberts' words pop into his mind: *Haven't I had enough trouble from you people?* He still finds them strangely unsettling.

'If our opponents want to stir things up, that's their problem,' Creed tells his audience. 'We maintain perfect discipline. Is that clear?'

There are nods all round. It couldn't be clearer.

Mike is standing by his bedroom window, looking out at the lights of the town. He is on the phone to Rabia.

'I'm missing you,' he says.

'Yes, me too,' says Rabia.

'Are you still on for Saturday?'

'Of course. I'm looking forward to the film.'

Mike smiles. Even at their most nervous and possessive, the Khans aren't able to see any problem in a Saturday afternoon showing.

'I wish I was seeing you tonight.'

'Mike, it's only the day after tomorrow. We've both got homework.'

'But two days! It's killing me.'

'Then you'll have to die in peace. Personally, I'm going to finish my homework.'

Even after hanging up Mike carries on smiling. He might be a little less happy if he knew that Liam is eavesdropping from the landing.

Late Friday evening, rumours begin to circulate round the Triangle. A large group of young men has gathered just up the road from The Gulam. Rashid peers out and shakes his head. One look at them and his customers will certainly think twice. Takings will be down tonight.

'There's no way we're going to let them hand out their poison unchallenged,' Tahir is saying.

'No,' says Khalid. 'I say we get down there early, around noon.'

Nasir is unsure about this. 'We don't even know if it's true though, do we?'

'We'll look pretty stupid if it is and we're nowhere in sight,' Tahir tells him. 'One thing though: don't go telling everybody. We only want people down there who are willing to get stuck in.'

'Stuck in?' says Nasir.

'Yes,' Tahir smacks his fist into his palm. 'Stuck in. So we don't want any elders and community leaders down there, just the youth. Got that?'

There are nods all round, even from the reluctant Nasir.

At breakfast time on Saturday morning Liam seems in a particularly good mood. There is going to be action. No need to think today, just act.

'What are you so chirpy about?' asks Sean.

'Oh, you know, I'm just looking forward to the weekend.'

Liam looks round at Mike. 'What about you, our Michael? What are you doing today?'

Mike scowls. 'None of your business.'

Rabia is the one good thing about his life. He doesn't want Liam coming within a mile of her.

'I'm only making small talk,' says Liam. 'There's no law against it, is there?'

Mike ignores him. He inspects his T-shirt and trackie bottoms.

'I'm going to have a shower and put some decent clothes on.'

'Does that mean you've got a date?' Liam asks.

Mike glares at him. 'What's that supposed to mean?'

'The last I heard, it meant are you seeing somebody? You know, of the female variety.' Liam traces an hourglass figure in the air and gives a wolf whistle. Sean splutters into his mug of tea.

'What, our Michael take an interest in girls? That'll be the day! He doesn't get his nose out of a book long enough to do anything normal.'

'Leave him alone, you two,' says Mary. 'Mike's a good-looking lad. He'll find the right girl when he's ready.'

Mike shakes his head and beats a retreat from the kitchen. 'I'm going up for my shower,' he says.

Tahir sees Rabia getting ready to go out.

'Where are you going?' he asks.

'Out.'

'Out where?'

'Since when was that any of your business, Tahir?'

Tahir is keen not to give anything away about the leafleting. He confines himself to a curt: 'I just wondered, that's all.'

'If you're that interested,' Rabia says, brushing her hair. 'I'm going to the cinema with Mike. Happy now?'

She is expecting Tahir to say something about Mike. Instead he simply asks which cinema.

'The multiplex. Tahir, what is this?'

'The one behind the community college?'

'That's right.'

'What time?'

Rabia laughs. 'The showing is about one o'clock. So what's the third degree in aid of, Tahir?' She waggles her fingers at him. 'Have you set up some sort of thought police, is that it? Do you want to come along and make sure we don't enjoy ourselves too much?'

Tahir shrugs and leaves the room. One o'clock. That shouldn't be too much of a problem. At least Rabia will be out of harm's way if there's any trouble.

By midday Tahir and his friends are sitting around Market Square in small groups keeping a watchful eye on the crowds. The minutes tick by. Half-past twelve passes. A quarter to one comes and goes. There is still no sign of the Patriotic League. At ten past one Tahir glances at his watch and smiles. Rabia will be watching her film by now. He feels less happy that she is with Mike, but at least she isn't in the town centre. Khalid appears a few minutes later. He has been keeping an eye on the bus station.

'Anything?'

Khalid shakes his head. 'It looks like it was a false alarm after all.'

'What do you think?' Tahir asks. 'Should we give it another hour?'

Khalid nods. 'I'll have another scoot round then report back.'

Tahir yawns. He's got himself all wound up over nothing.

Fifteen minutes later Colin Stone is parking up in the last space in the Moorgate car park.

'There are the boys now,' says Creed. 'Pop the boot for them, Colin.'

Eager hands pull out leaflets, placards and a loud-hailer.

'Right,' says Creed to the dozen or so party members. 'We're going to leaflet the shoppers in Market Square. Stick to the one simple argument: law and order, what are the police and the council doing about the attack on Councillor Roberts' car. You know the sort of thing – this town isn't a safe place to bring up kids, old people don't feel safe walking the streets, and we know whose fault that is, don't we?'

He glances at Stone. 'And positively no statements we might come to regret later, OK?'

The group set off in the direction of Market Square. They don't notice Khalid watching from the bus station.

The cinema is nearly empty. That's the way Mike and Rabia want it. They watch the movie. Their hands touch.

'This feels good,' says Mike. 'It's like being a proper couple.'

'We *are* a proper couple,' says Rabia.

'You know what I mean.'

A couple two rows back shushes them. Mike and Rabia smile at each other and their fingers interlock. They are happy.

'I'm fed up,' says Nasir, beating his gloved hands against the biting cold of the day. 'I think we should go.'

'Yes, you're probably right,' says Tahir. 'We'll just wait for Khalid to get back.'

'Anything doing?' asks Tariq, who has been sitting on the Town Hall steps.

'No. Oh, hang on, here comes Khalid.'

'They're on their way,' says Khalid.

'How many?'

'About a dozen.'

Tahir smiles. There are at least twenty-five Asian lads waiting around the square. 'Tell you what,' he says. 'They're going to wish they'd never come into town today.'

John Creed assesses the situation immediately.

'Well, gentlemen,' he says, 'it looks like we're out-numbered.'

'So what do we do?' Colin asks.

'Why, we go ahead, of course,' says Creed. 'If you hadn't noticed, there are more than enough police to deal with our friends from the Triangle. This will do our image no end of good. We'll be the beleaguered white tribe standing up to the Muslim tide. It's our version of the thin red line. Dish out the leaflets, Colin.'

Liam notices Tahir in the crowd. 'Hey, Daz, that's the one who broke your nose, isn't it?'

Daz looks across. 'Yes, that's him all right.'

Creed is holding the megaphone. He hops on to a bench and starts to address the crowds. One or two shoppers stop to listen. A few more take the leaflets. Most put their heads down and hurry by.

'Ladies and gentlemen,' Creed says, 'I would like to introduce you to the prospective candidate for the Moor-side ward, Colin Stone.'

He hands the megaphone to Stone, who launches into an impassioned speech.

'You will all have heard about what happened to Coun-cillor Roberts lately . . .'

'Yes,' Tahir heckles. 'He got exactly what he deserved.'

A policeman asks him to tone it down, but Colin Stone is keen to up the ante.

'There it is,' Stone retorts. 'The authentic voice of hatred. If you want to know who interfered with Councillor Roberts' car, then I think we need look no further.' He is looking straight at Tahir.

'You take that back!' Tahir yells. He is being quietly restrained by the policeman.

'Hear that?' Stone continues, warming to his theme. 'He

wants me to withdraw my accusation. Well, no, my young friend, I won't take it back.'

The shouts and boos from Tahir's group are getting louder. The police have started to move in in numbers.

'In fact I would go further. I think the police should interview this individual right here, right now.'

John Creed nods approvingly and leads the applause.

'Interview *me?*' yells Tahir. 'That's a joke! It's your lot the police should be talking to.'

He turns angrily to the police. 'Why don't you ask them about women and old men who are being harassed in the street?'

The exchange is getting more heated. The police have started to push the young Asians back. More protestors are arriving all the time.

'Now there's a welcome sight,' says Stone, seeing the police confronting the demonstrators. 'Finally *our* police are starting to do their job.'

Creed takes up the theme. 'A round of applause for the British bobby,' he says. 'What a pity they are continually stopped from doing their duty by political correctness.'

'*Your* police is right,' Tahir shouts. 'They spend all their time defending racists. Where are they when our people get attacked? Answer me that.'

The peace in Oakfield town centre has now been pulled so tight it could snap at any moment.

'**D**id you enjoy the film?' Mike asks.

'It was all right,' Rabia says.

She sees his face fall. It's obvious he wants everything to be perfect.

'But I *loved* the company,' she reassures him.

She squeezes his arm, attracting the disapproving attention of an elderly couple coming the opposite way.

'Ignore them,' says Rabia. 'We're going to have to get used to this.'

'Why should we have to?' says Mike.

'Because places like Oakfield have got a long way to go,' Rabia tells him. 'Miss Jamil told our class about a friend of hers from university. Her dad's black, her mum's half Australian, half Indonesian.'

'So what does that make her?' Mike asks.

'That's what I said,' Rabia answers. 'You know what Miss Jamil said? It makes her beautiful. She's got green eyes, dark hair and toffee-coloured skin. She's got a career in journalism, her own flat. People look at her and they don't see somebody who belongs to this or that community, they see a strong, confident woman who belongs anywhere. You want to know how I see the future? *She's* the future.'

'So how does that go down with Tahir?'

Rabia shrugs. 'Not that well. He thinks you lose something if you go down that road. He believes the communities should keep their traditions. Well, that's fine by me so long as *everybody's* culture is respected. The trouble starts when people want you to be British *instead of* Muslim.'

'What?' says Mike. 'The cricket test and all that? British-born Asians should support England?'

'Yes,' says Rabia. 'Why do people have to try to turn us into something we're not? What's wrong with British *and* Muslim?'

They walk down College Street until they are within striking distance of the bus station.

'You don't want to go home yet, do you?' Mike asks.

'No way,' says Rabia. 'Let's go round the shops.'

They are making their way through the crowds on the upper tier of the Market Centre when they see the disturbance in Market Square. Rabia rushes to the large plate glass windows that look down on the square. She immediately heads for the escalator.

'Mike, that's Tahir down there!'

———————

Suhail Khan has just dropped a fare at Oakfield Park and is heading for the taxi rank in Market Square when a police officer approaches him. Suhail stops and lowers his window.

'Is something wrong?' he asks.

'There's a protest in the square,' the policeman says. 'Things are getting a bit heated just now. We're advising taxi drivers to use the railway station rank for the next hour or so.'

Suhail looks across the square. 'So what's this protest about?'

'It's just a political group,' the officer tells him impatiently. 'Now could you park at the station please, sir?'

Suhail nods and drives on. He doesn't know that both Rabia and Tahir are already caught up in the protest.

Chants are starting to echo round Market Square. The police have put a cordon around the Patriotic League members.

'Racists out!' the sixty or so counter-demonstrators are chanting.

'Who is in charge here?' the senior police officer asks.

Liam directs him to the Patriotic League's national organiser. 'This is the man you want, John Creed.'

'Could I have a word, Mr Creed?' says the officer.

'Certainly, officer,' says Creed.

'I am sure you will agree with me that this is getting out of hand.'

Creed scans the angry protestors. 'If you mean *our opponents* are getting out of hand, then I quite agree. My members will continue to ignore the obvious provocation.'

The officer doesn't take kindly to Creed's answer. 'Then I will have no option but to start arresting your members.'

Creed glances at Stone, who starts speaking through the megaphone.

'Hear that?' he shouts. 'This rabble is allowed to shout us down but are we patriotic Englishmen allowed to exercise our right to free speech? No we are not.'

The press and TV have arrived just in time to record the moment. Encouraged by Creed, Stone repeats his speech for the benefit of the media. Satisfied that Stone's speech will be in the papers and on the screen, Creed crosses his palms in a gesture that says *That'll do.*

'If it is your advice that we leave,' Creed says, 'then I reluctantly agree.'

Rabia reaches Tahir just as the dozen members of the Patriotic League are about to be led away. The counter-demonstrators see this as a victory and applaud.

'I thought Mum and Dad told you not to get in trouble again,' Rabia cries.

'I said I wouldn't get myself arrested,' Tahir answers, 'and I haven't.'

He sees Mike behind her. 'Shouldn't you be with them?' he snarls, indicating the Patriotic League.

Mike is about to reply when he sees Liam looking in his direction. His flesh starts to crawl.

'Mike!' shouts Liam.

Mike Kelly just wants to get away. His brother's voice is digging into him, peeling at his skin from the inside.

'Hey, Mike, why don't you come and join us?'

Mike tries to ignore him but the voice won't go away, picking at him, jabbing into his chest.

'Don't you go pretending you don't know us, Mikey,' Daz joins in. 'You can take the boy out of the Moorside, but you can't take the Moorside out of the boy.'

Mike is shrivelling from the inside. His heart is turning to ash.

'Do you know them?' Rabia asks, eyes wide with horror.

Mike just looks straight ahead, wishing the earth would swallow him up.

'Mike, is there something you haven't told me?'

'Rabia, I–'

He is interrupted by Liam's voice. 'Hey, Mike! Whose side are you on, bro?'

'Bro!' cries Rabia. 'You're not telling me he's really your brother?'

It is an age before Mike can bring himself to speak. When he does all he can say is: 'Yes.'

Half an hour later Stone is driving Creed, Liam, Jason and Daz back to the Moorside. There is satisfaction all round.

'A job well done,' says Creed. 'I think you could say we're on the map.'

The younger men have other fish to fry.

'Did you see your Mike's face?' Daz says. 'It was priceless.'

'And is that really his girlfriend?' Jason asks. 'You didn't let us in on that juicy bit of gossip.'

'Drop it, eh?' says Liam.

He enjoyed baiting Mike at the time, but he is starting to feel uncomfortable. Guilt gnaws at Liam's insides. The derelict look in Mike's eyes has got to him. He remembers all the times his brother has stood up for him over the years – covered for him. He is wondering what to say to Mike when Creed starts speaking.

'You've nothing to feel ashamed about, Liam,' says the Patriotic League's leader. 'My sister's married to a Nigerian.'

'You're kidding!'

'No, they met at medical school. My parents were devastated, cut her off completely. The family haven't seen her in eight years. I'm afraid Louise is the black sheep, if you'll excuse the pun.'

Stone and the three lads in the back are all speechless.

'The little family secret doesn't stop *me* being a true patriot, now, does it?'

There are shaken heads all round.

'So there you go,' says Creed. 'Cut Liam some slack. Now, who's for a pint?'

Tahir and Rabia are halfway across the square before Mike can react.

'Rabia!' he cries. 'Don't walk away. Not like this. Please come back.'

But Rabia just wants to get away. Her eyes are filling with tears.

'I can explain.'

But no explanation will satisfy Rabia. She feels betrayed.

'Rabia!'

Mike starts to run after her. Tahir blocks his path.

'I think you've done quite enough, don't you?'

'Tahir, I've got to talk to her.'

'No,' says Tahir, laying a hand on Mike's chest, 'you don't.'

Mike tries to push back. Tahir reacts by punching him in the mouth. Mike staggers back against the wall, spitting out the blood from a cut lip.

'Now leave my family alone,' Tahir says before following Rabia.

By the time Mike's senses clear Tahir and Rabia are crossing the road by the station. They see their father's taxi and get in.

Mike runs towards them. 'No!' he cries. 'You can't go.'

Suhail is pulling away when he sees Mike.

'Don't stop for him,' says Tahir.

Confused, Suhail glances round at his daughter. 'Rabia?'

'Just drive, Dad. Get me out of here.'

Mike watches the car disappear into the Coronation Street-style houses of the Triangle. He feels as if the life has been sucked out of him.

PART THREE
A MOMENT OF HISTORY

1
The Dream Factory

There is fear in every part of the town. On the Triangle there is fear of young men rampaging down Clive Road, smashing everything in sight. On the Moorside there is fear of change, of a strange culture creeping up Ravensmoor Road. In better-off Old Moor and Shevington there is fear of anything which could shake the complacency of its neatly-hedged streets and avenues. Even in the shiny new malls of the town centre angry voices are to be heard.

Where there is fear there is danger. The usual ways of doing things fracture. The social fabric tears, soon people will start to lash out, desperate to protect themselves, shaken so far loose from their usual habits that they could turn on anyone who is different, anyone they can label, or maybe just anyone who is in the wrong place at the wrong time. No-man's-land is a risky place to be.

'Are you all right?' Ady asks Mike.

It is a quarter to nine in the morning and they are standing in a doorway at Moorside High, doing their best to shelter from the driving sleet.

'I've had better days,' says Mike.

In fact he means better weeks. He is red-faced and red-nosed but he feels about as far from the jolly Christmas reindeer as you can imagine. He has spent the last few days making calls to Rabia. She hasn't returned one of them.

'So what's happened, Mike? Is it girl trouble?'

'Yes, you could say that.' He is chewing the zipped collar of his jacket.

'You really want to know?'

'I wouldn't ask if I didn't.'

Mike starts to explain.

'Never!' says Ady. 'So all this time you've been dating an Asian girl without even telling me?'

Mike nods. 'Trying to. Have you got a problem with that?'

'No, each to his own, mate, but you're a braver man than me. It doesn't go down well round here.'

Mike nods. 'Don't I know it.'

Ady gives a sympathetic smile. 'So what you're saying is you're paying for your Liam's stupidity.'

'That's about the size of it. I tell you, Ade, he's playing with fire.'

'And you're the one who got burned.'

Mike nods ruefully

'What a clown though!' says Ady. 'Groups like the Patriotic League suck you in and spit you out. My cousin knocked round with them for a bit a few years ago. He told me that Colin Stone's a right weirdo. He actually organised a Happy Birthday, Hitler party one April. Strange stuff. You should tell your Liam he's being used.'

'Don't you think I've tried?' He squints against the thickening sleet. 'Our Liam's as dense as those hills.'

'So do you reckon this girl's binned you then?'

Mike feels a lump in his throat. Binned. It's such a brutal word. How can something have been destroyed when it has hardly even started to live? It can't have ended, not like this.

'I don't know. She won't answer my calls.'

'That doesn't mean anything, Mike. You know females – they like to keep you hanging. It's what they do.'

Mike shakes his head. He tells himself that Ady's view of women can only reflect the kind of girl he has dated.

'Rabia's not like that.'

Ady shakes his head. 'Mike, take it from somebody who knows. They all are.'

Mike lets it go, but he knows Rabia. Doesn't he?

Like Mike, Rabia is feeling anything but good. The last couple of times Mike's name has appeared on her mobile she has been tempted to answer. She misses him more than she cares to admit.

'Here comes Miss Jamil,' says Sofia.

'Oh, I'm glad I bumped into the two of you,' says Sumeara Jamil. 'I've got the date for your performance at the festival.'

She rummages in her bag. 'Here. I've made each of you a photocopy of the letter.'

Sofia looks excited, Rabia less so.

'Is something wrong?' Sumeara asks.

'No,' says Rabia, 'I'm OK.'

'Don't believe her,' Sofia says. 'She's got boyfriend trouble.'

Rabia glares at her.

'Well, you have.'

'If I can help,' Sumeara says, 'all you have to do is ask. I'm a good listener.'

'Thanks,' says Rabia. 'But I can deal with it.' She walks on towards the computer suite. Sofia gives her a sideways look.

'Are you sure about that?'

At ten o'clock John Creed and Colin Stone are sitting in Stone's car. They are listening to Creed's interview on the local radio news. They had to be at the radio station at six-thirty this morning but it has been worth it. It has been carried on the hour every hour.

'No,' Creed is answering the interviewer, 'I don't think there was anything provocative about our appearance in Market Square. Are you saying an Englishman has lost the right to free speech in this country?'

At the end of the item Councillor Mohammed Saddique appeals for calm.

'Calm!' snorts Creed. 'If he wants calm maybe he should catch the first flight back to Islamabad.'

'So what now?' asks Stone.

'More of the same,' says Creed. 'We'll carry out weekly leafletings in the town centre and mount other demonstrations as the opportunity arises. But we don't let the momentum drop, Colin. We keep up the pressure all the way through to election day. The tide of events is running strongly our way. I tell you, Colin, the future belongs to us.'

Mike and Ady are tucking into their usual dinner, gravy and chips followed by a Danish pastry. It's hardly healthy but they like it.

'You know what you should do?' Ady is saying. 'March right up to her house and demand to see her.'

'You're joking,' says Mike.

'No way. You want the girl? So go out and get the girl. There's no point sitting here pouring your heart out to me.'

Mike wrinkles his nose. He can just imagine the way the family will look at him. 'I don't know.'

'Well, I do. I don't mean to sound unsympathetic, Mike, but you're behaving like a right wuss.'

'Thanks, Ady. That's just what I needed to hear.'

'No need to be sarcastic,' says Ady.

'No,' says Mike. 'I mean it. You're right. This has gone on long enough. I'm going to see her.'

At half-past four Suhail is arriving home at the end of his shift. He finds Mike walking up to the front door.

'Hello, Mr Khan. Is Rabia in?'

'I'm sure she will be at this time, Michael. Do you want me to see?'

'Please.'

Suhail stamps the snow off his shoes. 'You know she was really upset about last Saturday?' he says.

Mike nods. 'I'm really sorry about that, Mr Khan, but I can't answer for my brother. He's big and ugly enough to make his own decisions, even if they make my stomach turn.'

Suhail nods. 'Rabia!' he calls. 'There is somebody here for you.'

Rabia appears at the top of the stairs. 'Who is it?'

'Mike. Do you want to see him?'

Rabia hesitates. 'I'll come down.'

As she walks to the front door, Tahir appears.

'Did I hear Dad say Mike was here? Oh, come on, Rabia! Don't tell me you're actually going to talk to him.'

'Tahir,' Rabia says, 'you're not helping. Go away.'

'You're mad.'

'Maybe, but it's my madness.'

Rabia invites Mike in. 'Let's go in the kitchen.'

'Sit down please,' she says. She is standing with her arms folded. Mike looks small and vulnerable sitting at the table.

'What about you?' he asks.

Rabia nods and sits opposite him across the table.

'I thought your dad might chuck me out on my ear,' Mike says.

'Dad isn't like that. He doesn't do what you expect. He doesn't care what people think either. I suppose that's how he came to marry Mum.'

It is Mike's turn to nod. He was so focused on his way down Ravensmoor Road. He even managed to walk past Khalid and a few of his friends without paying any heed to their taunts. Now that he is sitting facing Rabia he is lost for words.

'Wasn't there something you wanted to say to me?' she asks.

'Yes. I'm sorry about Saturday.'

'Is that it, you're sorry?'

Mike nods. 'Pretty much.'

There is a long silence before he adds. 'No, there's a lot more. Look, Rabia, I should have told you about Liam – but put yourself in my place. How could I do it? He isn't just an armchair bigot like the old man. He's a card-carrying member of the Patriotic League. I thought I was bound to lose you.'

'Mike, that's so stupid,' says Rabia. 'It had to come out some time. How did you expect to keep it a secret?'

Mike shrugs. 'I suppose I just wanted to live in the dream factory a little while longer.'

Rabia has already decided how to handle this moment. She smiles. 'Do you think there's room for one more in there?'

———

Fifteen minutes later Tahir is watching Mike crossing the street. He keeps on watching until Mike turns the corner into Clive Road, then goes into the kitchen.

'You sent him packing then?'

'No,' Rabia replies. 'I made up with him. I've made arrangements to see him over the weekend.'

'You what!'

'Just leave it, Tahir.'

'I will not leave it. His brother's in the Patriotic League. What does that say about your precious Michael?'

'It says he's got a stupid brother. I hope I won't have to say the same.'

'You can't compare me to that lousy racist,' Tahir protests.

'I'm not,' says Rabia. 'You're my brother and I love you. But please, Tahir, don't keep on at me. I really like Mike and I know he isn't like the rest of his family. He hates racism. I don't understand it, but somehow he's managed to survive the brainwashing he must get at home. Why don't you just give him a chance? I know you'd like him.'

'You *know* that, do you? Well, you know a lot more than I do.'

Rabia loves Tahir, but at that moment she half-wishes she didn't have a brother.

Mike has just arrived home to find Liam consoling their mother.

'What was it this time?'

'She burnt his tea. He threw it at the wall.'

Mike sees the stain. 'I'll get a cloth.'

When he gets back his mother is sipping a glass of water.

'I couldn't help it,' she sobs. 'He was so late home from

work. He had a couple of pints on the way. You know what he's like.'

'Yes,' says Mike. 'I know what he's like. He wants locking up.'

'Oh, come off it, Mike,' says Liam. 'This is Dad we're talking about.'

'So what would *you* do with him?' Mike asks.

Liam shrugs. 'What can you do?'

It is the first time the brothers have spoken since the confrontation in the town centre.

On Saturday morning there is another disagreement in the Khan household.

'Please don't go down there,' Diane is pleading.

'I've got to,' says Tahir.

'Suhail, speak to him. Tell him he can't go.'

'I'll do better than that,' says Suhail. 'I'll go with Tahir.'

Rabia stares at her father. 'Dad, what do you mean?'

'I'll join the protests against these people,' Suhail explains. 'Tahir's right. They must be opposed.'

Tahir is smiling broadly.

'It also means,' Suhail says, glancing at his son, 'that by being there I'll be able to keep him out of trouble. Councillor Saddique will be there. I'll help him ensure that it's a peaceful protest.'

'Then I'm coming too,' says Diane.

'No,' says Suhail. 'This is no place for a woman.'

'That's the last thing I expected to hear you say, Suhail.'

'Diane, you must understand. I can't be worrying about you and Tahir.'

'Don't worry about me then,' says Diane, more than a little nettled by Suhail's words. 'I'll take care of myself, thank you very much.'

'Maybe we should talk about this without the children present,' says Suhail.

'Why?' asks Diane. 'I'm not going to change my mind. If you and Tahir are going then I'm coming with you.'

'What about you then, Rabia?' says Tahir mockingly. 'Are you going to make it a family outing?'

'No,' says Suhail. 'You are not to come, Rabia. I forbid it.'

Rabia shakes her head. 'You don't need to worry, Dad. I don't intend to be anywhere near the town centre. Mike and I are going to Oakfield Park for a walk.'

Diane smiles thinly. 'Maybe Rabia has the best idea,' she says.

At noon that day opponents of the Patriotic League are out in force. In addition to groups of Asian men there are demonstrators from neighbouring towns. Altogether there are upwards of a hundred and fifty people in Market Square. Diane Khan is sticking close to her husband and son. She has a bad feeling about the day but she can't think of a better place to be, unless it is in Oakfield Park.

Three-quarters of a mile away, Mike and Rabia are looking at the silver pheasants.

'Beautiful, aren't they?' says Rabia.

'Yes, very.'

She knows he is looking at her. Most people would find the things he says corny. She did to begin with, but now she finds it refreshing. He never tries to be flip or cool, just honest. Where so many people want to be somebody they have seen on TV, Mike is happy to be himself.

'Is Liam going to be in town again?' she asks.

Mike nods.

'How do you feel about that?'

'How do you think I feel? It makes me sick to the pit of my stomach. I'd like to march down there and drag him home, but that would only make things worse.'

'Don't your parents care?'

Mike shakes his head. 'Dad's the reason he's like that in the first place. As for Mum, the old man has ground her down so much she hardly moves out of the house. You know what, Rabia?'

'What?'

'If I do OK in my exams I'm going to stay on at school and go to university. I don't care what it takes. I'll work two jobs. I'll study all night if I have to. Maybe I'll do French and go and live in the Dordogne. I've just got to get away from this stinking dump.'

He turns towards her. 'If we're still together then, if in spite of everything we can hang in there, would you come with me?'

Rabia isn't sure how to answer this. Eventually she says: 'It's all too far ahead, Mike. Let's enjoy what we've got. All I can say about the future is I do want to go to university. I've got Mum and Dad's support for that. I don't know if I could move away from Oakfield for good though. I can't imagine life away from my family.'

Mike snorts bitterly. 'I can. The only one I care about is Mum.'

'You don't mean that.'

Mike runs his hand through his hair. 'Don't I? Listen, if Dad said he was clearing off tomorrow I'd pack him a bag and wave him off with a big white hankie.'

'What about Liam?'

'What about him?' He looks at Rabia.

'You've got a soft spot for him, haven't you?' she says. 'I can tell.'

'I suppose I have,' says Mike. 'God only knows why. But why are you asking about Liam? I thought you of all people would hate him.'

'I don't know him,' Rabia says, 'but people do things they regret later. Look at Tahir. He always jumps in without thinking but I love him dearly. Is Liam really that bad?'

Mike shakes his head. 'No, that's what hurts. Deep inside he's a good kid. He hasn't had a great life, either. Living in our house is like being operated on without anaesthetic. The Patriotic League gives Liam easy answers to difficult questions. It's his way out, I suppose.'

Rabia smiles. 'His dream factory?'

Mike nods. 'Yes, his dream factory.'

John Creed has a dream factory too. He sees a Patriotic League group on the town council, putting the major parties under pressure, forcing the pace of debate and raising the party's profile nationally. This bitterly cold winter's day he is playing party strategist. He and Colin Stone have taken a dozen members down to Market Square. The leafleters are merely a distraction, however.

Liam and his friends are elsewhere reclaiming Oakfield from the foe. When the Patriotic League group arrive they are met with howls of derision from the counter-demonstrators.

'Is that it?' Tahir yells. 'A dozen of you.'

Creed and Stone look on expressionlessly.

'Is this what everybody is getting so excited about?' Diane asks. 'This tiny group?'

She sees Tahir looking around. 'What's the matter?' she asks.

'Mike's brother,' Tahir answers. 'I don't see him.'

'Does it matter?'

'Maybe not.'

The confrontation in Market Square lasts less than forty-five minutes. When the police offer John Creed an escort to the edge of town he willingly accepts.

Mike and Rabia are climbing the hill from Oakfield Park to the Triangle when they see a group of white youths coming in the opposite direction. Rabia recognises the two boys who pestered her that night on Ravensmoor Road. She also recognises Mike's brother Liam.

'Well, if it isn't Michael Kelly and his Asian princess!' Daz sneers.

'Shut up, Hughes,' Mike retorts. He has instinctively placed himself between the youths and Rabia.

'Go on, then,' says Daz. 'Try to shut me up, why don't you?'

Behind him Liam is looking uncomfortable.

'Are you going to let us pass?' Mike asks.

'Depends.'

'On what?'

Daz ponders for a moment. 'On which way you're going, Mike. I take it you're planning to carry on up Ravensmoor. I mean, you wouldn't be trying to accompany Fatima here back home, would you?'

'It's none of your business where I go,' Mike tells him. 'And her name's Rabia, you ignorant piece of—'

'Oh, it's definitely my business if you're going to the Triangle,' says Jason, breaking in. 'You should take a look at yourself in the mirror, Mike, and remember where you belong.'

That's one thing Mike doesn't know. He doesn't belong on the Moorside, that's for certain.

'Oh, go and get a brain transplant!' says Mike. 'I can hear the wind blowing through your ears from here.'

Mike can feel Rabia's fingers digging into his arm. 'Don't, Mike – they're only looking for an excuse.'

Mike looks straight at Liam. 'Are you going to let us through, or what?'

Liam knows what the others expect from him. The strange thing is, he seems to have lost interest in the whole thing. He suddenly feels very tired. He stands to one side. 'Go on,' he says.

Daz and Jason are furious. 'What are you doing, Liam?' they ask.

Liam waves Mike and Rabia past. But for them, everything would be so easy. Sick of difficulty, Liam chooses not to meet their eyes.

'Just go,' he repeats.

The counter-demonstrators are holding a short rally before dispersing. One or two speakers use the word 'victory'. They are not from the town of Oakfield. Councillor Mohammed Saddique merely expresses his relief that there has been no trouble. He reminds the young men of the Triangle that Islam means peace.

The Khan family are in high spirits as they set off home.

'So much for the master race,' says Diane. 'Their meeting was no bigger than last week's – smaller if anything.'

'Thank goodness for that,' says Suhail. 'Let's hope, *inshallah*, their influence is starting to decline.'

Tahir smiles. 'I'm glad you came, Mum.'

'Yes,' says Diane. 'Me too.'

They turn the corner into Caernarvon Road and come to a dead stop.

'Oh no!'

The wall of the mosque is visible from here. It is covered in fresh Patriotic League posters. The paste is still wet. They show a photograph of Councillor Roberts' crashed car and read: *Bring the criminals to justice. Peace wall now!*

There has been no victory. The battle-lines have simply been redrawn.

'I bet this is where Mike's precious brother was all the time,' says Tahir. He runs forward and starts ripping off the offending posters. Suhail and Diane join in.

'You've seen it, then,' says Khalid, arriving from the other end of Clive Road. 'They've covered half the shops with this stuff. They're pointing the finger at the whole community. Everybody is out cleaning it off.'

It is at this moment that Rabia and Mike arrive.

'See what your brother and his friends have done!' says Tahir.

He steps forward and pokes a finger into Mike's chest. 'Proud of your family, are you?'

'I think you had better go, Mike,' says Rabia sadly. 'I'll ring you soon.'

Mike nods and turns towards the Moorside. A quarter of an hour later he is back in its bleak streets. He looks around. Even though he has lived all his sixteen years on this estate he feels like a stranger here.

2
Loyalties

A fortnight later nothing has changed in the town. The weekly ritual is continuing in Market Square. Day after day rumours have been whipping through the Moorside and the Triangle like the wind off the hills, alerting people to new threats to their community. Old loyalties are being reasserted. Against it all Mike and Rabia have tried to keep something good going. They have tried to do what people are meant to do: talk, hold hands, fall in love.

It is Thursday night and they have just met on the steps of Ravensmoor Road library. The result of the Oakfield Book Award will be announced within the next hour. It will be one of the few pieces of good news in this week's issue of the *Chronicle*.

'How are things at home?' Rabia asks.

'Let's see,' says Mike. 'How are things? Well, Mum's depressed, Liam's out with his nasty little friends, Dad's drinking. It's all par for the course, I'd say.'

'And how are you?'

Mike grins. 'I'm surviving. I don't think I've got much choice, really. What's the old line? Been down so long it looks like up to me.'

They follow Sofia into the library. Just before they go inside Mike catches Rabia's sleeve.

'You really want to know how I am, Rabia?' he says hurriedly before Sofia can hear. 'So long as you're in the world, I'm great.'

They look around the library. It is set out differently this time. There is a buffet with wine for the dignitaries and fruit juice for non-drinkers and for the members of the judging panel. Councillor Mohammed Saddique is there, as is the mayor. The *Chronicle* is interviewing the Award organiser. The talk this evening will be of ideas and understanding.

'Hi there!' says Simon, seeing Mike, Rabia and Sofia.

Nobody thinks of him as Chubby Nerdy Guy any more. Now that they have got to know him they are able to see through the painful shyness. He is witty and intelligent. Simon himself, who goes to the selective Marshal school, is glad to make friends outside his usual circle.

'Hi, Simon,' says Mike. 'Who did you vote for?'

'The Morgan book, of course. It was head and shoulders above the others.'

He remembers he is supposed to be shy and adds: 'At least, that's what I think.'

It turns out that all four of them have opted for the same title so it comes as little surprise when the winner is announced.

'The winner of this year's Oakfield Book Award is *Love Song* by Chris Morgan. I am delighted to confirm that I have been in touch with Chris today and he will be attending our celebration event next month to receive his award in person.'

The conversation at the following function is still going strong when Suhail arrives to give Rabia and Sofia their lift home. Councillor Saddique recognises him from the demonstrations and comes across to greet him.

'Suhail, it's good to see you. What brings you here?'

'This is my daughter, Rabia. She is one of the judging panel.'

'Ah yes, we spoke earlier. You must be very proud.'

'I am,' says Suhail. 'Well, we must be going.'

'Do you think Mike could come back with us?' Rabia asks.

Suhail looks at his watch. 'Not tonight. It's getting late.'

Mike smiles despite the disappointment. 'Yes, I think you're right.'

Mike sees Simon getting into a black Audi and says goodnight. He turns and watches Suhail Khan's red Sierra pull away before starting the lonely walk back to the Moorside. Halfway up the hill he realises that of all the judging panel he alone has had to make his way home by himself.

Liam is sitting on a wall with Daz and Jason. 'Do you think we're doing any good?' he says.

'Yes, of course we are,' says Daz.

'So what are we doing?'

'You know,' says Jason.

'Yes, I probably do,' says Liam. 'But just go through it for me.'

Daz and Jason wonder why their friend is acting so weird. 'Well, we're getting our country back, aren't we?'

Liam looks across the boarded-up houses of the Moorside. 'This, you mean? Is this the country we're getting back? I'm not sure I want it.'

'Come off it, Liam,' Daz says. 'You know what we mean. We're going to send our friends from the Triangle home and make it a white man's country again.'

'So we get one of *their* houses, is that it? Funny, but I don't think the Triangle looks much better than here.'

'Are you trying to wind us up, Liam?'

Liam sighs. 'No, I was just wondering, that's all.'

Daz and Jason exchange glances. Liam's definitely got them worried.

'What were you wondering?' Daz asks.

Liam looks at his friends and realises that, pathetic as it might seem, they are all he's got.

'I'll tell you what I was wondering,' he says. 'Wondering how long it would be before you idiots realised I was taking the mickey.'

Daz and Jason jump on top of him. The three carry on mock-fighting all the way up the road. They part at the end of Boundary Road. Once Liam is out of their sight he runs a palm over his face. He wants to be as certain as they are. He wants his cause to be true. But once doubt has got hold of you it rarely lets go easily.

On his way home Liam has to pass Colin Stone's house. The lights are on and the curtains are open. Liam sees Stone standing very still in the window, staring straight ahead. Creed must be out, Liam tells himself, otherwise Stone wouldn't be acting like this. For a moment Liam catches Stone's eye. The look he gets in return gives him the creeps. John Creed can be quite intimidating, but Stone is beyond scary. In that moment Liam remembers the black uniform and wonders if there is any limit beyond which Stone wouldn't go. Looking away, he puts his head down and hurries on by.

Mike walks into the living room and drops down in an armchair. Mary is watching a game show.

'Mum,' he says, 'why do you stay with Dad?'

'It's the way I was brought up,' she says. 'Marriage is for keeps.'

'And that's it?'

'No,' she says. 'I loved him – *love* him.'

'You don't sound so sure.'

Mary smiles. 'I'm sure.'

'I don't get it,' says Mike. 'He hits you. He acts like a pig. How can you love him?'

'Wait till you meet someone special,' says Mary. 'Then you'll understand.'

'I *have* met someone special,' he says.

The moment he hears the words coming out of his mouth he wishes he could run back time. He's pretty sure Liam can't have said anything or there would have been repercussions before this.

'You have?' says Mary. Mike's news has come as a bright moment in a bleak year.

'That's wonderful! When can I meet her?'

Mike is wondering how to get out of this.

'You can't,' he says. 'She doesn't live round here.'

'Where then?'

Oh, what have I got to be ashamed of?

'She lives off Clive Road.'

Mary's eyes widen. 'Clive Road? Down the bottom of–?'

'Ravensmoor. Yes.'

'You mean she's–'

'Yes, Mum, she's Asian. Her name's Rabia.'

'Mike,' Mary says, 'you know this is impossible. Your dad–'

Mike snaps his interruption: 'Dad can go to hell!'

He glares back at her, steely-eyed.

'You know what? I'll even draw the old beggar a map.'

Mary reaches out a hand. 'Listen to me, son. You've got to forget about this girl. Can you imagine what your dad would say? It would tear this family apart.'

'What family? What sodding family would that be, Mum? I know exactly what Dad would say. I've been hearing it for years and now I'm getting it from Liam as well.'

'You mean Liam knows about this girl?'

'Yes. I'm surprised he hasn't blabbed it to everybody.'

On reflection, Mike is more than surprised. He is stunned. Twice in just over a fortnight Liam has done something halfway decent. Maybe there is hope for him yet. Mary is still looking at Mike with her pale, troubled eyes. 'Look Michael,' she says, 'you know I'm not pre-judiced—'

'Do I, Mum?' Mike retorts. 'And just how am I supposed to know that? When did you ever say anything? When did you ever stand up to the old man?'

Mary Kelly looks back at her son and realises how much he has been hurt. She wishes she could make it better. If only she could claim back the wasted years. But it's too late for that.

'Just promise me one thing, Michael,' she pleads. 'I don't care who you see but please, please don't tell your dad.'

'I'm sure he'll get to know soon enough,' says Mike.

'Maybe he will,' says Mary. 'But promise it won't come from you.'

Mike looks at her for a few moments. 'OK,' he says. 'I promise.'

Over on the Triangle Tahir Khan has to be home earlier than the Kelly boys. The Khans have strict rules. There is no control over making phone calls, however. He is speaking to Khalid.

'I think it's time we took the battle back to the enemy,' he is saying.

'Are you serious?'

'Definitely. They defaced the mosque, didn't they? They came on to our territory and now they're laughing at us. It's been two weeks and there have been no reprisals. They think they can do what they like. They must be feeling very smug.'

'I'm not going back to the Moorside. No chance.'

'We don't have to,' says Tahir.

Khalid is puzzled. 'I don't get it,' he says.

'You should,' says Tahir. 'You're the one who spotted them. Their organisers bring the leaflets and placards to the same car park every week, that's what you told me.'

'That's right, they do.'

'And you'd recognise the car again?'

'Of course.'

'Then this week we'll have a little surprise for them.'

When Liam finally gets home about half-past eleven he finds Mike on his own in the kitchen. He asks the inevitable question: 'Is Dad in?'

Mike nods.

'So how is he?'

'Quiet for once, thank goodness.'

Mike watches his younger brother swigging milk from a four-litre bottle. 'Liam?'

'Yes?'

'Why didn't you tell the old man about Rabia?'

'What, and start a civil war?'

'So that's all it was?' Mike asks. 'You were after a quiet life?'

'Yes, something like that.'

'And two Saturdays ago, when you let us pass?'

Liam frowns. 'What is this, Mike, an interrogation?'

'I just want to understand your motives,' Mike says.

Liam knows Mike wants to talk, but he isn't sure he knows what to say in reply. Until the last couple of weeks the Patriotic League seemed to have all the answers. Now he's starting to have doubts. He wonders if maybe there is something else he could be doing with his life. Then he remembers all the 'I told you so's', all the times Mum has told him to be more like Mike, and that's when he hardens against his older brother. No, he won't be second best. He isn't going to give Mike the satisfaction of being right as usual.

'You'll have to work it out for yourself,' Liam replies. 'I've nothing more to say.'

Mike walks to the door. 'I'm going to bed. Goodnight.'

'Yes,' says Liam. 'Goodnight.'

Mike isn't the only one who wants to talk. In spite of everything, Liam almost calls him back. Almost.

At twelve noon the following Saturday the stand-off between the Patriotic League and their opponents is continuing. This time Mike and Rabia have joined the counter-demonstration. Suhail still doesn't like the idea of his wife and daughter attending the protest – there are few Asian women present – but he feels proud nonetheless.

When the Patriotic League take up their usual position Liam is with them. Daz and Jason nudge him, pointing out Mike in the opposite camp. They are expecting Liam to lead the heckling, but he is unusually subdued. Daz and Jason start to shout at the opposition, asking Mike what he sees when he looks in the mirror.

'Still a white man, are you, Mikey?' Daz asks.

Mike doesn't respond, either to the catcalls or to the questioning looks of the Khan family. What he is feeling he will keep to himself.

'Your mate's here, I see,' says Nasir, joining Tahir.

'What? Oh, *Mike.* Yes, he's tagged along. He's trying to show Rabia he isn't like his brother. Well, he doesn't impress me.'

Nasir looks round. 'So where's Khalid? I thought he'd be here.'

'Don't worry about Khalid,' says Tahir knowingly. 'He's around.'

Khalid Hussain is crossing the car park on the edge of town. His heart is thudding. He wishes he had never let Tahir talk him into this. The carrier bag he is holding in his right hand contains the three spray cans used on the night of the meeting at Moorside Primary school. Crouching between the white Honda and Stone's car, Khalid pulls out one of the spray cans. He shakes it, listening to the rattle of the ball bearing inside, wishing it wasn't so loud. He takes a deep breath and starts to spray his message. He has just sprayed the word *Racists* when he becomes uncomfortably aware of somebody standing behind him, watching. He turns and sees a man in his early sixties, obviously the owner of the white Honda.

'What the hell do you think you're doing?' the man demands. He makes a grab for Khalid's jacket.

'I'll soon sort you, you young hooligan!'

'Get off me!' Khalid yells. 'It's not like it's even your car. What are you getting so excited about?'

But the Honda owner seems determined to be a responsible citizen. 'You're coming with me,' he barks, getting an even tighter grip on Khalid. 'We're going to have a talk with the police.'

They start to struggle. Khalid expects to be able to shrug the old man off easily, but he is hampered by the carrier bag he is holding in one hand. The spray can he was using has rolled under Stone's car.

'Let go of me, will you?' Khalid cries. 'Get off, you crazy old man.'

But the old man is set on making a citizen's arrest. 'Police!' he yells. 'Police!'

Panicking, Khalid swings the carrier bag. With the two cans inside it is heavy and connects with the man's head with a resounding crack. To Khalid's horror blood begins to pour from a large gash on the old man's forehead and he staggers back, shock registering in his eyes.

'I'm sorry,' says Khalid, reaching out to support the swaying pensioner. 'I didn't mean to do that. I'm so . . .'

But before Khalid can explain himself a police car pulls up at the entrance to the car park. Somebody has raised the alarm. Khalid has no choice but to run.

The demonstration in Market Square is over and the Patriotic League are dispersing. Liam, Daz and Jason are carrying the placards and loud-hailer back to Stone's car.

'Hello, what are the police doing here?' Creed asks.

'My car!' cries Stone. 'Have you seen what they've done to my car?'

'This is your vehicle then, sir?' says the policewoman who has been examining the car.

A male officer and a paramedic are talking to the man who tackled Khalid.

'Damned right it's mine,' says Stone. 'It's not even paid for yet. Just look at the state of it.'

While Stone rages about his vandalised car, John Creed is taking in the situation. He can see the face of the bruised and bloodied old man in the Sunday newspapers. He takes out his mobile and punches in a number he has called several times before and now knows off by heart.

'Roger Gray?' he says. 'Yes, it's John Creed. I may have

something for you for the evening edition. I thought you'd be interested.'

Khalid is being pursued through the Market Centre by two policemen. He's young and fit but he isn't shaking off the pursuing officers. What's more, one of them has radioed for back-up.

'Get out of the way!' Khalid yells as his path is blocked by two teenage girls.

He shoves them roughly aside and hurdles one of the concrete plant pots that are dotted about the central mall. He can hear the rattle of the spray cans in the bag and realises it's evidence. It's probably got the old man's blood on it. Up ahead is the point where Pennine View crosses Market Way. Khalid skids round the corner and dumps the incriminating carrier bag in a bin before racing on towards the down escalator which will take him into Market Square. Just another hundred metres, he's thinking, then I'm home and dry. He reaches the top of the escalator and feels a tremor of horror. There is another policeman waiting at the bottom. Khalid turns, looking round desperately. He sees the other two policeman behind him. One of them has retrieved the carrier bag.

'Stop right there!' they command.

But Khalid isn't finished yet. He sees the walkway to Market Square car park. If he can only make the stairs!

'We're going now,' Suhail says. 'Mike, I hope you'll be our guest this evening. Both Diane and I are excellent cooks.'

'I'd like that,' says Mike. He ignores the scowl from Tahir.

'I still don't see Khalid,' says Nasir.

'He'll be along any minute, don't you worry,' says Tahir. But when he does finally spot Khalid the smile disappears from his face. Khalid is racing across the square pursued by three officers. For a moment it looks as if he will reach Oakfield Park Road and stand a chance of giving the officers the slip. Then a burly middle-aged man in an Oakfield Town shirt steps out from the crowd and trips Khalid. Khalid staggers against the ornamental fountain in the middle of the square. As he scrambles to his feet, winded and holding his ribs, the police officers seize him and wrestle him to the ground. Councillor Saddique is on the spot immediately.

'What is happening here, officers?' he demands. 'Why are you arresting him?'

Before the police have the chance to explain some of the younger men in the counter-demonstration start to move forward.

'Let him go!' says one.

'Yes, let him go!' shouts another.

The chant is taken up by eighty or so people. Seeing the disturbance, more police officers come running. Soon Market Square is the scene of an ugly confrontation.

Colin Stone, John Creed and their three young foot soldiers are halfway home in the vandalised car when there is a newsflash on the local radio.

'*Trouble has flared in the town centre*, the reporter begins. *Skirmishes have broken out in Market Square. First reports suggest that the disturbances are the result of the arrest of a young Asian man. Elsewhere in the town an elderly white man has been attacked in what is being seen as a racially-motivated incident.*'

Creed claps his hands. 'You know what this means?' he cries.

Nobody else in the car knows what it means.

'This is it! The war has begun!'

Liam remembers a time just a few months back when he was shocked by the word 'war'. It seems a long time ago.

'It's the chance to put ourselves centre stage,' Creed is saying. 'Don't you get it? This is the moment we've been waiting for!'

All the way along the line what has kept Liam with the Patriotic League has been excitement. Now he can see something more in Creed's eyes. There is joy.

'Colin,' Creed says, 'the moment we get to the house you have to phone everyone. This is an opportunity we can't afford to miss. Liam, where did you and the boys stash that peace wall stuff?'

'The painted boards, you mean?'

'That's them.'

'They're in Jason's garage.'

'OK, boys, run over and bring them round to Colin's.'

'What for?'

Creed shakes his head. 'Don't you have any imagination?' he says. 'If we play our cards right, this town is going to be front page news tomorrow, and our party will be centre stage.'

By five o'clock it is looking like the trouble might just be dying down. There are groups of young men facing up to police officers on the front line at the end of Clive Road, but Councillor Mohammed Saddique is actively trying to calm things. The Khan family, accompanied by Mike Kelly, have left the scene. They think the worst is over. Two events within a quarter of an hour prove to be turning points. They will undo all Councillor Saddique's good work.

At eight minutes past five Tahir Khan and Nasir Ahmed are taken to Caernarvon Road police station for questioning. The police have prised their names out of a reluctant Khalid Hussain. Within ten minutes the rumour is circulating that they have been arrested in connection with Councillor Roberts' recent crash. The word among the youths on the street is that it is a frame-up.

At seventeen minutes past five twenty Patriotic League activists assemble outside the Lion. The Saturday afternoon edition of the *Chronicle*, featuring the bruised and bloodied face of the man hurt in his struggle with Khalid, has been pasted to ten placards. The rest of the demonstrators are carrying the Peace Wall boards.

By twenty-five past five Councillor Saddique's pleas have begun to fall on deaf ears. The Triangle's young men have seen the Patriotic League demonstrators not fifty yards from the mosque whose walls were so recently defaced. They are determined to defend their community.

At half-past five the first stones are being thrown. This time the Patriotic League return them. Within minutes police in riot gear are on the scene.

Mike and Rabia are alone in the house. Diane and Suhail are with Tahir at the police station.

'Did you see the look on Mum and Dad's faces?' says Rabia.

'Yes, I know,' says Mike. 'They seemed shell-shocked.'

'How could he do this to them?' Rabia cries. 'After everything they said the last time. You should have heard the promises he made.'

'You don't know the full story yet,' says Mike. 'Kids do get picked up for things they haven't done, you know. I think it's best if you just wait till they get back.'

'Will you stay with me?' Rabia asks.

'Yes, of course.'

Rabia walks into the kitchen. 'You never did get anything to eat,' she says, 'what with Tahir's arrest and all.'

'That's all right,' says Mike. 'I can wait.'

'No, let me get you something. It might take my mind off things.'

'OK, I'll tell you what. You can make me something just as long as you eat with me.'

'Oh no, Mike, I couldn't, not until I know what's happened to Tahir.'

'Humour me, eh?' says Mike. 'Go on, even if you just eat a mouthful.'

Finally Rabia nods. She knows Mike is trying to help.

The police have drawn up two lines, one facing the Triangle, one facing the Patriotic League supporters at the bottom of the Ravensmoor Road.

'You should be going after that lot,' Daz yells, confronting the police. 'How come you always take their side?'

'Give us a break, son,' says one policeman. 'We're always piggy in the middle in these situations.'

It's only when Daz starts to pass his words round that the policeman realises what he has said. The blush of embarrassment can be seen through his visor.

'Hey, Liam!' Jason says. 'Did you hear what that copper said to Daz?'

'Yes,' says Liam absent-mindedly. 'I heard.'

Liam is watching John Creed talking to the TV cameras, condemning the residents of the Triangle.

'Of course we in the Patriotic League deplore violence,' Creed is saying. 'Nobody wants to see disturbances like this on our streets.'

'You hypocrite,' Liam murmurs. 'You rotten, lousy hypocrite.'

'While we talk peace,' Creed continues, 'they declare war. I'm afraid our Muslim friends on the Triangle don't understand English codes of behaviour. Maybe now the people of this country will start to take notice.'

'Hey, Liam!' Jason calls. 'Don't leave all the hard work to us. Come over here and give us a hand.'

Liam continues to watch events from a few metres away.

'Did you hear what Jason said?' Daz asks. 'What's the matter with you, Liam? You've been acting really strange just lately, you know that?'

Liam stares straight into Daz's eyes. 'Daz,' says Liam. 'I've just resigned.'

He starts to walk up Ravensmoor Road.

'Resigned?' says Jason. 'You don't just resign from the League.'

'I do,' says Liam.

'Are you winding us up again, Liam?' Daz calls. 'Come back, will you?'

'Yes, come back here!' shouts Jason.

But Liam keeps on walking.

Suhail and Diane are sitting in a room in the police station with Tahir. They look up at the missing ceiling tile and the curling posters on the wall. They feel embarrassed and confused in equal parts.

'Just tell us, what's going on?' Suhail asks. 'What have you done? What's this about paint?'

'We went up to the Moorside ages ago, the night of that meeting. We spray-canned a few cars.'

'Why?' cries Diane.

'They were whipping up a lynch mob,' Tahir replies. 'We wanted to let them know they couldn't push us around any more.'

'But what's that got to do with what Khalid did today?' Suhail asks. 'I don't understand.'

Tahir explains about Colin Stone's car.

'And they're the same spray cans?'

Tahir nods. 'I'm sorry, not for what I've done, you understand – those racist scum deserve it – but for dragging you into it.'

'But what about this other stuff?' Diane asks. 'The police

asked you if you knew anything about Councillor Roberts' car.'

'They're making that up,' Tahir cries. 'We didn't have anything to do with it. We wouldn't!' He is almost in tears.

'They're trying to pin that on us just because we're Asians. Muslims don't get justice in this country.'

He turns to Suhail. 'Dad, you should know that.'

'Tahir,' Suhail says, taking him by the shoulders, 'I don't want to hear slogans. Just tell us what happened. The solicitor will be back in a moment. He'll ask you to tell the truth. Is there anything else we should know?'

Tahir shakes his head. 'It's the spray cans, that's all. I don't know how Khalid came to hit that man and I definitely don't know anything about Councillor Roberts' brakes. You've got to believe me.'

'Of course we believe you,' says Diane.

The family sit trying to make sense of the events that have engulfed them. They don't know that beyond the walls of the police station things are spinning out of control.

Rabia and Mike are sitting looking at their uneaten food.

'Sorry,' says Rabia, 'I just can't eat.'

Mike reaches for her hand. 'Me neither.'

He is about to say something else when there is a loud bang outside. 'What was that?'

Rabia shakes her head. 'I don't know.'

They go into the living room. There the shouts of the rioters and the sound of flying missiles are much clearer.

'There's fighting on Clive Road,' says Rabia. 'Mike, this is about Tahir and Khalid.'

Mike shakes his head. 'No, this is about Oakfield.'

Rabia opens the front door. At the bottom of the street she can make out running figures. The air is full of the smell of burning, and raucous shouting. They can hear the sound of the police beating their shields with their truncheons. Amid the scenes of battle, Rabia sees a familiar figure.

'Councillor Saddique!' she shouts. 'It's me, Rabia. We were at the book award together.'

'Yes,' says Councillor Saddique. 'Suhail's daughter. I remember.'

'What's happening?'

'The young men are beyond my control,' says Councillor Saddique. 'I did my best, they wouldn't listen.'

'But what's happening?' says Mike. 'Who's fighting?'

'The Patriotic League have really stirred it up,' says Councillor Saddique. 'They are on Ravensmoor Road. The moment our young men saw them . . .' He holds out his arms in a gesture of despair.

'Liam,' says Mike. 'I've got to speak to him. I've got to talk him out of this madness.'

'No, Mike,' says Rabia. 'Don't go. It's too dangerous.'

She is still trying to talk Mike out of going when the phone goes.

'That could be your parents,' says Mike. 'You'd better answer it.'

'Promise you won't go,' Rabia says. 'Promise.'

'Answer the phone, Rabia,' says Mike.

'Just stay here,' Rabia says. 'Please.'

But by the time she returns Mike has gone.

When Liam gets home Mary is waiting for him.

'Oh, thank God!' she cries. 'I thought you might be in the middle of all that trouble.'

'You know about it then?' says Liam.

Mary nods. 'Michael just called me to see if I knew where you were. Oh Liam, I was so worried.'

'So where's Mike now?'

'He's down there, of course,' says Mary. 'He's gone looking for you.'

Liam runs to the phone. 'He's got to get out of there, Mum! You should see what's going on. Somebody could be killed. It's madness.'

He rummages in the mess on the phone table. 'Where's that diary with our mobile numbers?'

'It should be there.'

'Well, I can't find it. Do you know Mike's number?'

'Just a minute,' says Mary. 'Let me think.' She stammers out a few digits then throws up her arms in a gesture of despair.

'I can't remember.'

'I didn't even put it in my directory,' says Liam. 'It's not like we ever had much to talk about.'

That sounds so stupid. They had everything to talk about.

'Let's check the whole place over again,' says Mary. 'The diary's got to be here somewhere.'

She has an awful feeling that time is running through her fingers like sand.

Mike is running down Clive Road. His presence attracts hostile looks.

'What are you doing here?' demands one Asian youth.

'Yes, wrong side of the line, aren't you?' says another.

'Look,' Mike says, slowing, 'I don't want any trouble. I'm trying to find my brother, that's all.'

He is feeling uncomfortable but not scared. He walks steadily past the group of youths. They seem suspicious of him but they don't follow.

Where are you, Liam?

Ahead of him he can see the flames thrown up by several overturned vehicles ablaze on the front line. Against the firelight he can see projectiles being thrown. Like firebirds, he thinks, seeing the dark shapes in the sky. There is a large crowd at the bottom of the road. No way through there, he decides.

Maybe if I cut down a side road.

But it is the same story there. Crowds of young men are pelting the police as they crouch behind their riot shields. Mike wonders whether he should go back to the Khans' house. After a few moments he decides to try one more route around the rioters.

Councillor Martin Roberts is sitting at the computer, trying to draft his letter of resignation from the Council, when his wife Yvonne comes to the door.

'Martin, have you heard the news?'

'No, what?'

'There's full-scale rioting between Clive Road and Ravensmoor Road. The police have arrested three young Asian men. They think they're the ones who interfered with your brakes.'

For a few moments Councillor Roberts can't make sense of what his wife has told him.

'Did you hear me, Martin? It's like a war zone.'

Councillor Roberts gets out of his chair and brushes past his wife.

'Martin, where are you going?'

'There's something I have to do,' he says. 'Something I should have done a long time ago.' He picks up the phone and dials.

'Hello,' he says. 'Oakfield police?'

———————

Rabia doesn't know what to do. The phone call was only Sofia asking if she had heard about the riot. By the time she got back to the front door Mike had gone.

'Oh Mike,' she says, 'why did you have to go?'

She looks at the glow of the fires then back at the telephone on the hall table. What would Mum and Dad say if they called and she was out?

'No, I can't go.'

Suddenly she wants the world to stop spinning on its axis, to freeze and take a moment's breath. It seems to be careering out of control.

'Stop,' she says, looking at the flames. 'Please stop.'

She is still willing the fighting to end when the phone rings.

'Hello? Mum! You're coming home? Yes, that's brilliant. What did they say about Tahir? They think he'll get away with a final reprimand? What does that mean? OK, OK, tell me when you get back.'

She is about to hang up when something occurs to her.

'Mum, are you still there? Listen, you know about the fighting, don't you? Oh, they did. Yes, see you soon.'

Secure in the knowledge that her family will be home soon, Rabia turns her thoughts back to the riots . . . and Mike.

3
Night of Fire

John Creed is standing in a doorway at the bottom of Ravensmoor Road, watching the fighting spread in a band of fire and rage three roads deep.

He casts his mind back to the night he arrived in this nondescript little town. It was half asleep then, he thinks, with its head stuck up its own backside. But look at you now, Oakfield! You know what you were then? In the popular imagination you were no more than a bag of nostalgic images, a Hovis-advert world of clogs and shawls. But it was a lie, wasn't it? There are more mosques than mills these days. You'd be as likely to hear the call to Friday prayers as the rising note of a brass band.

Then I came to open people's eyes. Deep inside they must have known the truth, of course, but it took a group of determined men to make them face it – men who wouldn't flinch from a challenge. *I* found those men. *I* fashioned them into a fighting unit. *I* chose to make history. He closes his eyes. When he opens them again Colin Stone is standing in front of him.

'Daz has just been arrested,' says Stone.

'Good,' Creed answers.

'*Good?*'

'Yes, good. You've got to get this clear in your own

mind, Colin. Boys like Darren Hughes are two a penny. Cannon fodder, that's all they are. The foot soldiers are always expendable. Half of them will fall by the wayside, no matter what we do. It's the leaders that are thin on the ground – men like you and me. Believe me, we can turn any arrests to our advantage. Every movement needs its martyrs. There's no such thing as bad publicity. Use your imagination, man. *Young Englishman arrested on vigil for peace.* Colin, we can't go wrong. We're not extremists any more. We're *saviours.*'

Alerted by another loud bang, Stone turns to see an injured policeman being dragged away. He has been knocked unconscious by a concrete block. Stone has taken another step into Creed's world. A few moments ago he would have seen an injured copper, now it's just one more expendable member in Creed's cast of hundreds. Even before the senseless policeman reaches the ambulance a snatch squad is going into Smith Grove to find the person who threw the missile.

'**M**um! Dad!'
Rabia is overjoyed to see her parents. Tahir slips into the house almost unnoticed behind them. That's the way he wants it. He still can't bring himself to regret what he's done, but he wouldn't mind lying low for a while.

'You didn't see Mike, did you?'

'Mike?' says Diane. 'Didn't he go home?'

Rabia shakes her head. 'He went to find his brother.'

'You mean he's out in the middle of all that?' Suhail asks.

'Yes,' Rabia answers. 'Dad, we've got to find him.'

'No, Rabia,' Suhail says firmly. 'You stay here where I know you're safe. *I'll* find him.'

'But Dad . . .'

Suhail looks to Diane for support.

'Your dad's right, Rabia,' she says. 'This time we really do have to say no. Let your father look for him.'

Rabia protests long and bitterly but eventually she has to give in.

'And you, Tahir,' says Suhail, 'you stay with your mother and sister. I think you've done quite enough this evening.'

'Got it!' cries Liam, reaching behind the table. 'It's fallen down the back.'

He flicks through the pages of the book. 'Here it is.'

He taps in Mike's number. 'Come on, *come on*!'

But he is unable to connect. He is put through to Mike's voice mail.

'Mike,' he says, 'if you get this message it's me, Liam. I'm home. You've got to get out of there. Mum's worried sick.'

Liam looks at Mary. 'I'll keep phoning every few minutes,' he tells her. 'He'll be all right. I know it.'

Suhail is in Clive Road. He pauses outside The Gulam. Rashid is standing at the door. His three staff are just behind him, watching events.

'Bad business, isn't it?'

Suhail nods. 'You haven't seen a white boy, have you?'

'A white boy? Here? Not tonight, Suhail. All my customers have been frightened away by the fighting.'

'I'm not talking about a customer, Rashid,' Suhail tells him. 'His name is Michael Kelly. He's a friend of my daughter.'

Suhail looks at the plumes of reeking tyre smoke that are hanging over the area. 'Rashid, I've got a bad feeling about this.'

'Me too,' says Rashid.

Suhail can hear the rhythmic beating of truncheon on riot shield. It seems to be getting closer. Bidding farewell to Rashid, he crosses the road and asks a group of youths on the corner about the white boy.

'Yes, there was one. Beats me what he was doing here. What do you want him for, anyway?'

'That's my business,' says Suhail. 'Now which way did he go?'

The youths point the way and Suhail hurries on. He's got a *really* bad feeling about this.

Councillor Roberts is giving a statement to the police. 'Why didn't you tell us this earlier, sir?' one of the officers is asking.

'I was terrified, that's why,' says Councillor Roberts. 'You don't seem to understand. This man is a complete psychopath. He was standing by my hospital bed. He kept talking about *Misery*.'

'Misery?'

'Yes, *Misery*. It's a movie, from a novel by Stephen King.'

'Oh yes, I know the one,' says the second policeman. 'That bit with the hammer. I can't watch it.'

That's when the penny drops. 'Oh, *Misery*!'

'Now,' says Councillor Roberts, 'you know the truth. Isn't there some way you can get this on TV or something? Those boys you've been holding are completely innocent.'

'They're not just being questioned about your crash, sir,' says the first policeman.

'Look,' says Councillor Roberts, seeming incapable of taking in what the policeman has just said, 'whatever they've done, they're not responsible for my injuries. You must see that. You've got to stop the riots.'

'I'm sure that's exactly what the uniformed boys are trying to do,' says the first policeman, 'but I don't think a TV statement would do much good now. Things have gone too far for that. Besides, our enquiries aren't complete.'

'Not complete! What more do you need?'

'Well, to begin with there's the matter of a statement from Mr Stone.'

'Then get it. We've got to make the truth known.'

'Maybe,' the policeman replies. 'You should have thought about that earlier, Councillor.'

Mike Kelly has got as far as the top of Oakfield Park Road. It is quieter here and he can see the Patriotic League supporters right up against the police lines. It almost looks as if they are sheltering behind their shields. Mike approaches the demonstrators. He notices a familiar face.

'Jason! Am I glad to see you.'

'What's this, Mike? Finally realised whose side you're on?'

'No,' says Mike. 'Nothing like that.'

He feels uncomfortable. He doesn't want to be seen in the company of lads like Jason and Daz, but he is desperate.

'Listen, I'm looking for our Liam. Have you seen him?'

Jason doesn't answer. 'Daz has been arrested,' he tells Mike. 'Not that you'd care anyway. That's great, isn't it? He turns up to fight for his country and the police pull him in.'

Mike almost bursts out laughing at the words *fight for his country*. D-Day this isn't. But Mike isn't interested in the rights and wrongs of Oakfield's self-appointed patriots and their pathetic demonstration.

'Look, have you seen our Liam or not?'

'Yes,' says Jason. 'I've seen the lousy sell-out, more's the pity. It looks like you've got yourself another race-traitor in the family. You Kellys are making a habit of it. You'll be wearing turbans next.'

Mike doesn't have time to tell Jason that Oakfield's Muslims don't wear turbans.

'Don't be stupid, Jason,' he says. 'I don't want a row. I just want to track Liam down.'

But Jason isn't about to give up. 'I don't know how you Kellys sleep at night,' he says. 'Go on, tell me that, Mike: how do you live with yourselves?'

Mike is confused by the exchange. Does this mean

Liam's seen some sense at last? In the event he doesn't get the chance to squeeze an explanation out of Jason. Mounted police have appeared at the top of Oakfield Park Road. They are about to charge.

Back at the Khan house Tahir is pacing the floor.

'This isn't right,' he says. 'I should be out there defending the Triangle.'

'Oh no,' says Diane. 'You should be right here where I can keep an eye on you.'

'Just think what would happen if you got arrested again,' Rabia cries. 'You could kiss goodbye to a decent career. Haven't you learned anything?'

'Yes, I've learned that Muslims won't get justice from a white police force. All that me, Khalid and Nasir were doing was standing up for our people.'

'Yes,' says Rabia. 'That's all well and good, but didn't you ever think that you might have gone about it the wrong way?'

Tahir snorts. 'Rabia, you're so full of–'

'Tahir!' Diane is standing facing him, her fists clenched. 'You shut your mouth now, Tahir, or I swear I'll shut it for you. You've embarrassed your family and you don't seem to feel one iota of shame. Don't you understand that? Are you so thick-skinned that you can't see how much you've hurt us all?'

Tahir doesn't say another word.

The mounted charge sends the Patriotic League supporters retreating up Ravensmoor Road almost as far as
Foulshurst Avenue. They fall back reluctantly, hurling
shouts of *Traitor!* at the police. The officers on foot quickly
move their lines up Ravensmoor Road. They have created a
significant gap between the two sides. In the confusion
Mike has been separated from Jason and the rest of the
demonstrators and has run into Smith Grove. Panting, he
sits down on the step of a house and switches on his
mobile. He wants to talk to Rabia.

'Hi Rabia, it's me.'

He hears her voice. 'Mike! Oh, it's so good to hear you. I
thought–'

'Don't you worry about me,' Mike says. 'Look, I don't
know what's going on, but our Liam isn't with his sick
little friends any more. By the sound of it, he's finally
walked away from trouble. Maybe he's actually started to
see sense.'

'So what are you going to do?'

'It's pretty hairy here at the moment and there's no way
home. The police have blocked Ravensmoor off.'

'You'd better come back here until it's all over,' says
Rabia. 'Dad's looking for you, by the way.'

'*Your* dad?'

'Yes, we thought some of the Asian boys might mis-
understand your presence.'

'It hasn't been that bad,' says Mike. 'Mostly they ignored
me. I was expecting a lot worse, to be honest.'

'Get right back here,' says Rabia. 'Where are you, by the
way? I'll call Dad.'

Mike looks up at the street sign. 'I'm in Smith Grove. See
you in a minute.'

L iam is getting desperate.

'Come on, Mike, switch the damned phone on, will you?'

Then, after half an hour's trying, he gets through.

'Mum, I've got him! Mike, it's me, Liam. Look, I've been leaving you messages all evening, you dope. What's the point of a mobile if you don't keep it on? I'll tell you where I am if you let me. I'm home. That's right, I walked away. I've told them where to stick their stupid organisation. Just get back here.'

He hears Mike saying he can't get through the police lines so he is going to hole up at Rabia's for a while.

'Sure,' says Liam. 'Anything. Just get off the streets.'

He lowers his voice. 'One more thing. I'm sorry about everything. Look, I'm putting Mum on.'

'Michael!' says Mary. 'Thank God you're all right. What time will you be home?'

Mike tells her things are still pretty scary on the front line. He doesn't know when it will be safe to make a move.

'Do what you have to, love. Take a taxi – anything. No matter how late it is, I'll be waiting up for you.'

Before she hangs up she adds: 'I love you, Michael.'

M ike has just put the mobile phone away when he hears the sound of running feet. Then the first police horse is galloping down Smith Grove straight for him. Mike joins the fleeing crowds. Feeling the breath of the lead horse on his back, Mike vaults over a low wall and runs along the tiny front gardens. Ridiculously, he thinks the decorative walls and knee-high picket fences offer protection. Something about an Englishman's home being his castle. But Mike Kelly's castle has been breached. He feels a sickening blow on the back of the neck and a sticky feeling on his cheek and shoulder.

'I'm bleeding!'

He hears a voice as if through a mist. 'Are you all right?'

He sees two Asian youths looking at him. He hears them talking as if about somebody else.

'We've got to get him inside. He's in a bad way.'

Are they talking about me? Mike wonders. Am I the one who's in a bad way? It is as though he is in a tunnel. All the sounds around him are reduced to a dull booming. He is trying to focus, but he is unable to claw his way back to reality.

'Do you hear me?' one of the youths is saying. 'You've got to get out of here.'

Then the dull boom is transformed into a loud roar. Mike is aware of something big and dangerous towering over him. Horse and rider are transformed into a single image of horrifying power. He feels as if he is about to be destroyed by it.

'Help me!' he cries.

J ohn Creed has left the scene of the riot, leaving Stone in
   charge. He walks up to the police lines, holding his
   hands in the air.

'Good evening, gentlemen,' he says to the line of tense,
suspicious riot police. 'I wonder if you might let me
through.'

'Where are you going?'

'My car is in Foulshurst Avenue. I just want to get home.'

'And where's home?'

Creed gives the address. The officer in charge nods and
he passes through. He takes the car keys he borrowed from
Stone and drives up to the Moorside. As he turns into
Boundary Road he gives the blazing barricades one last,
satisfied look.

'Mission accomplished,' he says.

Creed inspects Stone's cassettes. 'Elton John? Oh dear
me, Colin. That's not exactly the stuff an Aryan soldier
should be listening to.'

S uhail answers his mobile.
   'Dad, it's me.'

'Rabia? Is something wrong?'

'No, everything's fine. Listen, I just got through to Mike.
He's in Smith Grove. His brother's gone home so there's
no need for Mike to go on looking. Mike can't get home so
he's on his way back here.'

'Smith Grove, you say? His quickest way back is up Clive Road. I'll catch up with him there.'

'Thanks. Dad?'

'Yes?'

'Everything's going to be all right.'

'Of course it is, Rabia. Of course it is.'

The two youths are guiding Mike past the Halal butcher's at the start of Clive Road. Other young Asians have gathered in the side streets and along Clive Road itself. They see the police as an occupying army. They are determined to keep them out of the Triangle. Bricks and bottles are flying.

'Here they come again,' says one of the lads.

The mounted police are galloping down Clive Road, followed by officers on foot. Groups of youths are pelting them with anything they can lay their hands on.

'We're going to get trampled if we stay here,' says one lad.

'Look, mate, I'm sorry about this. You stay in this doorway. We'll try to get some help for you.' Then the two youths are running, pursued by a snatch squad.

Mike sits slumped in the doorway while the storm of brick, concrete and glass breaks over the Triangle.

Rabia is at the window. 'Shouldn't they be back by now?' she says.

'You only just phoned your dad,' says Diane. 'And who knows what's going on out there? Just be patient, love. They'll be here soon.'

'I could go and look for them,' says Tahir.

'You'll sit tight,' says Diane. 'It'll be a long time before I let you out of my sight again.'

Diane Khan is trying to be the calm centre of chaos. Inside she is terrified. She can't believe this night of fire will end without casualties.

Creed is met at the front gate by Stone's next-door neighbour, Mrs Littlejohn.

'Isn't Colin with you?' she asks.

'No. Why?'

'The police have been round asking for him.'

'The police?'

'Yes, two plain-clothes coppers. They showed me their badges. I don't take anything on say-so.'

'Did they say what they wanted?'

Mrs Littlejohn shakes her head slowly. 'No, they didn't. Not that I asked. Nobody calls Maggie Littlejohn nosy.'

Creed opens the front door. 'I'm sure it's nothing. Thank you, Mrs Littlejohn.'

'Think nothing of it,' she says.

The moment Creed gets inside the house he smashes his fist into a wall unit. Suddenly, suddenly it all falls into place. Now he knows what Councillor Roberts meant. *Haven't I had enough trouble with you people?* You can't have spoiled everything, Stone! Surely even a moron like you couldn't ruin things now.

Mike's head begins to clear. He looks around the doorway.

'I've got to get back to Rabia's,' he tells himself.

Hauling himself to his feet, he staggers into the road. It feels as if the whole world is tilting precariously and that the pavement is pitching at a strange angle.

'What's wrong with me?' he wonders.

He lays the flat of his palm against the wall of a restaurant. He reads the name Gulam.

'The Gulam,' Mike says, still reeling from the blow to his head. 'So which way is it to Rabia's from here?'

An idea flits briefly through his head, something he was told when he was little: if you're lost, ask a policeman. But the policemen in Clive Road are not bobbies on the beat. They are wearing crash helmets and visors and they are fighting a war. He can't ask *these* policemen.

Mike remembers that there were two lads a few moments ago. They were helping him. Where did they go? He looks around. There are so many people in Clive Road at that moment. Some are running, others are throwing stones and bottles at the police. Some are even moving blazing vehicles into the middle of the road. The Triangle is going up in flames, Mike thinks, and I'm at the heart of the flame. He has a comforting thought: you can put your finger into the heart of the flame. Mike smiles. I'm not going to get burned.

M ary and Liam are watching the television news when Sean Kelly rolls in. He stands swaying in the middle of the living room for a moment then glances at the screen.

'One of the lads in the pub told me the Islamics had kicked off,' he says. 'Those Pakis don't know how to behave themselves.'

Mary is surprised to see Liam on his feet, yelling at the top of his voice. For a moment it is as if Mike is home instead of Liam.

'Shut up, Dad! Just shut your stupid, foul mouth!'

Tears are running down Liam's cheeks. He is guilty, humiliated and scared. He doesn't even have a name for the other feelings that are boiling up inside him. The dream factory has fallen in around him.

'What did you say?' Sean demands.

'I told you to shut your drunken mouth,' Liam replies. 'Is that simple enough for you?'

'Why you little–'

Liam skips back from the swinging fists. 'You know who you sound like, Dad? Homer Simpson. Well, I don't plan to stand here and get throttled by some cartoon cut-out slob. Come on! If you want me come and get me!'

'Liam!' says Mary. 'Stop it!'

But Liam doesn't want to stop it. He understands it now, the way he became like his dad. Not any more, he vows. Mike's right. He's been right all along. I've been throwing my life away on people not fit to dirty the soles of my shoes.

'Come on, Dad!' Liam yells. 'Hit me! That's it old man, knock me flat!'

He sticks out his chin. Sean swings again and misses. This time Liam doesn't just skip away. He throws a punch of his own that snaps Sean's head back.

'I'll have you, you little get!' Sean slurs.

'Oh really, you and whose army? Just look at the state of you. You can hardly stand. Do you want me to get you a zimmer frame? I'm not scared of you any more, Dad. After tonight nobody in this family's going to be scared of you ever again.'

He lays into Sean, throwing punch after punch, pounding his anger into the blotchy, unresisting face and the thick, slab-like body. Sean stands bloody and weary, his hands limp at his side.

'Why, son? Why are you doing this?'

'You want to know why, Dad? Because you make me sick. Yes, and because you made me into somebody I don't like.' Liam wants to hurt his father almost as much as he wants to hurt himself.

'Now get to bed and sleep it off. Mum and I are going to sit up and wait for Mike. He's the only one out of all of us who's tried to do a thing with his life and – guess what? – I hated him for it. Well, it just shows what an idiot I am, doesn't it?'

He gives his father another shove towards the stairs. 'Don't just stand there. I've made myself clear, haven't I? Tomorrow everything changes. *Everything*. We're going to be a proper family, with or without you.'

Sean wipes the blood from his mouth and trudges off to bed.

'Listen, Mum,' Liam says, 'don't go in with him. You can have my room tonight. I'll doss down here on the couch.'

Mary stares at her son. Liam is right. Something has changed tonight, changed for ever.

Mike is struggling past The Gulam when he sees something bearing down on him. It is the great, dark power that came at him in Smith Grove.

'Get out of the way!' Somebody is shouting. Is it me they're shouting at? Mike wonders. He turns to look at the restaurant owner, Rashid.

'Do you mean me?'

Rashid makes a grab for the dazed young white man as he stumbles towards the mounted policeman, but he is too late. The galloping horse careers into Mike, trampling him underfoot.

Suhail is halfway up Clive Road when he sees Mike. He looks strange, as if drunk. But Suhail knows immediately that the rolling, pigeon-toed walk has nothing to do with alcohol. Mike Kelly is hurt, probably suffering concussion.

'Mike!'

Then Suhail sees Rashid making a grab for him.

'Rashid, get him off the street.'

But a mounted policeman is thundering down the street, pursuing two stone-throwers. He only sees the dazed teenager at the last moment. Mike is in the wrong place at the wrong time.

'Mike!'

Suhail is no more than five metres away when Mike goes under the horse's hooves.

'In the name of God, no!'

By the time the horse collides with Mike he is losing consciousness. By the time Mike hits the pavement he is in a deep coma. Neither Suhail nor Rashid know this. All they understand is that they have got to get him off this street. He is in desperate need of medical attention. Their hopes rise when the two youths who helped Mike earlier come running.

'Great, you've got him! Come on, we've found the paramedics. They're at the mosque with Imam Hussain.'

Suhail picks Mike up and starts to carry him across Clive Road. Rashid snatches a tablecloth from The Gulam and waves it. The two youths see what he is doing and take a corner each and help raise it to alert the police and the rioters that they are carrying somebody who is badly hurt. The TV cameras focus on the image of four Asian men bearing the badly injured white boy across the road. They hurry towards the paramedics, silhouetted against the fireball coming from an overturned van. The police rein in their horses and the stone-throwers pause for a few moments. When they are gone the fighting will resume, but in later days, when they understand its significance, it will be seared into the memory of everyone there.

Rabia can't wait a moment longer.

'I'm going to call Dad.'

Diane nods. 'OK. I'm getting a bit worried myself.'

Rabia listens to the ring tone then fastens on her father's voice.

'Dad, where are you? Have you found Mike yet?'

Suhail tells her that the paramedics are with Mike now.

'Paramedics? You mean he's hurt? Dad, where are you? The mosque? I'm coming.' She hangs up before Suhail can argue with her.

'Mike's hurt, Mum. I've got to go to him.'

'No, Rabia. I forbid it.'

Rabia stares at her mother. She has never disobeyed Diane in her life, not over anything important. But she will disobey her now. Rabia runs to the front door and throws it open.

'Rabia, no!' But Rabia is already running up the street, her face streaming with tears.

'Tahir, you stay where you are.'

Tahir nods. He watches his mother and his sister turn the corner. He is just beginning to understand the seriousness of the situation.

The seriousness is only too clear to Rabia.

'Oh Mum, look at him!'

Mike is being lifted into the ambulance. He has been intubated.

'Can you give us any news?' Diane asks.

'Are you family?' the paramedic asks, glancing at Rabia.

'We're friends,' says Diane. 'He was spending the evening with us.'

'OK,' the paramedic says. 'Get in.'

'Suhail,' says Diane, 'we'll call you from the hospital.'

Suhail nods and steps back as the ambulance gets ready to pull away.

'I don't give much for his chances,' one of the youths says. 'He doesn't seem to be breathing.'

Rabia turns first to the boy then to her mother.

'We've just got to hope,' Diane tells her.

But as the ambulance doors close behind her Rabia can feel hope going up in flames along with the overturned cars in Clive Road.

It is two o'clock in the morning before Colin Stone gets home.

He lets himself in quietly and starts to cross the living room to the kitchen. He wants a cold drink to slake his thirst. He can still taste the thick musk of the flames. He is walking back across the living room with a glass of milk when he sees a dark figure in a chair. He drops the glass and watches the milk soaking into the carpet.

'John! You gave me a fright.'

Creed switches on the lamp beside him. 'It's nothing compared to the fright you've given me tonight.'

Stone frowns. 'I don't understand.'

'No? Maybe you'd like to tell me what you've been up to lately, Colin.'

Stone's heart misses a beat.

'You see, the police have been round.'

'What did you tell them?'

'Oh, I didn't see them. Mrs Littlejohn was waiting to give me the news.'

Stone is trying to think of something to say.

'So what's it about, Colin? Would you like me to take a guess? Maybe you've been ordering operations without telling me.'

He examines Stone's face. 'That's not quite it though, is it? No, I ought to be able to do better. Let's see . . . I wonder if you're the one who's been giving Councillor Roberts driving lessons.'

Stone flinches visibly.

'Ah! I'm right, aren't I? That keen to become a councillor, are you?'

'You don't understand, John.'

'That's right,' says Creed, leaning forward. 'I don't. I don't understand how one of our leading members could put at risk everything we've been working for. So how about explaining it to me?'

Mary Kelly pounces on the phone.
'Mike?'

It isn't Mike's voice on the other end of the line.

'I'm sorry,' Mary says, sitting down heavily, 'what did you say?'

Liam frowns, wondering what's going on.

'No,' Mary tells the mystery caller. 'That's not possible. He's at his girlfriend's house.'

Liam sees his mother drop the phone and hurries across to take it. 'Hospital?' he says. 'Yes, we'll be there as soon as we can.'

Mary is sitting very still, staring into space.

'Get your coat, Mum,' Liam says. 'You call a taxi. I'll try to get Dad up.'

He runs upstairs. Three times he shakes his father awake. Three times Sean Kelly grunts and slips back into a deep, intoxicated sleep.

'It's no use,' Liam says. 'We'll have to go without him. Did you call the taxi?'

She hasn't. Liam realises that in some ways his mother is as far gone as the old man. He calls a cab.

'It'll be all right, Mum. Trust me.'

Rabia is sitting by Diane, waiting for news. Mary and Liam Kelly have been in with the doctor for the last ten minutes.

'It's bad news, isn't it, Mum?'

Diane takes her daughter's hand. 'We've just got to wait and see. That poor woman. Did you see Mrs Kelly's face when the doctor asked to see her?'

Rabia bites her lip. She can recall every moment of this

night of fire. She remembers the tortured look on Mary Kelly's face, the way Liam couldn't even look her in the eye. Sitting here in this hospital corridor, Rabia feels as if reality is breaking free of its moorings. Oakfield, until recently so dull and parochial, has gone up in flames. Mike, until a few hours ago so bright and alive, is fighting for his life.

'How did this happen, Mum?'

Diane shakes her head. 'I don't know, love.'

She is searching for something to say when the Kellys appear.

Rabia leaps to her feet. 'How is he?'

She only has to see the shattered look on Mary Kelly's face to know the answer. But Rabia refuses to accept what she knows to be true. She wants a miracle. She expects it. Meeting somebody like Mike Kelly, an ordinary event in so many other places but an extraordinary one in Oakfield, now seems like a miracle in itself. Just knowing him has proved that miracles can happen. Rabia stands waiting, *demanding* her miracle. But there will be nothing magical this night in Oakfield, no angel to pull a human life back from the brink, no turning back from the darkness. There will be an empty space in all the lives this young man has touched.

Because Mike Kelly is dead.

The Mastery of Fear

A poet once said that April is the cruellest month. This late winter's morning, just days after the night of rioting that claimed Mike Kelly's life, few people doubt that this year February has a stronger claim. The hills have a sheen of ice and snow, barely reduced by the morning sun. Across Oakfield people are out scraping the frost off their cars. Others, like Bobby McAllister, are mopping the condensation from the inside of their windows and wishing they had double-glazing to eliminate this chore.

In Old Moor Yvonne Roberts has double-glazing so she can sit in her dressing gown reading the newspaper while Martin, soon to be a former councillor, makes her breakfast. Colin Stone isn't doing either of those things. He is fastening his tie, getting ready to go down to Oakfield police station for his second interview about the damage to Councillor Roberts' car. The two-bedroomed terrace is empty this morning. John Creed moved out the day after the riots, distancing himself from his former deputy. Creed now has a room at the Station Hotel, where he is preparing the most difficult press conference of his career at which he will try to explain away Colin Stone's 'act of madness'.

The most obvious activity this Wednesday morning is in Clive Road, where council workers are putting the final touches to the clear-up. The burnt-out vehicles have gone, as have the stones, half-bricks and shards of broken glass. There is evidence of the night of fire. There are visible scorch marks on the road and, for the second time this year, Rashid is supervising the work of the glazier as The Gulam gets a new front window. The stone step at the Halal butcher's is being replaced after it was ripped out and broken up for ammunition. The newsagent is having security bars fitted on its windows front and back. There is work going on over on Ravensmoor Road too. The evening after the riots there was an attempt to torch the Lion. The landlord has given a statement to the *Chronicle* in which he gives an assurance that he knew nothing about the policies of the Patriotic League. He further declares that there will be no political meetings on his premises in future.

Finally, in small, quite similar houses, one on the Triangle and the other on the Moorside, two families are getting ready for Mike Kelly's funeral.

Mary Kelly assesses her appearance in the mirror, then goes to check on Liam. She adjusts the shoulders of his jacket then tightens the knot of his tie.

'There,' she says. 'You look quite presentable.'

The suit is Mike's, but it could have been tailor-made for Liam. There is little doubt that, though eighteen months Mike's junior, Liam would soon have outstripped his older brother. Yes, in future family photographs Liam would definitely have been the taller of the brothers. If only . . .

'Your dad should be here by now,' says Mary.

John Creed isn't the only one who moved out after the riots. Sean Kelly now has the spare room at his brother's place. Being in a drunken stupor the night his son died was the last straw. When Mary said he had to go, Sean barely raised a protest. He only had to look into the eyes of his wife and surviving son to know that something else had perished along with Mike, gone forever.

'Here he is now,' says Liam. 'The cars are just turning into the road too.'

All along Saxon Avenue people have drawn their curtains as a mark of respect. A shame about young Michael, they say. Such a polite, quiet lad. If either of the Kelly boys was going to go, it should have been Liam. No justice, is there?

The Khans are also waiting for their car. Tahir feels uncomfortable. Twice that morning he has tried to comfort Rabia. Twice she has rebuffed him. Suhail Khan has just got off the phone.

'Who was that?' Rabia asks.

'The *Guardian*,' Suhail replies. 'They wanted a quote for an article they're going to run.'

'What did you tell them?' Rabia asks.

'Oh, the same that I've told all the others. Hatred killed Mike. Love and understanding should be his epitaph.'

Rabia smiles. It is for moments like this that she loves her father so much. Tahir stands in the corner of the living room, wishing he had been able to find words like that.

Down at Oakfield police station Colin Stone is signing his confession. For two interviews he held out, but now that he has been expelled from the Patriotic League and has even been disowned by his own mother, there seems little point maintaining his innocence. This last time he just wanted to get it over with. A prison sentence is likely to follow.

Stone walks out of the police station and stands on the steps. The hearse bearing Mike Kelly is just making its way round the one-way system. Two older men remove their caps and stand in silent respect. Glimpsing Liam Kelly in the back seat of the leading car, Stone lowers his eyes before slipping unnoticed into the Market Centre.

The moment Sean Kelly gets out of the car he sees the Khan family and scowls.

'What did they have to come for?' he grumbles.

Mary Kelly walks across to him. For a moment it looks as if she is going to slap him across the face.

'They came,' she tells her estranged husband, 'because they showed him more warmth and friendship in a few weeks than his own father managed in his whole lifetime.'

The words don't touch Sean but they strike a chord in Tahir's mind.

'Look at Mike's father,' says Rabia. 'He hasn't learned a thing, even now.'

It's true. When Councillor Mohammed Saddique and his wife Aisha arrive at the crematorium Sean Kelly's eyes narrow.

'You're right,' says Tahir hesitantly. 'He hasn't, but there is somebody here who has. I'm sorry, Rabia. I hope that means something.'

Rabia squeezes her brother's arm. 'Thanks, Tahir. It does.'

John Creed is still working on his notes for the press conference. Six Patriotic League candidates will still stand, he has decided. Moorside ward, however, will not be contested as a mark of respect for Michael Kelly. Creed looks at the revised statement and screws it up.

'No,' he says out loud. 'It sounds as if we're admitting responsibility.'

There is a knock at the door. It is Daz and Jason.

'Hello, lads,' says Creed.

'Hi, John,' says Jason. 'We were wondering if the branch can do anything to pay Daz's fine.'

'How much is it?'

'A hundred.'

'I tell you what we'll do,' Creed says. 'The branch will pledge fifty pounds immediately. We'll organise a fund-raiser to get you the rest. How does that sound?'

'Great,' says Daz. 'You're the man, John.'

Creed sees them out. 'Yes, I'm the man.'

As the service at Oakfield Park crematorium gets under way, and Darren Wright and Jason Hughes set off to tell

Daz's mum the good news, Creed continues to wrestle with his statement. At the moment when Mike's remains are being reduced to ashes, Creed is wondering whether his party's prospects in the May elections have been similarly incinerated.

'Damn you, Stone!' he says. 'Damn you!'

'How did the funeral go?' Khalid asks Tahir. They are standing on the front step of the Khans' house. Tahir is grounded for the duration.

'Yes, it was good,' says Tahir. 'They didn't have hymns or anything. It was just memories of Mike, a couple of poems and some music.'

'What sort?'

'Old stuff, mostly. It finished with Bruce Springsteen. You know the one, *Philadelphia*? There was one strange moment though.'

'Yes? What was that?'

'Mike's old man walked out at the end of the service. Can you imagine that, storming out of your own son's funeral?'

Khalid shakes his head. 'That's what my dad says about the English these days: no sense of family, no tradition.'

'What did the police say to you, anyway?' Tahir asks.

'The same as you – final youth reprimand.'

Tahir nods. 'At least you're not grounded.'

'Who isn't?' says Khalid. 'I'm under curfew. In by seven o'clock every night, that's the rule.'

'Till when?'

'I've no idea. A few weeks, I think. See you in school, Tahir.'

'Yes, see you.'

John Creed is sweating. This is even worse than he has expected. Fielding hostile questions from the local hacks is one thing, answering the London journos is something else entirely.

One of them has just read a long list of convictions of Patriotic League members.

'Wouldn't you say this reflects badly on your claim to be a democratic organisation, Mr Creed?' she asks.

'Young men commit indiscretions,' Creed replies. 'I can only repeat what I have said before: my party is a law-abiding organisation.'

Then, just when he thinks things can't get much worse, in walks Councillor Martin Roberts.

'I've got a question for Mr Creed,' says Councillor Roberts.

'Yes, Councillor?' says Creed.

'Are you really expecting us to believe that all the time you were sharing a house with Colin Stone he didn't once mention what he had done?'

'That is exactly what I am saying,' says Creed.

It is the most truthful thing he has said in the last half hour. It is also the least believed.

It is late afternoon when Liam Kelly makes his way back to the cemetery. He has changed and is wearing jeans, a sweater and a thin jacket. He wants to pay his own private respects to his brother. But when he reaches Mike's tiny plot, Liam discovers that he isn't alone. She's there – the girl Mike was so keen on, Rabia. Liam looks around and sees Rabia's parents standing talking about fifty metres away. Taking a deep breath, he steps forward. He gives a nervous cough.

'Hi,' he begins. 'I just . . .'

Rabia looks both startled and uneasy.

'Look,' Liam says, 'I know what you must think about me. I'm not going to make any excuses. Whatever opinion you've got of me, it can't be any worse than how I think of myself.'

Rabia isn't even meeting his eyes. Liam feels like he is drowning.

'The things I did, they were stupid, wrong.'

Rabia isn't arguing. If Liam wants absolution it won't come from her. He holds out his arms, palms up.

'I wish there was something I could say.'

Rabia speaks for the first time. 'I don't think there is.'

'No,' says Liam. 'But there's something I can do.'

He takes his Patriotic League membership card from his pocket and tears it into little pieces before letting it fall, spiralling, through the dusk. Rabia watches the scraps of card tumbling to the ground, then turns and walks away.

'Isn't there anything I can do?' Liam cries. 'I want to put things right.'

Rabia stops and looks round. 'You've made a start,' she says.

Liam nods. A start. At long last he is beginning to understand something that Mike tried to tell him. He is better than the teachers thought, better than Dad thought –

yes, and better than he thought himself. But there are no ready answers. Not only does he not know where tomorrow is going to lead, he isn't even sure where the road begins. He stands alone in the fading light, watching Rabia picking her way towards her parents between a gravestone and an angel.

That Friday John Creed is leaving a meeting at the Black Horse pub, just along Ravensmoor Road from the Lion. The meeting has been booked under the name of the Skittles Club. Since the riot, local landlords aren't very enthusiasic about meetings of the Patriotic League. Creed is shaking hands with the League's new branch secretary and prospective candidate for the Moorside ward, a local scrap metal dealer by the name of Dougie Moyle. Creed has checked Moyle's background carefully. Moyle is a family man with three children, which is promising for starters. He likes a pint but he is not a heavy drinker. He has no criminal convictions and is a recent recruit to the League with no obvious baggage to bring along.

'I'll see you some time next week, Dougie,' Creed says. 'I need to spend a little quality time with the family, don't you know?'

Moyle winks. 'Don't I just? As soon as you get back we'll start planning the election campaign. After all, it's March next week. There's no point dragging our feet.'

'I quite agree,' says Creed, encouraged by the new man's enthusiasm.

Less than a hundred metres away the faithful are being called to Friday prayers. The cry of *Allahu Akbar* rings out in the still, frosty air. Suhail Khan and his children are among those on the way into the mosque. Creed frowns and pops in the *Lohengrin* cassette.

'Stirring stuff,' says Dougie Moyle. 'What is it, Beethoven?'

'Wagner,' says Creed. 'Do you like it?'

'It's OK,' says Moyle. 'I'm more of a Rolling Stones man myself.'

Creed sighs. You can't have everything. Giving the Triangle a last glance, he pulls away and heads for the northern hills.

The first weeks of March bring a thaw. Wild rain-laden winds scour the hills and send pinch-faced men and women scurrying through Oakfield's narrow streets. At five o'clock one Tuesday night Ravensmoor Road library is again throwing its doors open to host the Oakfield Book Award. Prize-winning author Chris Morgan has made the long trek from Somerset.

'I don't have that much to say,' he begins, addressing the packed room. 'I am very grateful for this Award. My book is called *Love Song*. I suppose that says everything. The way I see it, there are two great genres. There is the love story. Then there is the horror story – what happens when love fails.'

Rabia feels he is looking straight at her. He can't be. They have never met.

'My book is being reprinted now,' Morgan continues. 'There will be just one change to the new edition.'

He opens his copy of *Love Song*.

'It is a simple dedication,' he says, 'but I am sure you will all understand my motives in writing it. It says: *To Michael Kelly, in celebration of a life.*

Sofia glances at Rabia.

'I'm struggling here,' says Rabia, obviously fighting back tears.

Sofia squeezes her arm. 'You're doing just fine.'

Rabia smiles. She isn't now, but very soon she will be.

Winter continues to loosen its grip on Oakfield. In another few weeks there are signs of colour on the hills. On the Moorside, leaflets are being handed out. For once, John Creed has had nothing to do with them. They are in the form of an open letter to the local residents. A couple of sentences will give the flavour of the letter:

Two months ago, it says, *a young lad from this estate died in the worst riots Oakfield has ever seen. Michael Kelly didn't go looking for trouble; trouble went looking for him. Extremists had been whipping up hatred. Michael Kelly was simply a victim of other people's prejudice.*

The letter ends with an appeal.

There are people trying to stir up trouble for their own ends.

Think very carefully about how you vote in the forthcoming elections.

A week ago Councillor Martin Roberts held his last surgery before retiring into a meeting on the way forward for the estate. People who had remained silent while hatred gained a foothold started to find their voices. It was at this meeting that the idea of a leaflet was born. Among the people canvassing the Moorside are Liam and Mary Kelly, Councillor Roberts and his wife Yvonne, and community worker Bobby McAllister.

B efore long spring has turned to early summer and the arts festival is under way at Oakfield Town Hall. Rabia is waiting nervously in the wings while other performers finish.

'Come on,' says Sofia. 'You'll be fantastic. You always are.'

Rabia looks at herself in the mirror. She is wearing her hair loose. She stands barefoot in a costume of blue satin with beadwork. She never did get to dance for Mike.

'And now,' Sumeara Jamil is announcing, 'two wonderfully expressive dancers from Oakfield High School, Rabia Khan and Sofia Akhtar.'

Suhail and Diane Khan smile proudly as the girls walk on stage. They are even prouder when Rabia takes the microphone.

'Our dance is dedicated to Michael Kelly,' she says.

When the music begins the two girls dance, making circles of shimmering, electric blue under the hall lights. Watching them is a group of pupils from Moorside High. It includes Liam Kelly. Maybe one day kids from the two schools will do more than meet once a year, he thinks.

Maybe.